ASSIGNMENT:
EARTH

Lynne Armstrong-Jones

ISBN 978-1-63784-074-0 (paperback)
ISBN 978-1-63784-075-7 (digital)

Hawes & Jenkins Publishing
16427 N Scottsdale Road Suite 410
Scottsdale, AZ 85254
www.hawesjenkins.com

Printed in the United States of America

Other Books by Lynne Armstrong-Jones

On the Trail of the Ruthless Warlock (Book 1)

On the Trail of the Wind's Tears (Book 2)

On the Trail of the Unseen (Book 3)

On the Trail of the Mountains' Mysteries (Book 4)

Each book is written to stand alone. Readers do not need to read them in sequence.

Praise for Assignment: Earth

"Armstrong-Jones' novel works most of all because the premise seems almost plausible, mixing together social commentary, humor, and a well-crafted plot, for a layered and entertaining work of social science fiction." —*Self-Publishing Review*

"A warm, satisfying SF tale that intrigues and charms... The novel contains everything that makes the universe of this world appealing, including sympathetic, passionate characters, deadly conflicts, and a warm love story with depth...A must-read." —*The Prairies Book Review*

"Armstrong-Jones' creative imagination was well utilized, seamlessly weaving an invisible alien attack on earth into events that appear to be happening in our mundane reality. Realistic despite the fantastical elements, I could easily imagine it to be true...Overall, this is a unique story that is very well done." —*Reader Views*

Prologue

Perka. My name is Perka. At least, that is the way that *they* would pronounce it. It is actually a lot more like pp-KKK-uh. But they would never be able to say that—and, anyway, it would sound awfully strange to them.

Even Perka was too unusual, the KKK-stt had said. I must try harder to think like they would. KKK-stt is our sound for *representative.* The KKK-stt has said that each of these Earthers has at least two names.

My name on Earth will be *Andrea Perk.* I will certainly still feel like pp-KKK-uh inside, though, I am sure.

I have forgotten again! I must remember to use those—those—what are they called? Contractions, that is—that's it. My command of the language will sound more natural if I do, the representative said.

I shake my head as I consider the mission before me. How sad to think that it is—*it's*—even necessary. We must interfere as little as possible with their cultures, their lives. Yet we must also do whatever we can to help them. To protect them.

Before it is—*it's*—too late.

I'm gazing down at my fingers, thinking about how strangely unfamiliar this body feels. And how very different it appears, with these dull, lifeless colours. I must remember to use my pigment-suppressants weekly, or even more often if necessary.

I gaze out of the viewscreen of our little craft. We can see our destination now—the third planet from the sun in this solar system.

We have passed the lifeless ones that are little more than frozen rock. We have passed the large ringed one and the enormous one nearest to it, and are coming slowly closer to the one which some of the inhabitants call *Earth*. We have been assigned to the country called Canada.

We have now passed the reddish one which once supported life similar to ours but does no longer.

Am I truly ready for this assignment? I must be, or I would not have been chosen. And I must be successful in my mission to protect the Earthers—

Or I will die trying.

Chapter One

BAM!

Jared felt a bitter satisfaction as the door *slammed* shut behind him. Yes, yes, he had neighbours in the apartment building who might not be pleased, but the slam felt good. It was like his soul crying out…and it desperately needed to. He stepped onto the mat inside his front door and kicked off his shoes. Gripping the envelopes from his mailbox in one hand, his other went to the area over his heart. Just under his light jacket, he'd felt his phone vibrate in his inside pocket. Another email.

And he was positive it wouldn't be good news. It never was anymore.

Damn it to hell and back! Nothing but bad news. Didn't matter if it was email or snail mail. It was all *shit*! Every morning his hand trembled when he picked up his phone. He almost felt sick when he opened his inbox because he knew—he just *knew*—there'd be another rejection. He kept hoping that maybe one of his prospective employers might use good old-fashioned snail mail to send him an offer. So, he'd watch out the window for some clue whether the letter carrier had been here yet. If he saw someone come, he'd bolt down the stairs from his second-floor apartment, mailbox key in hand like an idiot.

Angry all over again, he threw the mail on his little kitchen table, as though his defiance could help him strike back at the fates, or gods of employment or whatever else had dealt him another unfair blow. Every day, the same damn crap. Rejection letters and junk mail. And in his phone, rejection letters and notices of unpaid bills.

How the hell am I supposed to take care of the bills if I can't get a frigging job!

Slumping onto the kitchen chair, he moaned as he held his head in his hands. With a shaking hand, he reached under his jacket and pulled out his phone. It took effort for him to keep his trembling fingers still enough to open his inbox. And there it was. What he'd expected all along—

Shit, shit and doubleshit! This time was worse. This time he'd felt that he really had a good rapport with the principal who'd interviewed him. And this time he'd *really* wanted the job, almost hungered for it. He'd *thought* he had an excellent chance!

What did a guy have to *do* to get work as a counsellor in a school or a treatment centre?

Sighing, he passed his jacket sleeve across his moist eyes and tried to pull himself together. He re-read the email. Yes, he'd made the short list, his qualifications were good—

But there'd been someone else just a little bit more suited to the position. There was *always* someone else just a bit more suitable!

He raised his arm to throw the damn phone across the room. But stopped himself. If he broke it, he might not be able to afford a new one...

Isn't there someplace that needs me? Maybe I'll have to try another city—or go back to being a research assistant.

He'd have to do *something.* There was still enough of the money his father'd left him to last a little while longer, but it sure wouldn't go on forever. Besides, surely the longer he went without employment the less desirable he'd appear to a possible employer.

Restless, he walked across the small living room to stand at the window. He gazed at the leaves as the breezes urged them to let go of their tethers and drift downward to the ground. *Ironic.* They were letting go of their tethers, and he was at the end of his rope!

Fall was here. Maybe the employment picture would start to look better now. *Maybe, maybe...*

A long sigh escaped him. A terrible sadness was beginning somewhere deep inside of him. It was like a huge, aching, emotional bruise in the depths of his soul, reaching up through his body, grasping upward at what remained of his mind.

No! "C'mon, Jar—snap out of it," he commanded himself. *Things will get better—they have to—*

Jared ran his hand through his short, curly brown hair and took a deep breath. For a few moments, he just stood there, focussed on his breathing. *In through the nose, out through the mouth. Slow and easy. That's it.*

Calmer now, he zipped up his jacket and returned to the doorway to put his shoes back on and head out. At the bottom of the staircase, he paused. He walked over to the row of mailboxes along the wall under the staircase and stared at his. He was unaware that his hand had sought the touch of his phone in his inside jacket pocket. If only there was some way of removing the curse that seemed to have been put on all his mail.

A bitter chuckle escaped him when he realized how ridiculous that might sound to someone else. Stepping out into the cool breeze, he headed to the parking lot and his dilapidated, old, green VW Beetle. *Make that green and rust,* he thought bitterly. He unlocked the door—with his old-fashioned key—and prayed that the car would start without a fuss.

Not long later, he guided the old car into a familiar parking lot, adjusting the manual choke as the VW coughed. The flashing yellow sign above the building's entrance told everyone that this was *MIKE'S BAR AND GRILL.* It had a pleasant, cheery look about it, and the few customers entering or leaving joked and laughed as though to confirm that this was a place of good times. He eyed the entry doors as he had many times before. Chuckling, he mused that the sign could say *JARED'*S considering the amount of time he'd spent here lately. If that were true, at least he'd have a reliable source of income…

Seated at a table for two, he sopped up a bit of slop with his denim jacket sleeve, then lifted the foamy mug to his lips and took a long gulp. The place was almost empty now that it was mid-afternoon. It was still too early in the season for the young faces of the university crowd. And the lucky people who had regular jobs and enough money to have lunch here had already left.

Jared put the mug back down, gazing at it in sudden alarm. That *had* been a big gulp! He'd have to drink more slowly and make it last. The money from Dad wouldn't go on forever. Dad had actually been his stepdad, but—with Jared's mom—he'd raised Jared. To Jared, the 'step' part had never really existed. He found himself reminiscing about happier days. Yes, though it seemed like a long time ago, there had been a better time. A time when Dad wasn't sick, and a time when Marjorie still loved him. A time when they'd been planning on a wedding sometime after university—

But now he was alone. Alone and unemployed. And he just couldn't seem to shake off the depression for all that long. He could forget for a little while, distract himself with something, and then that awful sensation deep, deep inside would begin to simmer again.

"Hey Jared!"

The cheery female voice startled him, making him jump a bit and slosh some of his beer on the table. *Betty.* Looking—as usual—as fresh and lovely as spring sunshine. Her pink sweater matched the glow of her cheeks. Jared nodded in her direction, silently envying her boyfriend. Returning his attention to his beer mug, he quietly traced finger designs on the cool, wet surface.

The pink sweater was suddenly right in front of him. It looked so soft. He ached to reach out and touch it, but managed to stop himself. As he gazed up at her beautiful, round face, she pushed a strand of dark hair out of her large, intense brown eyes. "You okay, Jar?"

He smiled. So concerned about him. She really was nice. Her brown eyes met his sky-blue ones. He opened his mouth to speak, then closed it again. Something inside of him was wanting to get out. The words were on his tongue, but he couldn't bring himself to give them life. How could he share his problems with *her*? Beautiful Betty who was going to start her career soon. Beautiful Betty who was happily in a meaningful relationship with handsome Tom—who'd already started an executive position with a large insurance company. The perfect, successful couple.

The perfectly lucky couple.

How could he share his failures with the likes of *her*? Already someone else had come into the bar and was calling her name from across the room. Someone else, no doubt, wanting to tell Betty that she, too, had found a job.

The newcomer arrived, nodded at Jared, and began to pull Betty away from his table. Betty smiled kindly at him. "Hang in there, Jar," she said softly, and followed her friend to another part of the bar.

"Yeah," Jared whispered to himself sullenly. Both hands were around the mug as he savoured the cool wetness of the thing.

Suddenly he had an eerie feeling in the depths of his chest. That ache was there again. The word *hang* echoed through his mind as though it were bouncing from one wall to another. Hands trembling, he lifted the mug to his lips. He tried to use the beer to wash down the lump which had taken up residence in his throat, but the thing wouldn't seem to budge. Blinking until the dampness in his eyes cleared, he rose and, sighing, made his way outside to his VW.

Shaking his head, he tried to reason with himself. He was a trained counsellor with degrees in psychology—and only too aware of the dangers of what he was feeling. The depression was a thick, deep mudhole, and one of his legs was stuck in it up to the knee as it threatened to pull the rest of him in and smother him completely.

He needed help. But whose? What would happen if he went to his doctor and asked for a referral to a social worker or psychologist? How could he do that without feeling like a fool when he had the qualifications himself?

Jared pictured himself for a minute, sitting in a little office like the one he'd trained in. A degree on the wall. A comfy couch. An armchair. Nice, calming neutral colours. He imagined the counsellor entering…

But he shook his head, trying to get the image out of his mind. Of course, in his fantasy the counsellor was one of his former classmates—

One of his classmates who'd found a job.

No. That was no good. He'd have to handle everything himself.

His heart was beating harder. *Hang, hang, hang.* Pills. Pills would be easier. He was so engrossed in his awful thoughts that he wasn't even aware of getting inside and starting his car, pulling onto the roadway—

He gasped. His foot slammed on the brake pedal as the back bumper of the car in front suddenly filled his vision. A squeal—loud and piercing. People were staring. He hadn't missed the car's bumper by much.

Jared ran a trembling hand across his slick forehead, grateful for the pause forced on him by the red light. He had a minute to collect himself again, sucking in deep breaths while he watched the light change to green. As the car in front began to move, Jared gripped the steering wheel much harder than he needed to, anxious to keep his mind on his driving this time.

The line of traffic was heading to the underpass not far from his apartment building. Jared noticed dully that the billboard had a new advertisement. The message, though, caught and held his interest.

The We Care Line. Lonely? Depressed? Just need someone to talk to? Our trained telephone counsellors ***care****—and we're waiting to listen and help.*

Jared found himself repeating the phone number over and over so he wouldn't forget it.

After he'd parked his car, he took a moment to put the number into his phone's list of contacts. As he turned to make his way to the building, he paused. From the corner of his eye, he'd spotted something orange. He turned in that direction.

"Hello, Freddy," he said softly, squatting.

A ginger cat made his way to rub against Jared, happy to have his ears scratched. The human sighed, grateful for the contact. He had no idea whether the stray had a name or not, but his strange overbite always reminded Jared of Queen's lead singer. They'd become friends of a sort—Jared no longer rinsed his tuna cans before he took them to the recycling area, as Freddy had a knack for showing up around those times. And the cat was always happy to do the rinsing himself.

Jared rose, still thinking about the advertisement, watched while the cat wandered away.

Chapter Two

I gaze upward, my eyes still looking at the spot where I last saw the underside of our little craft. The exterior of our craft has been treated in order to meld visually with its surroundings. This is so complete that it is virtually invisible to unaccustomed eyes. And, of course, it has been designed using technology similar to Earth's *stealth*, so that it is not easily located by these Earthers' RADAR. I sigh. The knowledge that it will not be *too* far away brings comfort to those parts of me which feel a bit of uncertainty.

My hair blows across my face as the breezes toy with it. I try to tuck it back behind my ear, but the wind stubbornly refuses to give up the game as the long grasses dance around us. I find myself yet again pulling my light jacket more snuggly around myself. This area of the planet is much cooler than my own, even in its warmer parts. But it was those of us with the greatest stamina who were selected to serve in these cooler areas. We cannot, after all, serve only those Earthers who live in warmer climes!

A few (what do they call them? I chastise myself for having to search for the correct term) *miles* away, or perhaps *kilometers* from here, we can see the outskirts of the city. Am I truly ready to go there and begin? My continuing hesitancy with correct usage of the language causes me uncertainty. If the need here had not been so great, I might not have been chosen for this project at all.

A voice distracts me from my thoughts. I listen and open my mouth to reply, but I must stop myself. I close my mouth once more as the votary reminds the voice's owner to please remember not to make use of our true names. We are now standing on the surface of our assigned planet, and therefore must only utilize our *Earther* names. This lesson, I reflect, is one that I have learned well, and it is an important one—

We must not risk causing any unease among the Earth inhabitants.

Now the speaker tries again. I smile in anticipation, as she is someone with whom I feel a sense of closeness. "Andrea," Georgia Lupoff says, the name sounding awkward, as though to confirm that her mouth is not yet completely accustomed to saying it.

I turn to face her, musing that her name sounds as strange as mine does. It is—*it's*—certainly not nearly as simple to produce as her true name, gu-p-FFF. Yet I am bound never on Earth to say that. "Yes, Georgia."

It is Georgia's turn to smile. We are enjoying the novelty of appearing so different!

There is no doubt that my colouring is closest to natural. The reddish hair and pinkish tone of my skin now are probably more similar to my true colouring than the pale skin and fair hair of Georgia.

We are all grinning at one another, excited to begin this challenge for which we have been learning and training. Unfortunately, only fourteen of us could be spared for this particular city. Some think it to be insufficient. But we know that all types of statistics, observations, and data have been utilized in coming to this decision. There are seven females and seven males of various shades from darkest brown with blackest hair to almost white with hair of gold. Seven of us will approach from here. Our little craft has left the other seven on the far side of the city.

We eye one another as we adjust the clothing and prepare in other ways to begin. I fumble in my pocket for my *wallet* and *key*. These are new terms for me, as we do not have such items on our own planet. But I recall clearly the functions of these objects.

Our representatives, who are now back on our home world, have organized all aspects of our visit. They ventured here a short time ago, with images of our Earther bodies. Although the artificial images were able to speak and move, they were only simple models of us. Our representatives and our images selected suitable vocations, and training, if need be, and made arrangements for our residences. Currency was removed from the economy at that time. That we now have in our wallets, to help us to begin. Only a small amount was needed by each of us for our furnished *apartments*. Nourishment we can provide for ourselves.

I have selected apparel which covers each leg separately—*pants*, or *leggings* these are called. Some females, I know, prefer, at least from time to time, to wear a different style which consists of one covering for both legs together. What is the name for these? Oh yes, *skirts* or *dresses*. But in this area only females wear them. *How strange this world is!*

I watch as the first of our group picks up his backpack and heads in the direction of the city. I watch as Martin Kramer (KKK-r-r, on our world), the votary for our group, continues through the grassy field, a slight spring in his step. His form is that of a large, dark-skinned male, and it seems strange, somehow, to see someone of his size step so lightly. He is eager to begin.

And I must admit that, despite my trepidation and uncertainty, I am too.

As we walk, I am fascinated by the view of all those stars overhead, gleaming downward at us from the vast night sky. How very strange to enjoy the sight of a sky so different, and yet so similar to, our own. Thinking of home brings memories to mind…

As I recall once more the rigorous training we have—*we've*—received, I wonder if we are really, truly prepared for such an important assignment. I have to shake my head in wonder as I remember the most recent viewings of the Earther cities. Shocking. Horrible. Signs of the enemy were everywhere, it seemed.

And so well do they manage to exist furtively within the Earther society that the Earthers still do not know of the plot against them, nor the threat.

I know that others of my kind are here already and have been for some time, yet I am—*I'm*—questioning my own readiness. I must try to be more relaxed—after all, I *did* successfully complete all of my training. And if the votaries and the representatives believe that I am prepared for success, then surely it must be so!

As we enter the city limits, we separate. Some head north, some south and west. Four of us travel towards the city's core. That is where we will be needed.

We stop. From here, each will proceed alone. We smile and nod at one another. We must rely on Earth types of communication, as we dare not do anything which could alert the enemy to our presence.

We are ready.

I watch as Georgia, Martin, and Franco head away in different directions. It brings me comfort to know that at least one of them will never be further away from me than a focussed thought. I realize that I am smiling. I wonder if I look exactly like an Earther. I certainly *feel* like one might, as I take the key into my hand. I walk up the steps which lead to the apartment building door and, inside at the next door, insert my key into the lock. I ride the elevator to the seventh floor.

I am *home.*

At my place of work, I observe that the training program has seemed to be adequate, although not nearly as thorough as the one on my own world. I try to appear as though much is new to me, but I find that challenging at times. I can see the value of having one of my own kind work her or his way to the level of instructor or supervisor. Perhaps I will do just that. It helps, of course, that the credentials I've been given include an advanced university degree in psychology. Because of this, I am expected to be better-prepared than some of the others, and I can be more helpful in the training of those who require more assistance.

The first seven days—*week*—goes well. My training program here on Earth has been completed. I have told the instructor that I am eager to begin. And I am to start tonight.

Chapter Three

Saturday night. Saturday night and nothing to do. Sighing, Jared put his sock feet up on the little coffee table and leaned his head back. True, there was MIKE'S, but it would be crowded as hell. He sat up and put his feet on the floor again, picking up the remote from the table.

Flick. Flick. Flick.

Impatiently he hit the off switch, tossing the thing beside him on the sofa. Sighing once more, he rubbed his blue eyes and passed both hands through the curls of his short, brown hair. *Damn.* Even his video games held no appeal right now.

He swallowed the lump in his throat. "C'mon Jared," he whispered. "Don't let yourself get down! Remember—a week without rejection emails and letters is a good sign!"

But he was too restless to just sit here. He rose and wandered slowly across the room to the window, letting his gaze travel across the lights of the neighbourhood. Everything out there seemed so full of life…

I'm twenty-six and I feel like ninety-six.

He knew damn well he could've been over at MIKE'S instead of moping around at home. Betty'd invited him to join her crowd. So being home alone and restless and angry about it was his own fault. He stood, staring out the window, arms crossed, and nibbled on the inside of his lower lip.

There was something strange going on with him. More than simple frustration about not having a job. There was something more than that. And he just couldn't seem to put his finger on what it was. It almost seemed like he *wanted* to be unhappy. And it seemed to be mostly on Saturday nights.

As he turned, his gaze travelled to his phone where he'd left it on the coffee table. His mind was on his memory of the conversation he'd had a week ago with the crisis line worker. It had really been helpful. He hadn't needed to give his real name, which had made the experience less threatening.

Although he doubted that he really would've seriously considered suicide, still the chance to share his misery had eased the pressure that had been building inside of him like boiling water inside a kettle. He walked back to the brown corduroy sofa and sat down again, still nibbling on the inside of his lip. Mind made up, he let go a long breath and picked up his phone. He hesitated just a second or two, then tapped the number—

Suddenly he stopped. He put the phone down and began to nibble on his thumbnail.

What if I get the same guy? What was his name? Oh yeah, Murray. He was a nice guy—but if I call him again, maybe he'll think I'm unbalanced or something. Or at least inept. Dammit, I can't call him all the time!

Heart pounding, he realized that he was attacking his thumbnail with his teeth again, like a tyrannosaurus finding its first meal in days. He withdrew his thumb and stared at it. *Hmm. Self-mutilation.*

"Okay, okay," he said softly to his thumbnail. "For your sake, I'll do it! At least, I'll call the number and find out if it's Murray again. Yeah. That much I'll do."

Quickly, afraid he'd lose his nerve, he tapped the number. A female voice greeted him before he could change his mind again. Once more he listened to the basic description of the service and was reassured that he didn't need to give his real name.

"You can call me Kay," she was saying. Her voice had a pleasant, smooth, and gentle tone to it. Just listening to it made him feel better.

As they talked, Jared began to like her more and more. She sounded concerned and sincere. Murray had, too, yet this young woman seemed like more than just a crisis line worker. There was much more to her…somehow. To Jared, it seemed as though her listening and talking with him was vital to his very existence. He found himself pouring out more than he'd intended. He hadn't planned to tell her about the talk he'd had with Murray—still a bit worried that he might come across as a nut case, yet everything somehow just flowed out of him.

"Jerry," she said. He'd chosen that name because it was close enough to his own to be meaningful yet allowed him to keep part of himself secret. "Jerry, I wonder if your concern about being rejected by potential employers could be tied in with other rejection that you might have experienced in your life. I am—I'm—wondering if your feelings about Marjorie leaving you surface when you feel rejection from someone else. Perhaps it's rejection in general that distresses you… Jerry?"

Jared gasped. It was as though she'd opened up his heart and looked directly inside. "I—I'm here, Kay." His heart was pounding so hard he thought it might crack a rib. Suddenly he had trouble breathing, like he'd just run a mile.

The word *rejection* seemed to echo from the walls of the little apartment. Over and over it came, whispered with each beat of his booming heart.

"Jerry? Jerry, are you still there? Are you okay? I am sorry. I spoke too quickly. Jerry?"

Jared sighed, eyes closed, searching for peace beneath the turmoil. Finally, he spoke. "Kay, it's all right. You—you didn't go quickly. I—I was moving too slowly. What you say makes perfect sense. And…it hit home. I should've realized all this myself. I guess I *did* realize it. I realized it enough to try to bury it with as much denial as I could."

Swallowing, he sighed once more. He listened as Kay spoke again. But she stopped, as though wanting to ensure that she wasn't rushing him. He continued in a soft voice. "Every time I get a rejection email or letter, it's—it's a statement that someone doesn't—doesn't want me. It might sound a bit overdramatic, but every time that happens, I think about the day that Marjorie broke it off with me." He took a long breath before he continued. "I guess I'm still mourning for her, in a way…"

There was silence for a beat, then Kay spoke again. "And mourning for yourself and feeling the depth of your loneliness."

"Yes," Jared breathed. "Yes."

"Jerry," she continued, "we all get lonely."

"Even *We Care Line* workers?"

"Yes," she laughed softly. "Believe me, we do."

For a moment, Jared had the urge to suggest that maybe they should meet. Then neither of them would need to be lonely. But it sounded too absurd.

When he hung up the phone, he finally felt some sense of peace within himself. Shaking his head, he wondered how he could have managed to have buried his feelings so deeply, despite his training in psychology. Sighing, he walked to the kitchen, once more nibbling on his thumbnail, although more gently this time. When he returned to the sofa, he was holding a can of Bud Light.

He sat down, leaning forward slightly. "To Marjorie," he proclaimed loudly, a *ffffsssst* sound accompanying his exclamation as he opened the can with a flair. He drank deeply, dragging a sleeve across his mouth, then sat back with a deep sigh. "And here's to remembering! 'Cause tonight I'm gonna remember it all, Marjorie. Then maybe I'll be able to forget." The beer was pleasantly cool in his throat.

Jared found himself doing a lot of remembering and thinking that weekend—about Marjorie and how his fear of rejection could have been affecting many of his interactions and relationships.

Sunday night. He wondered what his chances might be of talking to Kay again. His heart was pounding as he hoped that it would be her—

"Don't you *ever* have time off?" He spoke with exaggeration, and he heard Kay chuckle in response. "How come you got stuck with the weekend shift?"

"I don't mind, Jerry," she said, the tone of her voice suggesting that she might be smiling.

Much more comfortable this time, Jared had no difficulty in sharing what he'd been thinking about over the past twenty-four hours. Kay, as usual, listened with her seemingly unending patience and concern, adding insights where appropriate.

"Go on, Jerry, talk a bit more about your dad," she urged him.

"My dad? *He* never rejected me, Kay! Never. Maybe he was the one person who didn't! Always stood by me. He was actually my stepdad. But that never mattered. He was just *dad*."

"What kinds of feelings did you have when he died, Jerry?" Her voice was quite soft and gentle.

Jared frowned, wondering why she'd ask such a ridiculous question. His heart was starting to beat harder again. *How would anyone feel when they lost someone?* "Oh, the usual, I guess. Sadness. Anger at God…"

"Did you ever feel angry at your *dad*?"

"Sure. Lots of times. We had our disagreements—"

"Jerry, I mean after he passed away."

There was silence for several seconds. Confusion was once more sweeping through Jared. "What do you mean, Kay? Why would I be angry at *him*? It wasn't his fault!"

"No, of course not. But he left you. He left you, even though you felt closer to him than anyone else. Perhaps you feel that *that* was the ultimate rejection." Kay's voice was so soft that it was barely more than a whisper.

My God, Jared thought. *Imagine that. Angry at dad for leaving me—angry at him for dying!*

"Is that possible? I mean—I mean is it normal?" Jared's mouth was suddenly awfully dry.

"Of course, it is, Jerry. Perfectly normal and very understandable."

Jared's heart was pounding again as he suddenly began to comprehend. "And—and I refused to let myself feel that way. Tried to be strong and let my mother do my share of the crying. Tried to bury it. Tried to bury the feelings I thought were…were *wrong*. Part of *me* was buried when they shovelled the dirt on Dad's casket."

Then there was a huge lump in Jared's throat, and he couldn't seem to swallow it. His eyes were moist as he began to share memories of his stepfather. Finally, he thanked Kay, and again assured her that he was okay. More subdued maybe, but okay.

He put his phone down and sat silently, eyes unfocussed.

"Yes. Yes, I'm angry, Dad! Why did you have to go? I wasn't ready to be the *man* of the family! And I couldn't be *you*. Mom wanted me to, but I couldn't, so I only felt like a failure!"

Jared closed his eyes for a minute. When he opened them, he did something he should've done a long time ago but hadn't.

He cried.

Chapter Four

It is quiet now. I am at home—or, at least, in the apartment designated for me while I am on Earth. For now, my work is complete, and I am alone. For now, I need not be concerned about the enemy and the importance of helping the Earthers.

But doubts cloud my mind. The importance of helping the Earthers seems sometimes like an enormous responsibility. And it *is* mine.

Did I do the right thing? Did I say the right things? Did I handle that call in the best way possible?

So many questions, Perka. Yes, I know. I am not Perka. I am Andrea Perk—*Kay* on the phone line. Inside, though, I am, and always will be Perka. *pp-KKK-uh*, to be precise.

A sigh escapes me. Did I truly say the best things to help that last client, the young woman? She was so very depressed.

And at times it can be so difficult to give the needed assistance without the benefit of actually *seeing* the person. Visual contact with the Earthers would afford so many more cues about their inner feelings, their thinking. It would be so much more efficient to project my thought-images to each Earther and receive theirs. But, of course, such would not be possible. And a lot of projections in a short time would likely alert any enemy in the vicinity to my presence.

But inside I am aching to do *more*, to find some way of serving the Earthers in a more effective manner. I want to find some way of ensuring that the words are truly assisting them. I know that I am making the callers more resistant to the enemy's seductions...but still

I long to make certain that we are being absolutely as effective as possible against the nnn-Asi-t.

Have I forgotten the Earther word for the enemy? I do not recall one. For a moment I am angry at myself for such foolishness. Of course. The Earthers do not—*don't*—know about the nnn-Asi-t. They think the enemies are simply some of their own kind who have gone astray.

I *must* do more! I am assisting the Earthers through the phone line, but I must also spend more time actively searching for the enemy—

But not without nourishment first. I must be careful not to neglect this body. I must keep it strong. It is still *mine*, inside.

Sitting at my kitchen table, I take the tiny sphere into my hand. *Ah, how wonderful.* Immediately I can feel its warmth, its gentle pulsations. I close my eyes to savour the delicious sensation. For just a moment, I can feel a bit as though I am at my *true* home. As my fingers close around it, I open my eyes so that I can watch with pleasure as my crimson sphere becomes warmer still, until a beautiful scarlet mist begins to rise.

Closing my eyes once more, I inhale deeply, enjoying the sweet scent as it fills my nostrils, my throat, and my entire being. I am oblivious to my surroundings, conscious only of the tremendous feelings of relaxation, of increasing strength, mental alertness. Slowly the deep sensation of total relaxation fades, to be replaced completely by physical stamina and mental acuity.

I open my eyes. I am whole again. At peace, I watch as my sphere's glow fades to a more delicate hue of crimson, then pink, then white. Finally, it contracts once more to its original tiny size. Gently, I place it back inside the little pouch secured inside my belt. As I do, my gaze turns to the small kitchen with its cold, metallic appliances. The stove, the refrigerator. At least the countertop reminds me of something warm, with its simulated wood finish. All these things needed for Earther nourishment! How inefficient! Our way really makes more sense.

In my peripheral vision, I notice my hand. And I gasp. I had thought that the pinkish glow was from my little sphere. But it was not the fading of my LLL-nnnta sphere which was giving my skin the reddish hue. I have been tarrying too long! I must consume one of my pigment-suppressants, or my true identity could become obvious to any nnn-Asi-t who might observe me. And it would most certainly alarm any Earthers who saw!

I rise and move to the bathroom so that I can observe myself in the mirror. But when I gaze at my reflection, I wish that I could simply allow my pigment to remain what is normal for my people. How I miss that scarlet glow! I had always been rather pleased with the intensity of my colouring when I was at home.

But I am no longer at home. I am on Earth. And the importance of being able to move among Earthers as though I belong here outweighs other considerations or desires. I watch the pinker tone of my skin as it brightens just a bit more. I see a female of perhaps thirty Earth years, with skin suggesting quite severe over-exposure to this solar system's sun. My hair is almost as brightly coloured as it usually is at home, although many of the scarlet tones are a bit muted. I cannot help but grin when I regard my eyes. Earthers would no doubt be shocked and terrified if they saw this deep red glow! Their folklore is filled with references to *devils* whose eyes might be just like mine!

I hate to do it, but I must use my pigment-suppressant. After all, it is imperative that I look as much like an Earther as possible. I remove the suppressant from another section hidden in the inside of my belt. Delicately, I lift the tiny speck to my face. I hold it directly in front of my nose and watch in the mirror as it becomes just a splash of whitish mist. I welcome the feeling of the familiar acridity as it hurries through my nostrils and into the depths of me…

In a short time, I am once again facing Andrea Perk, the supposed Earther. She has pale pinkish skin and auburn hair. Her eyes are deep brown in colour. I am rather sorry to watch the scarlet fade from them.

How bland and pale I seem.

Sighing, I make my way to the armchair in my living room. Here I will sit quietly, eyes closed, and dream of home. I must rest now for the requisite amount of time, knowing that this body requires a chance to make the adjustment complete. I need to discipline myself to accomplish this, as I have already made the decision to venture outside soon to search more intensively for any signs of the nnn-Asi-t—or, at the very least, to try to offer direct assistance to any Earthers affected by them.

I am pleased when I finally feel the familiar tingle spread throughout my body. The process is now complete. I am ready. Eagerly, I rise from the armchair and step to the closet by the door. I pull the red jacket from its hanger and put it on, knowing well that I will need its protection from this world's climes, which are cooler than those of my own planet.

Anxious to make a difference for these Earthers, I hasten to pull the door closed behind me as I step into the hallway and use my key to secure the lock. It seems sad to me that such items as *keys* and *locks* are necessary here. We do not have them on my world. I make my way down the carpeted hallway to the elevator and push the button for the lobby. As I step into the elevator, a man does, too. I glance at him and let my senses, just lightly, feel for anything untoward. Fortunately, he does not seem to be involved with the nnn-Asi-t in any fashion. He turns and gives me a slight smile, and I return one.

I walk through the small lobby area and push open the doors to the outside. Already a chill makes its way through me as I am confronted by the usual coolness of the early evening. The wind toys with my jacket, threatening to pull it open, and I wrap it more snuggly around me in protest.

The sun is still beaming, although it is now descending toward the horizon. But the surrounding area is quiet and well-lit—

Too much so. This is not the area which the nnn-Asi-t tend to frequent, so I walk away from it, and head toward the busy streets with the many-coloured flashing lights. It is here that I will find the nnn-Asi-t, if at all.

I must be alert and careful. Should an nnn-Asi-t see or sense my true identity, it will most certainly attempt to remove me.

Despite my discomfort with the chill, these Earthers seem either well-used to it or unaffected by it, for the streets are quite busy. Most are clad in jackets or other coverings which appear much lighter in weight than mine. Despite my body's adaptations, I obviously feel the cold much more than they do.

I turn a corner and am struck by the sudden beauty before me, for there are beautiful, bright colours almost everywhere! I had not realized how much I had been missing vivid luminescence!

Flashing lights of every colour seem to surround me completely. Every direction in which I turn, I see more and more brilliant lights, many blinking on and off, which adds to the effect. Some seem to depict outlines of female Earther bodies. Most form letters and words, highlighting the purposes of the establishments. As I read these, I know that I must be in the correct vicinity. I have been trained to recognize the most likely areas in which to locate the nnn-Asi-t.

And this, undoubtably, is one.

Oh yes, certainly the Earthers themselves are responsible for a great deal of these businesses which feature sexual entertainment, but the ones that take this a step further—the ones designed to corrupt the children and lead them to the malevolence—are not of this world.

I take a deep breath. I know that I must be close. Close to *them*, which also means that I am close to an opportunity—and responsibility—to truly help these Earthers.

I walk past the windows filled with photographs of nearly naked females. I walk past the store whose words indicate that inside is '*every kind of sexual toy imaginable... and then some*'. I walk toward the darkness of the alleyway, for there I have already seen shapes moving ghostlike amid the shadows.

Now I can hear their voices more clearly. A chill runs down my spine, but this one is not due to the coolness of the air...

I am listening to my first nnn-Asi-t on this planet.

I have no doubt of this. I focus. I must keep my mental shield in place, to avoid alerting it through my thoughts. I am close enough to hear its words and my jaws clench as I listen. These words are encouraging a couple of young boys to try *smack*. I know only vaguely what that is, but I understand quite completely that it is a weapon to further the cause of the nnn-Asi-t. Anger warms my insides as I listen to it promise all sorts of delights and satisfactions. I am careful to temper my anger with calm and determination.

What would be the best course of action? Certainly, that would be to speak to the boys away from the influence of the nnn-Asi-t. I could wait, and then follow them. But that thought disturbs me because if I do that, I might be too late. They might then be already under the influence of the drug and the nnn-Asi-t.

I could interfere now. I have a shield which my mind can produce to keep my thoughts from being read by the nnn-Asi-t. I glance over my shoulder, though. There are people behind me, back on the sidewalk, and I cannot be certain that there is not another nnn-Asi-t lurking among them.

But now I see the nnn-Asi-t in front of me. It has changed its form so that it appears as a human. It grips an injector in its hand and extends this toward the first of the Earther youths.

I shout to the boys to run—

Fortunately, they do. Quickly they disappear among the shadows, toward the far end of the alley, likely assuming that I am a law enforcement officer.

For a brief moment, my eyes meet those of what I believe is an nnn-Asi-t. The deep, silvery flash from those eyes then confirms my judgement. I am grateful that I used my pigment-suppressant prudently. Had I not allowed my body ample time, a tell-tale reddish glow from my own eyes could have led the nnn-Asi-t to attack.

The nnn-Asi-t is slightly confused. It returns my stare, then suddenly flees.

Is there still time for me to reach the youths before it does? I call out to the boys once more, preparing to run after them—

Suddenly something from behind has grabbed my arm, restraining me. I turn. An older, dark-skinned man's deep brown eyes bore into mine. They seem filled with an immense sadness. "Don't bother. No use. You'll only get hurt. Get outta this place before you—*get out!* Get away!" He shoves me back, in the direction of the busy sidewalk. I watch him as he shuffles away, a long, tattered coat nearly dragging behind him on the pavement.

He is an Earther. I have no doubt of this. I wonder if he has had some kind of contact with the nnn-Asi-t. I begin to follow him but after only a few steps, I have lost sight of him among the shadows separating me from the busy, well-lit sidewalk. I gaze back into the depths of the dark alley and blink twice to store the image and experience in my memory. I look toward where I saw the tattered man and repeat the procedure.

Already this body is becoming weary, and I am quite aware that I must be prepared to perform as well as possible when I return to the telephone line tomorrow. As this day is on what they call the *weekend*, the phone centre needs well-qualified assistance during both the day and night.

After one more glance back into the alley, I begin to head in the direction of my apartment building. The contrast is quite startling as I leave the area with its crowded sidewalks and brightly flashing coloured lights. I am entering a place where only high, straight poles pierce the increasing darkness with their pale lights perched atop them. It would be very dull, indeed, if not for the accompanying lights from the houses along the streets.

The cool breeze is becoming stronger and now the air is what I would call *cold*. I smile at the thought of the warmth awaiting me when I see the welcome lights of the little variety store just ahead. It is here that I purchase the newspapers which keep me informed of so many of the situations on Earth. I only wish that they could say something directly about the nnn-Asi-t influence which leads to what Earthers might think of as *misfortune* and *accidents*. I rely on such things as I do not have a cellular phone, as do virtually all Earthers in this area. Information relayed through those devices could too easily be intercepted by the nnn-Asi-t, and, anyway, my kind communicates more effectively without such items.

The door creaks as I open it. It is old. The variety store is the front of an old house, its owner possibly living in the house section. I greet the spectacled gentleman behind the counter. He seems kind and gentle, and I genuinely like him. He speaks a bit of the weather and, again, I am a bit surprised when he uses the word *mild*. But I smile and speak the expected words. As I bid him goodnight and step once more toward the door leading to the cold outside, I am startled to see a tall man, standing in the open doorway, now approaching me—

"Kay!" Smiling broadly, he says that he recognizes my voice.

This cannot be happening! He must be someone whom I counselled on the telephone crisis line! All that I can think of is that this could cause problems. My heart pounding, I hurry away. We at the telephone line are to keep our identities confidential. In my panic, I have forgotten what I was told to do in this circumstance—

By the time I remember, I am nearly at the front door of my building.

My heart aches as I gasp for breath. I feel badly. I feel foolish. I do not know the identity of the man, although I recognized his voice rather vaguely. Now, if he calls me again at the crisis line, I must certainly apologize and explain the importance of maintaining a strictly counsellor-client relationship.

And apologize again. I feel so torn inside. This must be a person in need of emotional support. I can only hope that I have not made his situation worse!

Chapter Five

Jared's insides were raging, his heart *pound-pounding* so hard that he thought it might burst right out of his chest. Despite the chill in the air, after walking up only one flight of the stairs, he could feel beads of sweat on his face. Yet, somehow, he managed to control himself and not give in to the temptation to slam the door as hard as he could. Breathing heavily from exertion and anger, he stood, and let the door close itself behind him. He stayed where he was, in the entrance of his apartment beside the closet. His jacket was open and hanging half off his shoulders. Besides the anger, there was something else seething inside of him.

Hurt.

Sighing deeply, he pulled the light jacket off and tossed it to the floor, where it lay in a bluish heap. He kicked off his runners and stumbled like a blind man to the one chair, across from the sofa. As despair threatened to once more creep upward inside him from the pit of his stomach, he collapsed into the chair and held his head in his trembling hands.

How could she have *done* that? Dammit, she ran off like he was an attacker or something! And, to make everything worse, the older man behind the counter had stared at him like he was a criminal…

And Jared *knew* it was her. There was no doubt about it. He had been about to enter the little store, had been standing there with the door open. He'd been listening to her, attracted by the happy familiarity of that voice—so happy to *see* her—

But she had actually run away from him. Yes, okay, he had startled her. That much he could understand. An *excuse me* or something he could have understood. But he *couldn't* understand how she would actually run off down the street! *He* knew *that it was her!* It had been more than just her voice. He *knew* it.

Okay, Jared. Calm down. Get yourself together. You just scared her. Don't beat yourself up about it.

Sitting sat back in the chair, he took a long breath. Of course, in her profession she had to keep her anonymity. He'd still be able to talk on the phone with her. It was just professional distance, that was all. They had to keep the professional counsellor-client relationship. He *knew* that. But still…

Dammit though. That look on her face—that *keep away from me* look. *Keep away from me.*

Marjorie had said that, too, once. That awful day when she'd told him there was someone else. Jared sighed. That familiar ache deep inside was growing once again, sending tendrils crawling upward, reaching right inside of his heart.

His thoughts became a memory. *Marjorie.* Marjorie with her raven hair and wonderful deep blue eyes. Marjorie with her curvy figure and full lips. He recalled how turned on he could get just by watching her as she walked toward him. She had been simply the most beautiful woman he'd ever known. And she had been *his.* How he had adored her looks, but also her confidence, her outspokenness.

Hell and damnation! I hurt! I still hurt! Marjorie! Why? What in hell did I do wrong?

Staring at the window, with the lights of evening gleaming through at him, his thoughts drifted back to the memory of Kay's startled face. Not an attractive face like Marjorie's—at least, not with that terrified expression on it! With a different facial expression, she might have been attractive. At least a bit. In his memory, her skin had a pinkish tinge as though she'd just got back from a sunny beach holiday. He was seeing the deep reddish tones of her shoulder-length auburn hair sparkling in the light from the overhead fixture in the store. She was small and lean. Maybe an athletic build. Hard to tell with the jacket zipped up all the way to her throat. No, not really his type. Too thin. No curves.

He didn't know if he could ever forget those deep brown eyes, wide with surprise. And shock—

Shock. Why *shock*? *Unless she knew who he was, too.*

Of course. She might well have recognized *his* voice. But that would mean she knew who he was when she ran away—

And that she had *rejected* him. After all their discussions about rejection. The ultimate irony.

He crossed the room to his laptop and sat down with it on his sofa. He had to get her out of his mind. Thinking about her, and about Marjorie and rejection was simply going to do him no good at all. Manipulating the mouse, he scrolled through some of his favourite sites. But even his favourite sites about beautiful women failed to distract him. Not even his games. Still restless, he plugged in his earbuds and found some of his music. He lay back on the sofa, feet on his coffee table, focussing on the driving rhythms. It helped to keep the thoughts from torturing him, but his gaze began to focus more on the phone in his hand. It was a *phone*, after all. And phones had been originally created for one main purpose. Alexander Graham Bell. A long, long time ago.

Maybe she was working tonight. Maybe she was going to head over there after she'd stopped at her apartment or house to get changed or something. Maybe she was there. Right there. Within reach. He could talk to her again. He could explain what happened, tell her how he felt. And she would apologize. She would explain that she'd overreacted. She'd just been startled, that was all—

Or she would tell him to leave her alone.

Keep away from me.

No. He just didn't dare take that risk.

Suddenly he realized that he didn't even know anymore what song he was listening to. He took out his earbuds, turned the music off and closed his eyes.

He saw her face. Her startled face. And the back of her as she ran away.

"Dammit," he moaned, wishing that, somehow, she could hear him. Why couldn't he get her face out of his mind? There was nothing physically remarkable about it, yet there was something…something strange. And he couldn't for the life of him figure out what it was, or why it was important. But it *was* important.

Jared rose and walked to his balcony window to gaze out at the night again. His phone was still in his hand. He could feel it. His fingers toyed with it, savoured its touch. He gazed at it, suddenly fascinated.

He had no recollection of having looked up the number or pushing it. But suddenly, out of the blue it seemed, he could hear the usual greeting from the other end of the line.

I should just hang up. They won't know who it was—

But, somehow, he couldn't. He heard himself ask about Kay. His voice seemed to be coming from someone else. He heard the male voice tell him that Kay wasn't there, but that he would be happy to be of help. He heard his own voice reassure the other man that, no, he'd be okay, thanks.

Still gazing out the window, his eyes fixed on the sight of the streetlight at the top of its pole. Its light seemed to seep outwardly to dissipate into the night sky. How he wished that he could do that, too. Everything seemed to have taken on a dreamlike quality. He could just stand here forever, transfixed by that light reaching outward into the darkness.

Jared closed his eyes, scrunched their lids together and massaged the top of his nose between them with his fingers.

Get real, Jared.

Suddenly he turned and strode purposefully across the small room. He pulled on his blue jacket and then his shoes. Grabbing his keys, he shoved his phone into his inside jacket pocket and opened his door.

He headed outside to make his way to MIKE'S.

His head throbbed, and his mouth was dry. Moaning, he hated the sunlight for prying between his eyelids as his fingers rubbed at his eyes in an attempt to deny the morning. He sighed, detesting the incessant pounding of his head.

It wasn't because of the beer, he was sure. He was positive that his misery stemmed from the dreams that had haunted him, over and over again, all night long. He'd kept seeing *her* face. And it wasn't even a remarkable face. In fact, it was uninteresting. There was nothing about it, really, that appealed to him. Not like Marjorie's. Marjorie's beautiful heart-shaped face, black hair so dark that it almost gleamed deep blue in the sunlight. Her wonderful, jaw-length hair that framed that wonderful face so perfectly. And dark blue eyes…

When he thought of her, that ache—from somewhere in his soul's abyss—began all over again.

He sighed once more, pulling the pillow across his face to try to block out the vision. But, of course, it didn't work. The sight was still there. As he lay there, he wondered briefly if he could just smother himself with the pillow.

And he saw the vision yet again—Kay's rather boring face floating in the air like a balloon, and Marjorie's beside it. They would start out close to him, then slowly drift farther and farther away. And his father's too, as he had lain on the hospital bed, then slowly but steadily floating away, away, away.

Dammit. Pushing aside the pillow, he shoved the covers away with his feet. He rose and showered, determined to wash away all the awful feelings that seemed destined to haunt him forever. Plugging in the electric kettle, he stood beside it at the kitchen counter, feeling numbness and depression begin to nag him yet again. Sipping at his coffee, he finally made a decision. It was something that had to be done anyway, and it would get him out of his apartment and moving around.

Betty and Tom had given him a lift home last night. Although Jared hadn't thought that he was under the influence to the extent that he couldn't drive safely, fortunately, they'd insisted that he should be cautious. Jared had thought it rather absurd—he'd only had two beers. After all, he didn't really have enough money to buy more. But he knew that they were only being kind, so he'd consented. Now he needed to retrieve his Beetle. It wasn't far, but it was a bit more of a walk than he was in the mood for. He just needed to stop at the variety store for a bus ticket.

At the store, as his hand gripped the door handle, he paused, remembering the last time he'd been here. For a moment, he was frozen in place, almost afraid of opening the door and seeing her there again.

Suddenly the door opened, the handle being pulled out of his hand. A shiver ran through him…

It wasn't her. "Sorry," said an older lady with white hair.

"No problem," he muttered. He'd been startled, and now he felt downright silly as she gingerly made her way around him.

Jared shook his head to clear it and walked inside.

He retrieved his old VW and was relieved that it started on the first try. It was a rather beautiful day, with the sun beaming down and caressing his face with its warmth as he drove. Rounding the corner, he pulled into his parking space beside the apartment building, stepped out of the car and made his way inside the building lobby. Here he paused, giving his mailbox a glance. Empty. It dawned on him that he hadn't checked his email yet.

Inside his apartment, he pulled out his phone and checked for messages. Other than junk mail, there was just one, from Betty. He answered it, reassuring her that he was fine and that he appreciated the ride home. His fingers lingered, his index finger travelling through his list of contacts…

His heart pounded, then seemed to skip a beat completely when he heard the familiar greeting—

And *her* voice.

Suddenly they were both talking at once. As his apology tumbled out, he was surprised to learn that Kay was saying that she was sorry too! He laughed. It felt good.

"No," he was chuckling, "it's all right, Kay! It was *my* fault! I shouldn't have come up to you like that, especially out of the dark! It was thoughtless of me. Of course, you were startled—"

"No, Jerry. That is—that's—not good enough. I should have had more presence of mind than that. Yes, we're to remain as anonymous as possible, but I certainly did not need to seem as rude as I must have. I *am* sorry, Jerry."

A long sigh escaped him. It felt as though that awful ache from deep inside of him had left him for good. There was a bit of an awkward silence for a moment.

"So...how have things been going for you, Jerry?"

"Oh. Okay, I guess. Um. *No*! No—better than that, thanks to you. I—I'm definitely coping better with—with things in general, now that you've pointed out some of what's been happening to me emotionally. So... I guess I should be thanking you. Um. Thanks again!"

"You're quite welcome. That's why I am here, after all. Is there... anything else?"

"Um. Well, yes. Kay, I really like you. I—I'd like to see you."

The silence on the other end of the line felt like forever.

"Jerry. Jerry, that's all been explained to you. If I am going to help you to talk things out on the phone, it is not advisable—"

"I know. I *know*. I understand all that. Really. It's just—it's just that I really like you, Kay. I'd really like to get to know you better..." He wanted to shout at the top of his lungs that he couldn't get her out of his mind.

"Jerry." She sounded very businesslike. Her voice had lost much of its softness, its gentleness. There was a firmness to it that hadn't been there before. "You think you want to see *Kay*. You're forgetting that *Kay* does not—doesn't—even really exist. She is someone carrying out counselling responsibilities, and that is all. You—you do not really know *me* at all. It could be that you are transferring to me feelings that you had for Marjorie—"

"No! Dammit, Kay, or whoever you are, I know enough about counselling to know that this isn't simply me transferring feelings for someone else to you! Please—"

"Jerry, I am sorry that this has happened. Please. Think about this. If you examine your feelings closely, I'm sure you will see that this must be related to transference. Jerry, you *don't know* me. I am trying quite hard to word this carefully. I don't want you to think of this as rejection. I am your counsellor and that is all you know me as. Jerry, you understand what I am saying."

"Yes." His voice was suddenly cold, just as he felt inside. "I know what you're saying. I thank you for all your help. But, believe me, you *don't* understand. Bye." He looked at the phone still grasped in his hand. Yes, she was theoretically right. But, somehow, he couldn't—or wouldn't—accept it. Something had happened when she'd looked into his eyes.

I'm not a romantic fool! But there was something. Something so very different—and I have no idea what it was.

He had to see her again. And the bit of trembling in her voice had confirmed for him that she really did care.

Another cool evening as the sun began to set. A slight breeze was rustling the leaves. The woman was trying to pull her dark red jacket more tightly around herself to ward off the chill. She opened the door to the little shop, relieved to feel the warmth from inside against her cheeks. After selecting a few newspapers from the rack, she reached inside of her wallet for the correct amount of money. Suddenly she frowned.

She did not see the man behind her at first, but rather sensed the dimming of the overhead light to her left when his tall form blocked the illumination from the ceiling fixture.

"I'll take care of that," the familiar voice said softly, extending a few bills to the man behind the counter.

She gazed up at him and thanked him before she tried to step around him to make her way to the door. But he was there first. His hand was on the doorknob and he pushed the door open, waiting for her to go through the doorway before he did. She stepped onto the sidewalk just outside the store. Although he half-expected her to hurry away, she stayed where she was, her eyes downcast…

He watched the scarlet highlights of her hair as the glow from the streetlight danced among them. She was opening and closing her mouth as though she was trying to say something. There was a vulnerability about her at that moment that touched him inside. For once, it was a good feeling.

Jared reached his hand to touch her chin and, gently, tilted her face upward so that their eyes could meet.

Her brown eyes seemed huge. There was a veiled look about them, as though she was prepared this time. He didn't see that—that *something* in them that he'd seen last time. But there was a wonderful depth to those eyes that he'd never experienced before. It was almost as though this woman held the very secret to life itself.

She wasn't beautiful. Yet she was.

And she smiled. He felt like he was watching a new star being born—a brightening and intensifying glow somewhere out in the vastness of space. She touched his hand, then, gently yet also quite firmly. Then she turned and walked away, giving him one last glowing glance over her slim shoulder.

Jared stood, unable to move. He stared after the small figure as it headed through shadows, then re-emerged in the light. He couldn't tear his gaze from the reddish brilliance of her hair gleaming now and then as she passed beneath the glow of the streetlights.

He felt no sense of rejection this time. No anger. No loneliness.

Only a wonderful, deep sense of peace.

Chapter Six

Have I, then, done the right thing? I have explained to him that he is experiencing transference, as he surely must already have realized. I have been firm. Yet I have also been kind. And I also used my ability to leave him immune to the seductions of the nnn-Asi-t, *and* I have left him with the deepest sense of peace that I could convey. Surely all of that was correct.

I have served as a responsible counsellor for this client, although it had become a bit more challenging as time passed.

So…why do I still see his face whenever I close my eyes? An unremarkable face, to be certain. A simple nose, eyes, mouth, chin. Not much different from any other Earthers. It must be that I am experiencing responses from the Earther-like parts of this body.

I close my eyes for a moment in order to clear my mind. I must focus on more pressing thoughts. I must analyze what occurred tonight at the schoolyard. The young man I saw had so much anger locked inside of him and did not know how to set it free. He did not realize that he was directing it at himself. He did not know that he was experiencing the agony of failure. He had been prepared to cause as much damage to the school building as he was able. The brick was already in his hand when I approached him—

And I also saw the nnn-Asi-t as it had drifted away once more into the shadows of night.

I recall the turmoil in the poor boy's mind as he responded to the urgings of the nnn-Asi-t—until he felt the peace of my own thoughts. I feel as though as I will never forget the anguish in the boy's eyes as he turned to look at me. We talked. He cried as he became aware of what had been going on inside of him.

But when I left him, he was at peace with himself. Stronger. And immune to further interference by the nnn-Asi-t. Yes. It had gone well. It would have been better, though, if I had arrived in time to destroy the nnn-Asi-t. Yet I must be grateful for the little bit that I have accomplished.

What was that? A sound I had not heard earlier. An unfamiliar one. I stop walking, remain still, and listen—

And the noise stops too.

Nnn-Asi-t? No. I think not...although I cannot be absolutely certain without sensing for one or seeing it. Should I be more concerned? Should I perhaps be alarmed? Is there something that the representatives failed to teach me? No. I do not believe that that could be possible.

Still, I am concerned. Surely there must be dangers and challenges here for which I am not completely prepared. After all, even our representatives cannot be expected to understand *everything* there is to know about this third planet from its sun.

All around me is quiet, save for the occasional traffic sounds from streets a little way from here. I begin to walk once more and yet again I hear the unfamiliar sound. Footsteps? It could be footsteps from somewhere behind me. Someone might be following me. It must be an Earther, for it lacks the stealth which would suggest it to be an nnn-Asi-t...

But why should some Earther follow me? I am not dressed as the sort to attract attention. And why would he or she choose to be out of my sight? I stop again to listen. Perhaps it is Jerry. No. I dismiss that thought. I do not believe that he would attempt to follow me secretly after our encounter.

Yet I cannot hear footsteps. The wind has come up so suddenly that all I can hear is its rush in my ears as it blows my hair and feels as though it wants to blow my jacket right off me. How I wish that I could adjust to the chill of this place! Holding my jacket as snuggly around me as I can, I continue walking again. This is a more open area, and I hurry to get to the next block where houses line the street and—I hope—will block this wind! Even as I make haste, crossing the street to reach the next block, the rain begins.

I try to look over my shoulder to see if there is, indeed, someone following me, but all that happens is that the awful wind has pushed down my hood. Now I try to pull it up once more and secure it as I walk as quickly as I can. We knew about the weather in this area, and yet I feel so unprepared. I should have purchased a warmer and more rainproof jacket! I try to walk faster, yet doing so is more difficult as the rain and wind seem to work together against me—

I must get to the warmth of my apartment as soon as possible! I am not accustomed to this type of horrible weather and now I worry about the added stress on this body—outwardly Earther yet inwardly very much not.

I am looking downward to try and avoid the next blast of freezing wind and rain on my face, and I struggle to walk quickly as the gale fights me at every step. Frustration is creeping in now, for I thought that I heard footsteps behind me again. I tell myself that I could not have detected anything like that over the din of the winds. But I think that I saw the shadow of something over my shoulder. Surely not! How could any Earther think of pursuing anyone through a gale such as this! It just couldn't be.

I hasten my steps as much as I can toward the glimmer of lights from the building ahead. I pull my hood down lower over my face as the driving rain feels like cold needles piercing my skin. Just ahead now, just across the street.

I gasp. In front of me is an apartment building, with inviting lights glowing in the lobby area—

But this is not my building! It had certainly looked like mine when I had stolen glances at it from further away. But now I see that it is only a three-storey building, not a tall one like my own. The tops of the blowing trees had hidden the fact that the building was not taller. Still, I hope that the front door is not locked, as, regardless of anything else, I must get away from what is now an awfully cold downpour.

Suddenly, a light from a second-floor window catches my attention. A face—a surprisingly familiar face appears and then is gone—

Another blast of frigid wetness smites me mercilessly across the cheek. I turn my cold, wet face away from it. It is impossible for me to focus as I struggle against the gale again to pull up my soggy hood. The wind is brutal—it seems determined to knock me down. I manage to stagger to the glass door and fumble for the handle…

The door has opened! A warm hand firmly grips the arm of my sodden jacket and pulls me inside to a wonderful, heated alcove. The contrast is incredible, for the cold wind and wetness have ceased their torture. It is still in here as I stand and drip water onto the floor…

After a few seconds to catch my breath, I look upward and into the face of my benefactor, knowing already whom it is that I will see.

Jerry.

"Come in," he says. "Come away from that terrible wind!" He frowns over my shoulder at the door which, the noises behind me say, struggles to stay closed against the onslaught.

I have no choice in the matter, as he has my hand in his and is pulling me in the direction of the staircase. But I stop. I turn, gazing back through the sight of the gale beyond the glass. Leaves and debris are swirling as the rain is blown almost horizontally.

What about my responsibilities? What if there are Earthers out there who even now need my assistance? "But—I have to—"

Jerry, putting a hand on my shoulder, comes closer. He, too, stares through the glass at the cruelty of the gale. "You can't do anything out there! And neither can anyone else. Come inside and get warm. Then I'll drive you home."

I look into his blue eyes and give a little gasp. He has responded incredibly deeply to our encounter of the other evening. His spirit, his presence is strong. Very strong. Especially for an Earther…

For a moment he has projected, without any knowledge of having done so, his own peace into my being through our physical contact. My conflicted emotions are gone. Already I feel a warmth inside as I follow him up the stairs.

Now that I have experienced contact which *he* has initiated, I understand what has occurred. He would have felt my approaching presence as I struggled in the direction of his building. That is why he looked out through his window just as I drew near. In all probability, he has no idea what has happened—

And I must not tell him, although my insides are in a turmoil as they struggle to understand *how* this could have occurred.

He opens the door to his apartment, holds it open for me as I step inside to stand on the mat. "What're you doing in this area, Kay?" He takes my dripping jacket from my shoulders. It is so wet that it appears to be a much darker shade of red than it really is. Jerry's forehead is puckered in a frown as he studies just how wet it is. I feel badly about the little pools of wetness that gather on the floor…

"I—I was heading home when the storm came up. It came up so suddenly! I—I guess in my haste to escape it I must have taken a wrong turn. I saw the lights from this building and thought that this must be *my* building…" Suddenly I feel rather foolish. This sounds so simplistic, but I cannot tell him about thinking I was being followed. He would not understand.

"Well," he says with a sigh, "I'll hang your jacket up in the bathroom for now. C'mon in and I'll get you something nice and hot to drink. Coffee okay?"

I nod, still standing on the now rather damp mat by the door. I have never tried this 'coffee'—this social drink of theirs. I push off my wet shoes and take a step toward the small table he gestured to in the kitchen, but my socks make squelchy noises. I stop and pull them off, watching the water drip onto the mat beneath my soggy shoes. Barefoot, I walk to the table and sit down on the nearest chair. I feel badly because my black pants, too, are wet, and will no doubt be leaving dampness on the chair.

Jerry returns with several towels, which he extends to me. I put one on the chair for me to sit on. It feels good to dry my soaked hair while I watch him pour hot water from the kettle into mugs. Just the look of the steam helps to stop my shivering.

"What d'you take?"

I pause in my towelling to ponder the meaning of the strange question. I have no idea at all what he is talking about. I must have appeared puzzled because when I look at Jerry, his eyes are twinkling, and he has an amused smile on his face.

"In your coffee," he says gently.

I wonder if he considers me to be feeble-minded. "Oh, of course." I force myself to feign a chuckle. "Um—the usual."

He is smiling broadly now. Suddenly I notice what an endearing smile it is. "Milk and sugar then."

I return his smile. It feels quite natural to do so. I close my fingers eagerly around the steaming mug. No matter what type of liquid is inside of it, holding the warmth of the mug itself is a delicious sensation. I sip the contents, not wishing to appear ungrateful. This body does not require the nourishment depended upon by Earthers, but small amounts will cause it no harm—except that I find the odour and taste rather unpleasant. I put forth my best effort, not wishing to offend, as I understand how popular this drink is among Earthers, especially when the experience is shared with others.

I do not manage to swallow very much of the drink, but it is quite peaceful sitting here in Jerry's kitchen. I know that part of this sense of peace is related to his unexpected sensitivity to my encounter. Although he is unaware of it, we are communicating. We are sharing this deep peace. Were we on my planet, it could be a first step toward bonding…

Shaking my head slightly, I push the thought from my mind. I am not at home. I am on an assignment. I sense Jerry watching me. I look up to meet his blue eyes.

The experience is wonderful. Yet disquieting.

"Thank you so much, Jerry. But I really must go." I put the warm mug back down on the white table.

He opens his mouth to protest, but I shake my head firmly. Resolutely, he rises to get my jacket from the bathroom. I am grateful that he is not near me at the moment. As I sit on the chair, I am struggling to pull my wet socks back on my feet. It seems an impossible task. The material is simply not easy to maneuver when soaked!

He returns, and we exchange glances. The jacket which he is holding is also still quite wet. He regards me with raised eyebrows.

"With or without your jacket on—socks or no socks—you can still accept a ride home from me."

And so, I gather my wet belongings and we make our way back down the staircase. We pause at the bottom of the stairs. Outside, things look formidable. If anything, the wind seems even stronger now. The rain has not let up at all. Jerry steps forward and, just as he is reaching to grasp the door handle, the gale suddenly decides to help, and forces the door inward. A cold spray greets us both before the door closes once again. Puddles on the floor confirm that this is not the first time that this has happened recently.

I had thought my shivering to be imperceptible. But suddenly Jerry's long arm is around my shoulders. Sighing, he gives me a little squeeze. "I'm afraid you're not going anywhere tonight, Kay."

We turn and head once again to the staircase. "Andrea."

"Pardon me?" He stops on the first step and faces me.

"My name is Andrea. Are you really Jerry?"

He steps back down so that we are on the same ground level. Still, he must look downward to meet my eyes. Small dimples appear in his cheeks as he grins. "Not quite. I guess I didn't have much imagination when I chose my name for your program. I'm Jared." He extends a hand as a broad smile begins to light his face. Taking my hand in his, he shakes it. "Pleased to meet you," he says and bows his head slightly in my direction. "Now let's get away from that cold doorway!"

As I follow him back up the stairs, I am thinking that I truly have no other choice. There is no other place for me to go. And, if Jerry began to drive me home, we might not be able to continue in such a strong wind. It would be rather difficult for any driver to see adequately in such an onslaught.

As we re-enter his apartment, he directs me to his bathroom while he fetches me some dry clothing. Standing in the bathroom doorway, he explains apologetically that I will have to roll up the sleeves on the sweatshirt and legs of the sweatpants, as these will be too long for me. But I smile in gratitude. It does not matter to me at all, as long as the clothing is warm and dry.

I make my way to the living area, where he sits on the brown sofa, sipping coffee. I decline his offer of some, knowing that this beverage is not something that I wish to try again. His mouth twists, though. It appears that Earthers are not contented with their beverage unless someone else is drinking, too. And so it is that I accept a glass of water and sit on his big, cushy chair. Gratefully I let myself sink into it, happy that the socks which he lent me—although large for my feet—are dry, warm and soft.

Jared talks. He seems very pleased to have someone with whom he can share his evening. And it is a pleasant, relaxed conversation, not the continued counselling session which it could have become…

As night falls, we gaze at the continuing wind and rain. He asks about me. I am, of course, careful with my answers. I must not give away any information about my assignment. If Earthers knew anything about the true nature of the serious difficulties on their planet, a terrible panic would almost certainly ensue.

And that would be exactly what the nnn-Asi-t would hope for.

We nibble on sandwiches which he has made for us, although he eats much more than I would ever be capable of. The tuna inside is tasty, but I have no need of it, and so I nibble sparingly. I find that I am enjoying conversation with this young man. He is humorous and entertaining. It is very relaxing to forget, just for awhile, the true nature of my business here. I talk a bit and listen much. I smile much. I know that night is growing deeper, and I am thankful that I am not scheduled for the phone line until the day after tomorrow.

I do not recall at what point we agreed that we should both get some rest. I do not remember all that much about the discussion regarding who should sleep in the bed and who the sofa, except for my pointing out the logic of the smaller person occupying the smaller surface.

It is *cold.* At least it seems quite cold to me. I shiver and shiver and draw the blanket more tightly around me. Yet my teeth continue to chatter. I try to lie quietly, but such is impossible when one's body is constantly in tremors.

I did not know that I had disturbed his rest. But dimly I become aware of something wonderfully warm. I am not consciously aware of what it is. In the haze of my fatigued mind, everything seems to revolve around physical sensations. Something warm is touching my arm, my shoulder, and I feel myself finally begin to relax once more as the terrible shivering lessens. Then I am vaguely aware of the delicious nearness of the other body as it holds me close until the chattering of my teeth has finally stopped completely.

The nearness begins to intensify. Lips reach down to caress my own and I find this body—Earther and yet not—responding naturally and easily. There is no conscious thought. Only sensations of wonderful warmth and gentle—yet exciting—touching.

As the caresses increase in intensity and our hearts beat more quickly and harder, other sensations develop within this body. From somewhere deep inside of my mind, I know that this must not occur...

But it is too late.

Chapter Seven

Dammit. If she stays silent much longer, I'm going to lose what's left of my mind!

Trying to be patient, Jared took a deep breath to try to relax. Then he found himself drumming his fingers irritably on the arm of the chair. His gaze was on the woman. She was sitting as she had been for what seemed an *awfully* long time, staring out through the balcony window. At nothing, he was willing to bet. He watched as the late morning sunlight gleamed, ferreting out the beautiful scarlet strands hidden among the more brownish hairs. He'd never known that so many wonderfully different shades of red existed...

Until now. Until Andrea.

And what had he done? Gone and blown it all, that's what. *Dammit! You'd think I might have learned a little self-control by now!*

He was furious with himself. But even as he was thinking again about what an animal he was, he was remembering once more the poor creature she'd seemed as she'd lain there, trembling with cold, teeth chattering. Suddenly he was reliving the compassion he had for her when he'd begun to touch her, trying to help her get warm. And he savoured the memory of how wonderful it felt to hold her against him, how natural and right it had seemed to brush his lips across her brilliant, soft hair and then her lips and skin...

And how her tender responses had provided him with what seemed the most tremendous moments of his life.

Yes. He was an animal. No better than a tom cat. But he also knew he'd give anything in the world to have it happen again, just the same way. How could anything so perfect have been so wrong?

And it *was* wrong. There was absolutely no doubt about it. Somehow, he didn't even have to look at her to feel what she was feeling. The whole damn room seemed to be filled with guilt, confusion, anger, dismay.

Great, Jared. Terrific lover you *are.* He buried his head in his hands.

Andrea had apologized, prepared to accept all the blame. She'd seemed absolutely devastated.

And she still did.

Maybe it had been impulsive. Maybe it had been wrong. But Jared still found it impossible to understand the great depth of her remorse. *She'd* caressed *him* at times! It must have seemed right to *her*, too.

Jared raised his head and looked through his fingers at her. So incredibly different from Marjorie. Andrea was beautiful. *Colourful.* He'd never been involved with a woman who had reddish hair before this. Other women seemed pale and bland in comparison. No other woman had ever possessed the great depth of character that seemed to define Andrea. He stared, transfixed by the image of this creature with the endless shades of red running through her hair, her eyes fixed straight ahead as though focussed on something in the distance. But he knew that her eyes were blank. Focussed on nothing, focussed on something inside of herself.

Jared just couldn't understand this. She seemed to feel so guilty, so sure it was all her fault. And *wrong*. But—if she was determined to blame herself—he was more than willing to forgive and—*no*. Not forget. Never forget.

He didn't want to forget.

So why couldn't she forgive herself? And forget, if she wanted to? Maybe she'd been a virgin. Maybe she'd been saving herself for her wedding night—

He shook his head at the thought. That just seemed ridiculous. *Nobody thinks like that anymore!* Maybe there was someone else. That had to be the explanation. Yeah. Maybe she was afraid that she'd hurt someone else. If that was the case, why didn't she just *say* so?

Why had she simply said *I cannot explain* when he'd asked?

He'd apologized over and over again and even said he forgave her when she'd been so horribly remorseful. But then she'd lapsed into this overwhelming silence, no longer responding to his questions or comments. Jared was getting downright scared. He had strong feelings about this little lady, and he wanted desperately to see her again. He didn't want to lose her.

Yet, somehow, he felt like he'd never really had her in the first place.

He began chewing on his thumbnail again, over and over, even though it was so short now that there wasn't much still there. But then he stopped. She was rising from the sofa, her eyes still facing something beyond the window. Jared sat, frozen, thumb slowly moving away from his lips, uncertain. He'd spent so long hoping for some sort of reaction from her. And now that there was one, he was afraid to move.

Eyes downcast, she stepped slowly away from the window. She was once more dressed in her shirt and red jacket, black pants. As she crossed in front of him, she began to move her hand in his direction, but stopped herself. His eyes were on her face as she mouthed the word *sorry,* but she made no sound. At the door, she slipped on her shoes. She said nothing at all, although she gazed at him sorrowfully for a few seconds.

Agony seemed to seize Jared inside. Somehow, he knew that he was experiencing *her* dismay, and it almost overpowered him. He couldn't move or speak. He was helpless. And he hated himself for it. Finally, he managed to stand as he watched the door close. Tears stung his eyes.

"Andrea," he tried to call out. But his voice was nothing more than a hoarse whisper in the heavy silence of the room.

He blinked back the tears, his eyes fixed on the sight of the closed door. Now he turned and stepped to the window. Staring down at the slight figure, Jared gazed after her as she moved along the sidewalk, away from the front of the building. The storm of the night before had left a bright and sunny day in its aftermath. He watched the small woman, the sunlight caressing her as though the weather was begging for forgiveness after attacking her previously.

She stopped. Jared held his breath as she turned slowly, then stared upward at the window. At *him*.

He found himself transfixed by those deep, brown eyes. Somehow, he was feeling their tremendous warmth all the way up here. And there was something more. Something incredible, something that seemed vastly important. As he drank in everything those eyes extended to him, he knew that something was tremendously different.

Something had been exchanged between them—something wonderful.

And he had no idea what that could be.

For a time, Jared had just stood there looking out the window, as though he were incapable of moving. His inner being was still filled with a wonderful sense of peace, of warmth, of serenity. The image of her remained in his mind like a picture in his phone. It was as though she had never left at all. Still, he stood, feeling the breath flow in and out of him, his heart beating slowly, rhythmically, in a completely relaxed manner…

And it made no sense when he allowed logical thoughts to have their say. How in the world could he feel such deep contentment when the greatest love he'd ever known had just walked away? This was crazy. Yet it was true.

He had watched her leave. She'd felt terrible about what had happened between them. Yet she had left him with this strange sense that everything was quite okay.

But I should be miserable…

Whenever he thought of her—of last night—again he experienced the wonder of total love, passion, contentment.

He raised his mug to take another sip of coffee. It had gone cold. Pulling himself away from the window, Jared walked to the kitchen, where he dumped out the cold coffee, plugged in the kettle, and added fresh instant to the mug. When the water was hot, he finished making his fresh mugful. Somehow, the clicking sound of the spoon against the mug was regular, relaxing, like his heartbeat. Stepping across the living room to his small computer table, he sipped the hot drink while he looked through the latest news items. He realized that he hadn't yet checked his emails. But there was nothing startling there. No job offers.

For once, he didn't care. The sunlight bounced off the laptop's screen, forcing him to adjust it to avoid the glare.

Turning his head toward the window, he gazed at the sunshine. So strange that last night had seemed like a typhoon, yet today was beautiful. A metaphor for his life, perhaps?

He closed his laptop and rose. Today shouldn't be wasted. It was time to get some air. Grabbing his blue jacket, he shoved on his runners at the door. It was Monday. As he made his way down the stairs, he cast a glance at his mailbox. Empty. But that no longer seemed important. Jared made his way outside and pet Freddy as he passed by, the cat giving him a purr and a nudge in response. The air was cool despite the glorious sunlight. The passing storm seemed to have accelerated the move from summer's passing to true autumn, yet the warmth and brightness of the sun offered reassurance that there was still a bit of heat to come.

Jared had ventured outside with the intention of sorting out his thoughts as he walked. But the relaxation that flowed through him dominated everything. He found himself simply drifting, savouring the twitters of the birds as well as the honks of the geese, as they soared through the azure sky in their V formations. His eyes were drinking in the glory of the yellow and orange shades of the leaves fluttering gently to the ground. It was comfortingly quiet in this area, which suited the calmness of his spirit just now. Many of the residents of this community would be at their places of business, and the children in school.

After a time, though, he headed in the direction of the more commercial area, for no conscious reason.

A raised voice in the distance began to attract his attention—so discordant with the quiet and peace. Curious, he moved in that direction. When he'd come close enough to make out some of the content of the confusion, he saw a gathering.

About twenty or so people. Another bunch of protesters in front of the women's clinic. This was one of the newer clinics, he recalled, and the pro-life people had vowed to be there every day until abortions were no longer performed. There were frequent demonstrators on the weekends, of course, but they seemed able to get a few to come out on weekdays as well—

Maybe they're unemployed like me.

He stopped on the sidewalk across the street to watch for a minute or two. Jared had no strong feelings either way about the issue, but there was something interesting—something *different*—about this particular speaker. It didn't seem to be his voice, as it was not especially commanding or compelling. And his choice of words wasn't that stirring either...

Yet there was something unusual, something almost *magnetic*, about him, despite an unremarkable appearance. He appeared to be around forty or so, although he had one of those faces that could be almost any age. The man had light brown hair, a clean-shaven face and maybe brown eyes. It was difficult to see this from where Jared stood. It might have been difficult to determine the colour of his eyes, but there was certainly an *intensity* about them that couldn't be missed.

"This is nothing but a licensed death house," said the man through the microphone at the podium. "In here, countless innocent lives are taken every day. We ask those of you watching now to join us. Help us to save these poor, unborn souls!"

"Thank you, thank you, sir." A gentleman beside the speaker now moved close and turned the microphone towards himself. This man was a bit taller, with thinning hair. He wore the collar of a clergyman. Apparently, it was he who was in charge and not the strange, brown-haired man. The clergyman began to speak as the other man stepped aside. "We appreciate your words and support, everyone, but please, if anyone else would like to come forth and say a few words, advise us first of your intentions. Although our numbers are not great, we *do* have a prepared agenda. I thank all of you for your co-operation. Now, let us return to the words of our loving Father in Heaven..."

With that, the clergyman opened the Bible and began a scripture reading. The people in the crowd appeared to be listening, some attentively and others simply in a polite manner. The reading was interrupted, though, as a car pulled to the curb and three young women emerged. The two on either side were obviously intended as escorts through the group of onlookers and demonstrators. The young lady in the middle appeared to be rather frightened as she took the arm of her companions.

As the trio made its way toward the clinic, some of the demonstrators began to wave their placards and shout, turning towards them. A few, although not actually interfering with the trio, walked alongside and behind them, directing accusatory comments at the nervous-looking young woman in the middle. Undeterred, the threesome entered the clinic as a door was opened from inside and then closed firmly behind them. The protesters who'd followed continued to shout comments, but gradually ambled away from the door and back to join the rest of the crowd.

The clergyman shook his head solemnly. "Let us pray for another murdered child," he said softly into the microphone while the demonstrators bowed their heads. Some of the people stood quietly but were obviously praying.

Jared was watching the man who had been speaking when Jared had first arrived. For this man was not standing quietly like so many others. When the prayer had begun, he'd initially bowed his head like they had. But now, although his head was still slightly bowed, those intense eyes were busily scanning the faces of the people around him. Jared wondered why. He was a slightly built man, and as he began to move, Jared could see how strangely fluid and graceful he was, moving among the people almost as a professional dancer might.

Fascinated now, Jared couldn't take his eyes from the man, who seemed to *flow* from one person to another. He almost appeared to pass *through* each one as he glided along with the fluidity and grace of a cloud drifting gently through the sky.

Now Jared shook his head. He *couldn't* be seeing what he thought he was. As the slight man snaked his way through the small crowd, Jared was sure he saw a misty trail of some sort flowing from him. And when the man stopped moving, Jared could see the little trail begin to dissipate, like water vapour into the air.

But it wasn't vapour. It couldn't be. It seemed to come from the man—

The strange man now once more approached the front of the crowd to stand beside the clergyman and the microphone. But he waited patiently for the clergyman to finish speaking. Several in the crowd were murmuring, nodding in agreement with what the clergyman had been saying.

Now the strange man moved a bit closer so that he could be heard through the microphone. The clergyman glanced sideways at him as though to protest—

But the strange, slight man began to speak. As he did, he lifted his arms to gesture toward the heavens. He didn't seem to be saying anything of great importance, or anything much different from what had been said before. Some of it seemed garbled and unclear to Jared, but the little crowd was becoming more and more agitated. The more the little man spoke and gestured, the more upset the people appeared to become, even the clergyman.

Jared gasped, as now some people in the crowd were crying. Some even started screaming, and some ran to the clinic door and yelled death threats! Others began banging on the door, kicking it. Many were walking quickly around now, yelling loudly, waving their placards as though they might use them violently. A passerby began to hurry as he made his way along the sidewalk in front of the crowd, but was shoved inadvertently, and turned to mutter something at the woman who had jostled him.

Jared was astounded to see the woman, who only a moment before had her head bowed and was deeply in prayer, strike the man hard across the mouth. The passerby put a hand to his lip and looked at the blood on his fingers. Angry, he stepped toward the woman, but backed away and hurried once more past when others in the crowd shouted and jeered—

The people seemed to have gone quite mad by now. Although he was across the street from the scene, Jared found himself backing up until he felt the window of the storefront behind him. Still, he was unable to tear his gaze from the now violent mob. Some had begun heaving rocks and stones at the clinic. A few rushed into the street, threatening passing cars with their placards. Some cars stopped, horns honked, and angry drivers opened their windows to yell, but then sped away when confronted by what seemed like total chaos.

With a trembling hand, Jared reached inside his jacket for his phone to call the police, totally confused by what had just occurred. He'd never seen a gathering change completely in such a short time. *How can this be happening?* But as he prepared to punch in 911, a squad car pulled up at the curb in front of the mob. Two officers emerged and attempted to intervene with the crowd, two more patrol cars pulling in behind it.

Off to his left, Jared saw something moving. He glanced in that direction to see the strange, slight man almost gliding as he slipped away from the scene. Fascinated, Jared stepped after him. The gliding man turned left again, into an alley.

Jared followed. Suddenly the man stopped, hesitated. Turned. Their eyes met. Jared's spine felt like an icicle. He was staring into the *intensity* he'd noticed earlier. But then the man's eyes changed. Jared was sure he saw fear. But he couldn't be sure—

Because somehow the man seemed to simply slip away and Jared suddenly couldn't see him anywhere…only the greyish, silvery, misty trail as it slowly began to dissolve.

Chapter Eight

I am sensing the presence of an nnn-Asi-t. This is two consecutive nights that I have sensed it. I must act soon. But not until I have more knowledge of my adversary. Such a challenge is not something to be taken without planning and thought. Carefully, *carefully*, I lift my mind's shield just a bit, closing it quickly before the enemy might sense my own presence. It can be, as the Earthers say, a two-way street. We are fortunate, though, that they are not as skilled in detecting our presence as we are theirs. Tonight, I am not required for work with the phone line. Therefore, it must be tonight when I will approach and seek to learn more. Perhaps I will also intervene tonight. I do not yet know for certain…

I gaze in the direction of the place I have felt it to be. It is near the city's centre in a run-down section. This is the typical location for the malevolence of the enemy, for this is the type of setting—away from well-lit areas and prying human eyes—which they prefer. And where the vulnerable Earthers upon whom they prey frequently gather.

As I approach the area, it is not without trepidation. For the closer that I come, the stronger is the malevolence which I detect. This nnn-Asi-t is not likely to be as easy to deal with as some of the others have been. This much I have sensed already.

Were I to use utmost caution, I would send my signal to one of the others of my kind and request assistance. I do not, however, wish to do so without ample cause, as they are likely to be preoccupied with other nnn-Asi-t—and sending such a signal would increase the risk of a perceptive enemy sensing my presence.

I take a deep, cleansing breath in preparation and square my shoulders. As I walk, I take careful note of the details of my surroundings. Broken glass seems to lie everywhere. The always-cool wind seems to be constantly sending dirt and discarded bits of paper in my direction. In some of the spaces between old, abandoned buildings I see small whirlwinds comprised of dust and dirt.

Pausing in my steps, I sense the strong presence more clearly. I must shield my mind, though, so that it does not detect my nearness. Moving forward carefully, I stop at the corner of the building and listen. Although I can hear voices, I am not yet able to discern many of the words.

Cautiously, with complete silence, my mind totally shielded, I take a furtive look around the corner. I can see them—a group of perhaps fifteen youths. They are listening attentively to someone who is speaking in the middle of the small crowd—

The nnn-Asi-t.

It has taken the form of a tall man with a long, wiry frame. Its hair is dark but streaked with silver. On its face is a few days of beard growth. This is a typical form for them to adopt when dealing with youth. Someone older suggests experience, although not so old as to be perceived as weak by the young followers. It does not need to appear to be a strong man, as its strength comes from within.

As though to confirm their respect for the enemy, the young people cheer every now and then, but with restraint, as though it is imperative that their venture remain a secret, at least for now. As they raise their arms in enthusiastic agreement with what is being said, I can see weapons of various sorts clutched in their hands. Some are firearms, while others are of a cruder sort—knives, clubs, broken bottles, rocks.

I am grateful for the cover of the darkness which surrounds me, for the nearest light fixture is broken. Still, I must move in more closely if I am to be as effective as I need to be, for, although these young people are not aware of it, they need me.

There is an overturned garbage can just around the corner, which is several feet closer to the group. I concentrate on blending in with the shadowy darkness as I turn the corner, and step carefully in that direction. I crouch down with the garbage can to conceal me, breathing deeply to slow my heartbeat, so that I can hear the nnn-Asi-t's words above the heavy pounding. As I exhale through my mouth, the first audible utterances reach my ears. The words are what I had expected, more or less.

"We're not going to let those bastards push us around. Right?"

The youths respond with hoarse whispers and murmurs of such expletives as *no fucking way, hell no!*

"That's right!" The nnn-Asi-t continues in its mesmerizing voice. "Fuckin' assholes. That's all they are. We're gonna show them just who runs this neighbourhood. Right?"

As the prattle goes on, of course it is not really the words which work the Earthers into their almost hysterical state. It is the power of the nnn-Asi-t which seduces them—on this planet through use of the voice. On other planets, this might vary, although their presence alone has a profound effect.

The talk continues, and I am able to make some connection between the words of the nnn-Asi-t and some of the news programs which I have followed through the city's newspaper and through the TV station. They have, apparently, been creating a hellish life for the residents of the surrounding neighbourhoods as well as for the law enforcement. This nnn-Asi-t seems to have been quite effective in its efforts.

And, therefore, its efforts must be stopped—quickly.

But this group will soon be too frenzied for an easy intervention. I must begin, and also be prepared to send my call for assistance should it become necessary. There is only a slim chance of my affecting these youths without the nnn-Asi-t becoming aware of me at all. Yet I must act *now*. I cannot risk allowing this gang to continue. There is too much at stake.

The group is large enough that I can begin to give its members assistance before the enemy realizes that I am here. Bending to keep myself as concealed as possible, I move to the outer ring of youths.

I will be able to influence the boys and girls on the outside of the group before the nnn-Asi-t senses my actions.

I am close enough now to several of them. With as little movement as possible, I silently touch the arm of the tattered jacket beside me and let my fingers gently slide to the inside of the boy's thin wrist. Quickly, I send my essence to flow deeply within this youth at his pulse point. This direct physical contact allows me to influence him effectively without lifting my mental shield. I try to work as quickly as possible but also concentrate on sending as much of my strength and peace into the boy's spirit as I possibly can...

And I must do so before the others are aware—especially the enemy in the middle of the crowd.

I move to the next boy, allowing myself one glance back at the first one to ensure that I have achieved the desired effect. There is a look of slight astonishment in his eyes, which tells me that he has sensed the difference inside of himself. Even as I do this, I am locating the place I require inside of the next boy's wrist. Almost instantly this time, my important message and essence are directed inside. But I feel some degree of resistance with this one. The nnn-Asi-t has had a very strong effect on this one. I must push harder, harder still, to send more of my essence inside. I am aware of sweat forming on my forehead, despite the always-present chill. *At last.* Finally, I feel him beginning to understand and accept...

Next, I move to a young girl. She is smaller and easier for me to reach. I save some of my energy by whispering my message into her ear. These are not words that will at first have meaning to her. But when they have reached her deep inside, she will understand their intent. I can feel her as she starts to respond.

These three have ceased their enthusiastic support for the nnn-Asi-t and appear a bit confused. But inside they feel peace. They will most certainly begin to move slowly away from the crowd and leave the area.

I step to the fourth. My fingers slide to his wrist—

Perhaps I have rushed the process. I am not sure why, but abruptly he jerks his hand away. The tall, fair-skinned youth mutters something and I see him suddenly stare down at my face through greenish eyes filled with surprise, then questions—

Then anger.

Hastily, I utter the words that can change him forever, and shield him from further interference from our enemy—

But I fall back, the side of my face stinging and hot from his slap. As I stumble backward, I see his hand still in the air just above me. He is saying something to me now, in a much louder voice than necessary.

Obviously, I am in trouble. Immediate action needed, I close my eyes and concentrate on sending my plea for help to anyone who is capable of receiving it—

But suddenly I am yanked to my feet, so I cannot be certain if I managed to send my message effectively. Two hands are roughly gripping the front of my red jacket. As I try to catch my breath, I stare into the face of a dark-skinned young man who appears darker because of the dirt on his cheeks and the black stubble on his upper lip and chin. His deep brown eyes seem almost overflowing with anger and fury. We stand thus for a few seconds as he trembles with hatred. Perhaps he is wondering what to do with me. He does not yet realize it, but already I am sending my essence to him through my eyes, focussing on bringing to him the all-important sense of peace—

Which will also give him immunity to the influence of the nnn-Asi-t.

But I am uncertain whether I can successfully complete this mission. Our exchange has likely caught the attention of some of the others. Although I am capable of performing my duty with more than one at a time, such requires a rather tremendous amount of strength and concentration—which I do not have at this moment…

The dark youth seizes me by the shoulders. "What the hell is going on?" He glances from me to the tall, fair youth who is now shaking his head and scowling.

The nnn-Asi-t is now watching and listening—and sensing. I *feel* it rather than see or hear it. I am deeply committed to this situation now. Had sufficient time elapsed, the first three youths might see and recognize clearly what is happening, perhaps to the point of assisting me. But this could not have occurred yet. It might not occur at all. Sometimes, all that I can do is make them immune to further interference and bring them the beginning of insight into their actions. The nnn-Asi-t is aware. And that means that this situation will now involve only myself and the enemy, and perhaps others of my kind who will have received my plea for assistance.

I am in, as some Earthers might say, a *pickle.* A predicament. I can feel the strength of the nnn-Asi-t, just as I recognize the physical strength of the youth who still holds me by the front of my jacket. But he is not the greatest problem for me right now.

This nnn-Asi-t is likely to provide the most formidable challenge I have had since my arrival on this planet nearly five weeks ago. I close my eyes and summon all of the power that I can still find inside. All of my concentration and mental force collect inside of my head like a swirling sphere of energy. Of course, it is deep scarlet. It is, after all, my true self. The youth who had been holding me must be wondering what could be happening, as he has released the jacket. I feel the enemy attempt to scrutinize me, gauging its chances. I am fully shielded, of course, and will not allow it to know just how great its chances might be.

I turn toward it. It appears far from formidable in its Earther adaptation. Of course, they always do, not wanting to arouse any suspicion. Our eyes meet, but I will not allow myself to feel the vastness of its strength. I am, instead, concentrating on preparing to use my *own* strength.

Suddenly, I can feel its power focus into a narrow beam. I am prepared, having anticipated this, for such is not an unusual form for a first attack. My barrier surrounds me.

If their Earther eyes were able to perceive this, the youths no doubt would be quite amazed. They would see two people who resemble Earthers facing each other and not moving. And, *if* they were able to perceive it, a silvery blast from the male toward me. Then they would see the bright flash stop abruptly, only a couple of their 'inches' from my body.

My peripheral vision tells me that the group of boys and girls has moved away from us, as they doubtlessly sense something quite unusual about this strange encounter—something telling them that they must not interfere at this time.

We are all surrounded by eerie silence.

Now I direct my essence toward the nnn-Asi-t and into its grey eyes. I push as hard as I can, willing my power to penetrate deep within it. Of course, it resists, and its resistance is strong. Yet I persist. I must. More. I focus still more of my energy into the being. And then I visualize myself as physically pushing narrow beams of scarlet inside, through the pupils of its eyes. It will be aware of this image, too. As long as I can concentrate as I am, it cannot escape that mental picture.

More and more. Still more of my essence is directed from my consciousness and into its. I can feel it begin to buckle slightly. I have made some sort of dent in its energy reserves.

Suddenly it shifts. All too quickly it has reformed its power into another silvery beam of its energy and malevolence. I have no time to focus my attention on adjusting the strength and distribution of my protective barricade. I must move *quickly.* I redirect my two scarlet beams into one and meet the silver one head-on. My still slender filament of crimson somehow manages to hold off the larger silver threat.

But, after accomplishing that, I can feel the end point of my energy reserves! For the first time, I feel fatigue. I must use my energies more sparingly if I am to last very much longer...and last I must!

I concentrate more determinedly. I visualize my slender, reddish thread as tremendously stiff and strong, fashioned of the mightiest material in the universe, which does not even exist here on Earth. Nothing can break it! Nothing can sever it! I put all of my mental and spiritual energy into maintaining this image...

Sweat runs into my eye, stinging. I cannot allow this to distract me. I must let nothing at all distract me.

But now *its* beam is stronger too. And larger.

And so thus we stand. Beams directed at one another, yet neither powerful enough to accomplish more than that. I *know*, though, that it has greater strength than I. How are *its* energy stores?

And what has it left to try?

I do not have long to ponder, for suddenly that silver beam moves! It shifts downward, and I find myself scrambling to find the strength required to redirect my own little beam to match it. Now it moves to the side slightly, and faltering just a bit, my crimson filament manages to go with it.

The Earther parts of my body have begun to tremble with exertion, though, and I am finding it even more difficult to continue matching this enemy's adjustments and relocations. And it must know this now. The truth of my inferior strength must be becoming clear to it. I can hear an almost imperceptible hiss of satisfaction. Still though, I must focus. There must be a way…

But it toys with me now. We both know that it is only a matter of time. It likely takes some delight as it manipulates its beam, teasing me, tormenting me as I constantly try to redirect my own flow to maintain what I have. Breathing heavily, I push harder, still *harder* against that silver threat, all the while knowing that my increased strength right now comes from the desperation of a being dreading its likely defeat. I push, push outward with my energy, and am rewarded for my efforts. That beam of silver has been moved back toward the nnn-Asi-t. My filament, although still as narrow as it has been all along, is now longer.

So much effort! And I have gained—what? A little more time, perhaps? Yet now there is suddenly more to it—

I sense more energy! *Yes!* Now I can feel my power being supported by one who can assist me in this altercation! My plea for help has been answered! It is with tremendous joy that I feel another's energy stores join with mine…

But *no*. Now I am confused. For this new energy is *not* joining with my own. It is simply *there*, allowing me to take what I need. The presence is certainly there, though. With the other's bank of energy near enough, I am free to augment my dwindling reserves. How will we defeat this nnn-Asi-t? Not simply through strength. My kind is more prepared than that. Now that more power is available to me, I can be more creative than to rely on power alone.

I take only enough strength from my friend to perform one more transfer of energy. The nnn-Asi-t seemed prepared for an outward attack comprised of sheer force. Its assumption that I am depleted, and therefore about to lose this battle, will be its downfall. More slowly this time, I increase my focus while maintaining the image of my scarlet filament. Inside of my filament I inject an even tinier—even finer—thread. This one, too, has the strength of the mightiest substances known throughout the vast galaxies of the known universe.

And this one I direct, to be well-hidden, down through the inside of the outer one. Swiftly, within only a fraction of a second, it has already travelled the full length of the crimson—

And it penetrates the encasement of the nnn-Asi-t!

There is a bright flash of red energy, but no sound. The force knocks me backward, to land hard on the pavement. I shield my eyes against the glare.

A voice penetrates the pinkish haze which I see within my own mind. The voice is certainly familiar, but I cannot as yet identify it. I open my eyes. I have to blink several times to clear away the remnants of the battle from my mind…

There is white light from somewhere. It seems to come from everywhere. When I try to find the source, I recognize the headlights of an automobile, so bright against the darkness. Vaguely, I can make out the silhouettes of many of the youths as they drift away to seek the anonymity of the night's shadows. In front of me I see the dwindling remains of the nnn-Asi-t, now not much more than a fading silvery, mist-like substance. They are, of course, not Earthers, and this one's remains resemble nothing more than a dissolving puddle. It becomes foggy as it dissipates.

Footsteps. I turn, wondering about the identity of my benefactor. Had it been gu-p-FFF—Georgia—I would most certainly have sensed this, for we were very close companions on our world.

But the individual who kneels by my side is not one whom I would in any way have expected. I am gazing into a confused and concerned face framed by curly brown hair. And staring at me in alarm are two very blue eyes, the colour of the Earth sky in daytime.

Jared.

Chapter Nine

Jared was lying on his back, as he had been for some time. Yet still his heart *pound-pounded* in his chest. Still, he couldn't seem to take deep breaths as he turned from one side to the other, then rolled onto his back again. *Sleep* was becoming more and more of an abstract concept rather than anything possible for him to find. He sighed. His eyes open once more, he simply stared at the ceiling, the shadows constantly shifting and changing as the headlights of passing cars lit his living room ceiling, then faded. He was so stressed, so *confused...*

It was no use. He sat up, his fingers seeking contact with his aching eyes. Shoving back the blanket with his feet, he turned to let his long, thin legs drop over the side of the sofa. Straightening, he stretched the cramped muscles of his back, massaging it through his tee shirt with his fingers.

This little sofa really *was* too small for him to sleep on. Hard to believe that he and Andrea had—

Jared shook his head to force the thought from his mind, the memories of that night. But the image of Andrea's face refused to leave. He rose, hand still on the small of his back which ached beneath his striped pyjama bottoms. Yet again he found himself wandering in the direction of his bedroom. Silently, he stood in the open doorway, only vaguely aware of the sound of the heating system coming on...

His gaze was on the mound of bedcovers and the lump beneath it. Softly, he moved into the room, grateful that his sock feet made almost no noise at all. Then he eased himself down into a kneeling position so he could watch her face once more. His knee made a cracking sound. Jared grimaced, holding his breath, hoping that she wouldn't wake up.

Only too clearly, he remembered how she'd been when he'd approached her. She'd been lying on the pavement, and she'd seemed totally and completely exhausted...spaced out, almost like a drug addict.

What had she been *doing* there? At first, he'd thought that she'd been attacked. But there were no marks on her, no ripped clothing. Just a scratch on her cheek. That was all.

A shiver rushed through him, from his head and down his spine. He shivered despite the warmth, reliving his concern and fear for her when he'd had that—that *feeling*. Somehow, he had known that she needed him, that she was in some sort of danger, and he'd arrived to find her with a—with a *gang* of some sort. At first, he'd been terrified that he was too late when he saw them moving off into the night's darkness. And then, in the glow from his VW's headlights, he'd been able to just barely see what looked like the shape of a man. Yet, right in front of his eyes, he'd seen it sort of *melt* or something...

But that was impossible. He rubbed his eyes and sighed.

And gazed back at her face. She looked okay now—at least compared to what he'd found at that—that place.

Against his better judgement, he gave in to his urges, just a bit, and reached over to stroke her soft hair. In the moon's glow peeking between the two sides of the curtains, he could see that her face still looked a bit pinker than usual. She'd seemed to develop a flush in her cheeks after he'd brought her here. Ever so gently, he stroked her forehead, hoping that she wasn't getting a fever.

Andrea moaned in her sleep. And the sound felt like an icy knife cutting him lengthwise. He stayed as still as he could, kneeling on the floor with one arm stretched across the top of the bed, his head resting on it while his other arm kept close to her. In his misery, he forced himself to take slow, deep breaths. Jared was sure that she must be mixed up in something terrible. Why else would she be so secretive? Why else would she be hanging around places like *that*? Maybe she was into drugs...

If she was, what the hell was she doing working as a counsellor for people who had problems!

And, whatever she was doing, she was obviously out of her depths, over her head. What would've happened if he hadn't shown up?

I just can't believe this—it's too awful—

And then there was that other question too. Jared pulled in another deep breath as he recalled how strange it'd been. He'd been watching the news on his laptop. They were summarizing the report about the mob scene outside the women's clinic. He shook his head again at the thought of how the mood of the crowd had changed so abruptly—

And how quickly the strange man had seemed to simply vanish into thin air.

Then, later, suddenly—just out of the blue—he'd heard *her* voice. He'd been watching the news report on his laptop and heard her voice. He'd even looked around himself at the inside of his apartment, thinking that—somehow—she must be here. Of course, she wasn't. Yet he was sure he'd heard her.

And then—and this seemed even crazier—he'd *felt* her. Not her voice. *Her*. At that moment in time, he'd known that she needed him.

Jared didn't think he would ever forget the bizarre walk out to his car, his conscious mind telling him that he had no idea where to go. And yet he kept walking, got inside, turned the key, and started the car. Putting it into first gear, he had *known* where he should head. At that point he didn't really even know if she'd be there. It was like he just got into the car, and it took him to her. Just like that. Sort of. There was still some kind of fog inside of his mind. A wave of exhaustion suddenly swept through him, leaving his eyelids feeling heavy.

What he was about to do seemed like the most natural thing in the world…

Jared dragged himself around to the other side of the bed—*his* bed—and lay down, very gently so that he wouldn't disturb her. He pulled up the covers, then reached over to cover her hand with his.

And finally fell into a deep sleep.

He had no idea how long he'd been asleep. But the room was brightly lit when he finally opened his eyes. The sun was beaming through the slit where his light blue curtains didn't quite fit together. Gradually, vague tatters of memory came together like a jigsaw puzzle, and he could remember what had been happening, as bizarre as everything was. Closing his eyes again, he reached over for her...

She was gone.

Moaning, Jared pulled himself into a sitting position and shifted his legs over the edge. His heart was beginning to pound harder. *Did she leave?* If she had, he'd still have no idea what was going on. What if she went away and he didn't see her again? The feeling of his thudding heart was becoming panic, climbing up inside his chest. Yet, as soon as this began, something stopped it.

Andrea! He could feel her now as surely and fully as though she was right beside him, talking to him, touching him, right now. The feeling of *Andrea* was a sensation of incredible, deep, wonderful peace. A sense that all was well, everything was just fine...

And more.

For the first time, he had a sense of—*how could this be?*—her *colour*. With the awareness of her peace and...whatever...came some sort of a mental—*spiritual?*—image of wonderful, glowing, comforting scarlet.

And that was Andrea. He didn't *see* it, but he sensed it. *Felt* it. And it was as sure as the sun coming up in the eastern sky.

Jared shook his head. *It can't be true.* He told himself it was just the memory of her auburn hair's highlights in the glow of last night's moonbeams.

Rising, feeling half in a trance, he stepped to the doorway. Before he had even turned to the left, he knew exactly where she was right now. For some reason, as he turned, he kept his eyes down and averted while he took the next few steps. Then he raised his eyes and gazed into the living room, where he already knew she was sitting in the chair nearest the window.

That more pinkish tinge to her skin that he'd noticed last night was less pronounced now. She looked more like her usual self, so his concern that she might be developing a fever hadn't come to pass.

When she turned and smiled at him, he was sure he was watching the sunlight form a beautiful, crimson halo around her head. He closed his eyes and shook his head a bit to clear it.

Somehow, he knew, even with his eyes closed, that his feet were already moving in her direction. She rose from the chair and put her cool hand over his. His heart was starting to *pound-pound* again and he had a million questions. Yet her nearness and her touch brought him instant reassurance that whatever she was involved in was quite appropriate and good. He wanted to maintain his mental discipline, determined to get answers *now*. But as he opened his mouth to tell her this, he was already lowering his face to hers. His lips touched hers lightly, ever so gently. Barely a touch at all. He leaned his cheek against hers, then moved his mouth to hers once more. And kissed her fully, lovingly, while all of his concerns faded into nothingness. He was aware of only one thing—no. Two. The complete and utter *rightness* of holding her in his arms...

And the tremendous sense of communion between their spirits.

When they pulled apart, his questions didn't seem to matter anymore at all. He embraced her once more, knowing he didn't want her to be away from him again.

Andrea was speaking, but he had no idea what she was saying. The soft tones of her voice didn't penetrate the depths of his contentment at first. She pulled herself further away from him, but not far enough to break the physical contact of his hands which were now on her shoulders while her fingers lingered at his waist.

"You have questions," she whispered, "and you deserve answers. But before that, I must thank you with all of my being for responding to my need last night. Your presence enabled me to accomplish more than I ever could have done alone. I am—I'm grateful."

Jared kissed the top of her head, stroking her hair with one hand. "I—I'm just glad you're okay!" His throat suddenly tightening, he had to work to get the words out.

She stepped back from him once more, this time holding each of his hands in one of hers. Smiling at him, she pulled him after her into the kitchen. She plugged in the kettle while he sat down, unable to take his eyes off her. A moment later, coffee mug in her hand, she turned to him. Placing the steaming blue mug in front of him, she placed her other hand where it could caress his shoulder.

"Ask," she said softly as he sipped the coffee.

As she pulled the other chair around the side of the table, she sat kitty-corner to him rather than across the table. The way that both were feeling, they needed to be within touching distance of each other.

As he put the mug down on the table, his forehead began to pucker in a frown. "Um. I don't know where to start! Uh—who were those *kids*? And what in hell were *you* doing in there?"

She thought silently for a moment, then shrugged. "Well, they were, just as you said, a bunch of kids. Teenagers. I was there to keep them from...from getting out of hand."

"But *why*? What the hell are you—some sort of undercover cop?"

She looked puzzled for a few seconds, Jared wondering why this question seemed so hard to answer. Finally, she spoke. "Yes. In a sense. Sort of."

"*Sort of*? How can you be *sort of* a cop?" He paused, his eyes on her face, then continued. "What *are* you?"

A deep sigh escaped her, as though she was not pleased to have to explain. "I—I am on a—a special assignment. No, I do not—don't—work for your city police. But my work entails...the—um—*prevention* of crime. I am assigned to—to recognize when your... um—people are about to—to get mixed up in something harmful. Then I intervene and try to prevent this from happening."

"Dammit Andrea! Isn't that awfully dangerous?"

Again, there was a pause before an almost painfully brief answer. "Yes."

That *pound-pounding* was beginning again in Jared's chest as he moved his ragged thumbnail to his mouth. He had felt so *good* only a short time ago, and now anxiety was rearing its ugly head again. He took a deep breath, trying to remain calm. "Andrea, I didn't even see you with a weapon or anything. If you do this kind of work, where in bloody hell is your *gun*?"

Her brown eyes met his blue ones. "Oh, I have a weapon, Jared. But my work is very, very secretive. Please be patient. I really am not free to tell you a great deal more than that. Something wonderfully special has happened between us. And, somehow, that has gotten you involved in all of this, which it shouldn't have. But you must be patient, Jared." She reached over to put both of her hands on his forearm. "I am—I'm simply not at liberty to give you all of the details."

And there it was again. That tremendous sense of calm that seemed to come directly from her to him when she touched him like that.

Jared took another sip of coffee as he tried to take all of this in. *Dammit! CIA? FBI? RCMP?* He shook his head, wishing that this stuff didn't have to be true. "Okay. Fine. I won't ask for details you can't give. But—but I saw some sort of shadow or something. Really weird. It looked like a man at first. But—and I know this sounds totally insane—I was sure he looked like he...like he *melted* or something. What the hell was *that*?" He gazed downward. Then he raised his hand to his mouth and continued nibbling on his thumbnail.

Andrea was watching his face, her hands now folded in front of her on the table. She was rubbing her thumbs together as she thought—

When she didn't say anything, Jared lifted his eyes to study her face. She looked as worried as he felt. The fingers of her left hand made their way to touch Jared's right. The sensation was one of warmth. Then there was more to it...and suddenly he understood.

She wants to tell me. But for some reason, she can't.

Jared turned his hand palm-up so their fingers could intertwine. "Okay," he whispered, "how in hell do you do *that*?"

Andrea smiled slightly. "You've heard of—of ESP? Extra Sensory Perception?"

In response to his nod, she continued: "Well, this is something like that. A special type. At least, that's the best way to explain it for now. You will—you'll understand it more completely as time goes on."

She lifted a hand to touch his cheek. Savouring the contact, he gazed at her face. Her brown eyes, somehow, seemed to contain all of the knowledge and understanding in the universe. "Jared," she was whispering. "Something—something unplanned and unexpected happened between us. And that has awakened something important within you. You, too, have a tremendous power inside of your mind. That is—that's what enabled you to see what you did. I sensed this, a bit. But I really didn't realize the potential that you have." Gazing downward, no longer certain of what to say, she opened her mouth, then closed it again. When she spoke next, her voice was even more hushed than before. "A strong bond has formed between us, Jared. Although it was totally unintended and definitely a surprise, it *is* there."

Jared was finally smiling, his worries no longer great. Surely, she didn't think she was sharing some sort of great revelation! He'd known this already!

He loved this most unusual woman.

Chapter Ten

How much should I tell poor Jared? How much *can* I tell him? This inadvertent partial bonding is, in itself, a violation of our regulations. I simply can*not* add further complications by telling him who I *truly* am or why I am here! Yet this unusually sensitive ability of his makes it so difficult to keep the truth from him! It would serve no purpose to simply stay away from him—he'd only receive more of my thoughts than intended whenever I needed to project them…

As a receiver, he seems so strangely strong.

It would quite likely be Jared who would receive projections which I would be intending for others of my kind. How awfully strange. And how completely unexpected.

It seems that I have no choice but to continue this ruse. I must somehow keep him convinced that I am some sort of international crime-fighter. But, then again, I guess that, in a sense, *is* what I am.

Oh, Jared. I must be so very careful. It would certainly do our cause no good whatsoever if you were destroyed.

I have completed another evening of telephone counselling. One more evening of attempting to make more of these poor, vulnerable Earthers a little more resistant to the influences of the nnn-Asi-t. Even over the phone, I can project some degree of my essence.

The representatives must have been correct. They had researched our methods extensively. By using telephone contact, I should be able to influence a fairly great number of Earthers. Yet still I feel frustrated, as this is a much less effective method than face-to-face contact. I must console myself with the knowledge that I *am* helping a *large* number to become a *bit* more resistant to the nnn-Asi-t, and then when I am off-duty, I can concentrate on face-to-face work with a smaller selection.

There is so much work to be done! But we *must* stop the enemy!

Not tonight, though. Not this night for me. I am still weakened by that recent battle. I can feel inside myself that I still lack the depth of energy stores needed in case I make the same mistake again…

That enemy had been more powerful than I was able to accurately determine from a distance. This must not happen again, as the result could be disastrous, at least for me.

If it had not been for Jared—

But I have to stop and chuckle. Here I am, my newspapers under my arm, standing on the sidewalk not far from my apartment building.

And here *he* is.

My heart beats just a bit faster as I admire the brightness of those blue eyes where the glow from the setting sun is caught. I like the curve of his lips and the slight upturn of his chin. Jared might be quite attractive if his skin did not have the pallor typical of the Earther Caucasians. We stand silently. His lips turn upward at the corners as he continues to gaze at me.

I open myself to him. This should be a safe move, although I really do not know if he can send his feelings—or, if he can, how much control he might have over such projections. But it would be highly unlikely that even a sensitive nnn-Asi-t could pick up our exchanges when we are in such close proximity. I feel free to project to him my feelings, touching his arm with my hand to make this sharing even more effective and safe. I can feel him receive, and then react to my weariness, as well as my joy at seeing him once again. He steps even closer, placing his hands on my shoulders as he leans towards me to kiss my forehead.

"I hope you don't mind, Andrea," he breathes into my ear. "I know how—how tired you've been. I—I just wanted to be with you..."

I gaze up at him and smile. There is no need to speak. He knows how I am feeling now—that I do not mind his being here.

"Then—then it's okay I'm here? I didn't want to interfere if you were going to be busy...um, in the field or on call, or whatever you call it."

Although I can express my feelings without speech, I know that speaking is what he is accustomed to and comfortable with. "It is—it's all right." I reach my hand up to touch his cheek. Our lips are touching now. How natural it seems. Yet, even so, there is a part of me that knows I should not be responding to this Earther. I shield that feeling from him with care, knowing how easily he receives.

I am gazing upward at the night sky as we walk, my arm through his. How beautiful the sight is, now that the moon has risen among the twinkling stars. One of the stars in that sky is my home, although it is not visible in this area at this time. My apartment building is just ahead, and it does *not* look like the one where Jared lives. It seems so strange in retrospect when I think of my confusion during the storm when I mistook it for mine.

We enter my apartment together. How peculiar it seems to be bringing an Earther here. Yet when I look at him, it doesn't feel peculiar at all. It feels *right.* It feels right, too, when we've removed our outdoor clothing, to embrace like we haven't since that first night when everything changed. I savour his touch—so gentle, yet so sure. My fingers want to drink in every aspect of his pale skin, his body. It is so fascinatingly different from and yet similar to mine, in some ways. And so gloriously warm!

My bed is much more comfortable and welcoming now that he is in it too.

I have slept wonderfully, dreamlessly. No nnn-Asi-t taunting me. No failed contacts. No fear. No calls for help. Only the comfort and peace of lying entwined with Jared's long form. Such wonderful warmth.

It is still quite early in the morning. The sun has not yet begun its upward journey. The moon remains the brightest celestial body as I gaze at it through the space between the unclosed curtains. I watch how its glow brings to light more and different curves and angles of Jared's face. How strangely colourless he looks when his blue eyes are closed! If not for the pale pink lips and brown hair, he'd be completely colourless!

I cannot resist touching a finger to those lips…softly, as I do not wish to disturb him. Even suppressed, my own colouring is much pinker than his lips are—

I gasp. In the excitement from the nnn-Asi-t and the exhaustion that followed, I have neglected to use my pigment-suppressant! I study Jared to make sure he is still deeply asleep. I must be extremely calm. If I move too hastily, I take the risk of waking him. I must not do that now! Gently, slowly, I ease my body from the bed and tip toe in my bare feet to retrieve my pouch from the dresser, grateful for the guidance provided by the moonlight.

As quietly as I can, I pull the bathroom door closed behind me, remove my fingers slowly and carefully from the doorknob. Sighing, more relaxed now, I take my little sphere in my hand. I must have nourishment before I use the suppressant. But something is wrong. My concentration must have been disturbed by my anxiety because I find it difficult to focus. I take another deep breath, yet still I am unable to find the relaxation I require.

I need to sit down. And the toilet simply will not suffice in this situation. Slowly, gently, I turn the doorknob and open the door. Taking a moment to glance toward the partially open bedroom door and listen for Jared's deep breathing, I step into the living room.

Seated on the comfortable soft chair, I move aside the curtain and let my gaze travel upward toward the stars. I think of home. My peaceful world where there are no locked doors because we have no need of them. I think of my kind with our brilliant colourings and our love. The relaxation comes more easily now.

Soon I feel my sphere begin to expand and grow warmer. I am feeling stronger already, although I know that I am actually experiencing the anticipation of what is yet to come…

My LLL-nnnta begins to gently pulsate. I look downward at it as it becomes crimson, almost as crimson as my skin has now become. The familiar scarlet mist has begun to emanate from the little ball. This surrounds me, saturating the room with a fog the colour of Earther blood. It is wonderful. The peace and joy of my world seem to embrace me as, at the same time, it fills me inside, completes me. All conscious thought leaves my mind. I can feel myself becoming physically stronger and more spiritually powerful than I have been for days.

A tinge of regret strikes me as I feel the sphere's throbbing begin to lessen in intensity. My eyes take in the wonder of the sphere's colour changes as they switch from deep pink to pale pink and then to white. I cannot help but smile. It always seems so very strange when it contracts to its original small size so abruptly, after the rather gradual nature of the colour changes.

I tuck my LLL-nnnta back inside its pouch and find the all-important pigment-suppressant. This tiny thing which is now on the tip of my finger is so vital to my work. There is just a hint of a hiss as it explodes. And the tiny, white cloud slowly disappears as I inhale as deeply as I can.

My gaze now turns to the sight of my skin as it slowly fades from its wonderful scarlet to Earther-acceptable paleness.

If only I could share my true self with you, Jared—

I gasp. The thought had struck me so quickly that I was unable to shield it in time. I force myself to breathe calmly. I reassure myself that he was sleeping. If he received the thought, it will be as part of a dream, and, after all, he *knows* that there are things which I am not free to tell him.

And so it is with a feeling of contentment that I slip quietly back to the bedroom. I move as silently as possible, while I put the pouch back into its hiding place.

Jared has rolled onto his side, now facing away from me. Good. Perhaps I will be less likely to waken him as I slide back beneath the covers…

I lie quietly and become aware of his irregular breathing. It must be a dream.

Is he dreaming of me, I wonder? I want to touch him, move him back so that he faces me. I want to feel our bodies locked together once more. And his delicious warmth. I am tempted to sense him, to reach into his mind…but no. I must allow him to have his privacy.

I do not wish to disturb him—especially, I think, if he is dreaming of me.

I fall asleep once more with only the memory of his sweet caresses to keep away the chill.

Chapter Eleven

Jared wasn't quite sure whether or not he'd been asleep since she had come back to bed. But he certainly felt like he'd been lying there more than long enough. He waited until the evenness of her breathing suggested that she was slumbering once again. Quietly he eased himself into a sitting position and then off the bed. Stepping to the window, he ran his hand across his mouth and chin, then began to nibble on his thumbnail as he stared through the window. As he moved the curtain aside a bit, he could see a faint, orangish hue beginning to light the horizon. It might have been a beautiful sight to see if he'd been in a better frame of mind.

He didn't want to look at her. But the shades of pink intertwined with the orange only made the awful memory all the more vivid. He turned, his eyes drinking in the vision of her sleeping figure. She looked...normal. *Normal.* Pale pink skin and auburn hair. As though nothing had happened—

Maybe it'd been a nightmare. A horrible dream and nothing more. But he shook his head again, knowing somehow that it hadn't been. Grabbing his clothes from the chair in the corner, he slipped on his pale green shirt, doing up a couple of buttons as he headed toward the door. He stopped there and gazed back at her as she lay in her bed. Staring at her, he compared this image with the one he'd seen last night. A lump formed in his throat. He was almost afraid to look into the living room at all, even though he knew that she wasn't there.

Standing in the doorway, he watched as the reddish glow of the sunrise began to light the room—

Dammit. Even the fricking sun is trying to remind me.

As though he could even hope to forget! Closing his eyes, he could see the vision again, just as he'd seen her last night. Had she really thought she could move so silently she wouldn't wake him up?

There she'd been, in the dim light of the streetlights and the moon, holding some sort of tiny reddish light in her hand, a look of ecstasy on her face as the light seemed to make her face and her entire body red, too. That was just plain *weird*. But he could accept that. If she was an international crimefighter, he knew she'd have all sorts of secret weapons and things he couldn't even imagine. That part was okay.

But what he *couldn't* understand—what he could find no possible Earthly explanation for—was that, once the little light had faded and stopped its glowing, she—she…

Was still red. All over. Not just pinkish like she was now, but vividly, brightly, totally—deep red. Crimson. Scarlet. Ruby.

And he was positive that it hadn't been just due to the dimness.

"Oh, dear God, help me," he was murmuring to no one, or maybe he really meant it as a prayer. He'd never been religious, but maybe he *should* be.

Because that wasn't the worst of it. As bizarre as that sight had been, it hadn't been the reason he'd cried into the pillow. It was the vision of her opening her eyes and focusing them on her fingertip. *That* was what did it for him. Did him right in.

Even her *eyes* were red, even the irises of her eyes, standing out like hot coals against the dim background of the room. *Her eyes were deep scarlet.* And they glowed in the dark shadows of the room like a cat's—

She was the personification of every horror movie about possession, satanism, exorcism…

The devil himself. *Could that be what she is?*

That could explain some things. It would account for why she'd been in the middle of that gang. *She* must've been the one trying to incite a riot—

And he'd made love with her! Nausea formed in the pit of his stomach. Stepping further away from the bedroom door, he moaned.

I should've left last night. Why did I stay? God forgive me—I've been seduced by the devil!

He had to get out of here—had to get away from her. His shirt half-buttoned, he yanked up his jeans, fiddling with the belt. But his trembling fingers made putting on his socks impossible—

"To *hell* with it!" Jared tossed them aside. Suddenly shocked by what he'd just said, he clapped a hand over his mouth. Rushing to the apartment door, desperately he tried to jam his bare feet into his shoes. Biting his lip to be silent, inside he was crying out with all the despair in his heart, tears filling his eyes and obscuring his vision. He leaned over to pull on a shoe and a tear splashed onto the bricklike tiled floor—

It was red! The floor was red here at the door, just like she was—

And then she was there. She'd heard his calls, even though he'd uttered barely any sound. She still heard him…

Through the tears in his eyes, he saw her. Her pale pink face and body, for she hadn't worn anything at all to bed. She stepped closer. He stood, not wanting to move, and studied her face. Her *brown* eyes—*her false face*. They were almost at eye-level, as he was still bent awkwardly over his shoe. But now he straightened up.

"What—what on God's good Earth *are* you!" Although he had intended this to be a demand, it croaked out as little more than a desperate sob.

Andrea reached a pale pink hand toward him. But he pulled away, as though she could destroy him with a touch.

Suddenly he felt her *inside*. She was love, peace, kindness, and goodness. But he shook his head, determined to resist. He would *not* be taken in again by her evil seductions! Jared fought back, filled his mind with an image of her being knocked back, away from him, while he reached his hand toward the doorknob.

No. Not this time—

Suddenly astonished, he stopped. He had felt her presence inside of him waver, ever so slightly. But, in the second or two he'd been registering his astonishment, she was renewing her attack.

He shook his head, tried to fight it.

Sweet, deep peace filled him entirely. It filled his whole being, taking away his desire to fight it, even though he knew it was a false front for her evil. It was inside of him and enveloped him, surrounded him. How could he resist something so beautiful, so wonderful? He had no desire to. His shoulders drooped, his body relaxed, his hand dropped away from the doorknob as his arm swung limply to his side. His sob broke the silence. "What *are* you?"

Suddenly her arms were around him, supporting him and keeping him from falling to the floor in the narrow space of the apartment entrance. Her presence was so warm, wonderful. Yet, even as he embraced her in return, a flash of fear penetrated the blanket of peace and serenity which both filled and surrounded him.

Together they sank down to the floor, she guiding him a bit farther away from the door to where there was more space. It was as though they were melting into each other. They sat as one where the floor met the carpet, she holding him against her and saying nothing. Everything that he wanted to believe seemed to be entering his mind directly from hers. Gradually, his breathing slowed, and he felt contentment just sitting, exhausted, in her arms.

Now he *knew* she wasn't Satan. She wasn't evil. She *couldn't* be, not with all the love and peace she was giving him, like a wonderful gift. He pulled away from her just a bit and gazed into her deep, brown eyes. Unafraid now, he cradled her cheek with his hand. He opened his mouth and closed it again, trying to find his voice. "What—what *are* you, Andrea? I—I need to know."

Returning his gaze, she gently put her hand on the one that held her cheek. Then Andrea pulled his hand to her lips and kissed its palm, closing the fingers as though not wanting the kiss to escape. She nodded, a serious look on her face. "You have a *right* to know."

Seated on her sofa, he took the glass of water from her gratefully, although he would've preferred coffee. She had apologized for having none. But he hadn't been surprised, recalling her reaction when he'd offered her some at his place. Of course, she didn't drink the stuff.

Andrea sipped her own water and placed the glass on the nearby table. She sat on the chair he'd seen her in last night, but everything was so different now. Her eyes were downcast.

Jared watched her, studied her. The rapport between them seemed even stronger now. It was as though every emotion inside her was being shared directly with him. He jerked slightly, startled by the wetness on his hand. He'd forgotten that he was holding the glass. He felt, rather than heard her chuckle as she rose and returned to hand him a paper towel. More carefully, he set the glass on the coffee table in front of him. Waiting for her to say something, he still felt nothing but peace inside.

Finally, she spoke. Her voice was soft, quite gentle, as it had been when she'd been his telephone counsellor. "Jared, what has happened with us is something that has the potential to be extremely important. You have an unusual ability—something quite different and totally unexpected—"

"Wait just a minute, Andrea." Although he continued to feel peace inside, he was becoming more confident, surer of himself. "Andrea, first I want to know about *you*." Jared *felt* nothing from her. He frowned, wondering what this meant.

"Very well, Jared," she said with a sigh, as though it was something that she would rather not share. "First of all, my name is not really Andrea—"

He snorted. "Somehow that doesn't really surprise me."

She raised her eyes to meet his. Still, he felt nothing from her. Then a slight smile upturned her lips on one side. "pp-KKK-uh," burst suddenly from her mouth.

Jared blinked. He stared at her, frowning, wondering if she had something caught in her throat. But, then again, how could she? She never seemed to eat anything. She'd only had water. He sat, still confused.

Suddenly it struck him. Or maybe she had sent him the thought. "That's your *name*!"

"Yes, Jared. Only you might pronounce it more like 'Perka'."

He frowned again, thinking. "Where are you from?" Part of him was dreading what the answer might be. He wanted to know, yet he didn't.

Again, her eyes met his. "From—from far away from here." Andrea was silent a moment, then added: "A planet outside of this solar system."

Jared found himself shaking his head again. But not in denial. It was an effort to somehow understand this information and store it as fact.

She continued. "Any information I have—I've given you already is true. My people do not tell falsehoods. I *am* a crimefighter, for lack of a more appropriate term."

"But how? Why?"

She raised a hand, signalling him to be patient. "Jared, for several years there have been—um, *aliens* on your planet. Many of your people have suspected this, but no one could prove it. These aliens—"

"Your people."

"No. Not these. We have only been here a few of your years."

"You mean—you mean there're *other* aliens here besides yourself?"

"Yes. Many."

Jared's heart seemed to skip a beat. Suddenly he coughed, finding it hard to get his breath. "I—I'm okay. Go on!"

"They are known by our people as *nnn-Asi-t*. And they want your Earth, Jared." She leaned forward, her hands on her knees. Her brown eyes were wide and bright with intensity. "They—they are doing whatever they can to encourage social, emotional, political, economical, ecological…turmoil."

Jared was only too aware that his heart was again pounding hard. "But—but why are they doing this?" A surge of anger at this unknown enemy struck him like a lightning bolt.

"So that your people will destroy themselves. Or, at least, to lead your kind to be open to guidance from *them*. They *want* your people to be bitter, angry, confused. They want you to kill off each other and the more the better." She reached across the coffee table to touch his forearm, trying to give him some sort of comfort, of reassurance.

"Because—because then it will be easier for them to step in and gradually take control of your people and your world."

Jared was dumbfounded, gaping. For a moment, he felt nothing but shock. Andrea said nothing, giving him the time he needed to try to process all of it. His heartbeat had slowed in response to Andrea's touch, but a bit of despair was growing inside of him now. He rubbed a hand across his mouth, his chin. Gazing at her face, he struggled to find words. "Andrea. I think—I think I saw one. The other day."

There was silence for a minute. Andrea/Perka's eyes were wide when she spoke. "*Saw* one, Jared?" There was a hint of a tremor in her voice.

"Yes. I saw—I saw a demonstration in front of the new women's clinic. There—there was a bunch of people in front, protesting. Everything seemed fine until this weird little man somehow got them all worked up over almost nothing. They went nuts. It was crazy! And the man. The man…" Jared stopped and licked his lips, his eyes fixed in a glassy stare as he saw the scene replay in his memory. "Andrea—*Perka*, the man didn't—he didn't *move* like one of us. He almost seemed to glide. *Dammit!* He almost looked like he was gliding *through* the people in the crowd! He seemed to leave a—a trail of some sort behind him. Something like mist or something. It *was* one, wasn't it."

When she didn't reply, he studied her face. Her eyes had a blank look about them while her mouth hung partly open. His heart in his throat, he reached across to take her hand. "Andrea? Um—Perka?"

She nodded, her eyes still staring at nothing. Her free hand was on her cheek. Finally, she took a breath. "It almost certainly *was* one, Jared. But—but Jared. As an Earther, you should *not* have been able to see it for what it was. Not at all. When you saw the other one—the night that you helped me—you said that you saw it *melt*. Seeing that is one thing, but to see it while it is active is a different matter entirely. Earthers should see it as it wishes to be seen, not as it really is. Jared…when did this happen?"

The sense of urgency in her voice set his heart pounding once again. He tried to concentrate, to focus, to remember exactly how long ago it'd been. His thumbnail was back in his mouth as his teeth worked away at what was left of it. "It was—it was the day before I heard you call out to me from where the gang was." He was certain of that.

"Jared, this is highly unusual. When we—when we made love that first time, I responded to you much more than I should have. You were so—so sensitive...*mentally* to receiving my mind's images and emotions. And that helped us to communicate in a way that I had thought only my own kind capable of doing. It's becoming clear that it's even stronger than I had thought. You have developed some of the skills of *my* people. That's why you responded to my call for assistance and that is why I was able to use your energy to defeat the nnn-Asi-t. But...if you can actually perceive them for what they are, you are more gifted than I had imagined!"

Jared licked his dry lips. Hands shaking, he picked up his glass and took a quick sip, sloshing water suddenly down the front of his shirt and automatically wiping it with his sleeve. "Is—is that good? What you just said?"

She was watching him, a slight smile on her face. She shrugged her shoulders. "I—I am not altogether certain. But it *could* be. It could be quite good. You see, my people—and there are many of us across your planet—are here to push the nnn-Asi-t out, to let you Earthers develop as you will...with a little guidance. There are two ways we can do this. We can render Earthers resistant to the ploys of the nnn-Asi-t and we can make them totally immune. We can use our influence when we do this to help Earthers to find the kinder, gentler aspects of themselves, so that they can live a better life. When we do that, of course, it becomes simply too difficult for the nnn-Asi-t, and hopefully they will leave your planet."

"And the other way?"

"We can destroy the nnn-Asi-t. Like we did the one with the gang."

Jared nibbled again on his thumbnail as he nodded at the memory, quite aware of the fact that she'd said *we*. "You want me to help."

"I... I am not quite certain yet. This is most unusual. We are here to protect your people, not *use* you. We are your liberators. That is our purpose. That is the reason that we are here. The idea of having one of the Earthers involved is—is rather unheard of. Jared..." She began to speak but closed her mouth once more, still leaning forward towards him. Now she rose and stepped over to the sofa. She sat down beside him, turning so that they faced each other. Her fingers sought contact with his upper arm, his shoulder, then reached over to touch his cheek. "Jared, to even *tell* an Earther about ourselves is forbidden. I could be sent back home."

His cheek felt wonderful beneath her touch. What would he *do* if she were sent away? "What about me?"

Sighing, she sat back against the sofa. "I—I do not know what they would do about you! If this has ever happened before, I do not know when. Earthers simply haven't shown the strength and sensitivity that you have." She became quiet again, in thought. Rising, she stepped across the small room to the window, gazing outward, her fingers over her mouth. Jared moved to stand behind her, wrapping his arms around her shoulders, leaning his cheek against her hair. She was trembling—

No. She was *chuckling.*

Suddenly he was angry. "What are you laughing about if there's a chance that you'll be sent home?"

"Oh, Jared, my dear one." Turning in his arms, she faced him, reached up to lay a hand on his cheek. "We have some experimenting to do! If what I suspect is true, they will *not* be sending me home. If what I think is really the case, the nnn-Asi-t will not have an easy time with us. Because we have a new weapon—new strength they have never seen before."

She stopped, breaking their eye contact, and gazed downward, once more in thought.

"Tell me," he whispered, tilting her face upward, his fingers beneath her chin. "What do you mean? What weapon?"

The smile faded from her face, leaving gravity in its place. "*You,* Jared."

Chapter Twelve

I do not believe that I will ever forget the look of concern on Jared's face when I told him of his potential, and of our need for him. His feelings of fear and confusion were very vivid and easy for me to read. And all this, too, in addition to the continuing shock of his having seen me as I truly am. Poor Jared! There has been so much for him to deal with so suddenly. I only wish that I had had more time to help him to truly understand.

But events did not occur that way. And there is nothing to be gained from wishing for something that cannot be.

He knows now. Oh, no—he does not know *everything*. Not quite. I do not think that he has a realistic picture of the nnn-Asi-t as yet. But he will soon. He will most certainly *need* to soon.

I too was shocked to have found that Jared saw my true self. He believes that this occurred because my movements in the bedroom woke him. He does not realize that it was his own extreme sensitivity as a receiver which was sensing my changes as I was replenished. Even I had not suspected that he was so strong…

And, now that I know and understand more completely, I also see just how much assistance he might provide to my people. I no longer feel confused about the correctness of that. After all, assisting *us* will mean that he is actively involved in protecting his *own* kind.

Jared is not the first Earther to have learned of us. There have been a few others, although certainly none who possessed talent the likes of Jared's. In the past, we simply needed to block the memories of the Earthers once we realized all that they had come to know about us.

Jared. Will I block his memories of us—of me—when we are ready to leave? Will I even be able to, for that matter? Considering his great strength, I certainly could not without his willingness. I had been dreading the necessity of informing my people, especially the votary, about my involvement with Jared. But now I feel confident that they will understand the situation once they sense how talented he is.

I hope so. If not…

But there is no point in speculating. Tonight, all will be shared. Tonight we—Jared and I—will meet with my people. A tingle of excitement shoots up my spine, although the still-present apprehension tries to drag it back down. But I feel strongly that I will be bringing them good news.

It is time to go. I slip on my jacket—the newer, warmer one which I recently purchased—and head out of my apartment's door. My jacket is new, but of course it is another red one. No other colour feels right for me. I will head to Jared's place. From there we will walk together. Even before I have reached the lobby, though, I sense him. A few more steps and I can see him, too. He has just come through the outer door of my building and is about to push the button to tell me that he is here. Jared stops, his finger still raised. I watch him turn his head, and his blue eyes meet mine through the glass. Although I have not sent him any images, thoughts, or feelings, he has sensed my nearness. *Such sensitivity!*

I open the door from the lobby and smile at him as he lowers his hand once more. *He* is *not* smiling. I understand, as I can easily sense his anxiety, as well as see it in his azure eyes. Instantly I send warm reassurance, and place a hand on his. Physical contact makes sending so much easier.

Finally, with a hesitant sigh, he manages a wry grin. His eyes look deeply into mine. "Let's go," he says softly with another sigh.

"Let us—let's go," I repeat, that shiver of excitement once more scurrying up the length of my spine. He gazes at me questioningly, having sensed my positive feelings but not understanding the reason why I would have them. I hold his long fingers with my shorter ones as we walk, and I try to explain. Yet still I can feel the fear simmering inside of him. I understand, though. He has never met any others of my kind. I continue to send him feelings of reassurance. So easy to do when we maintain physical contact. To try to help, I also send him visual images of the Earther-like bodies which my comrades use. I must keep these images minimal, though, to avoid my messages being intercepted by possible nearby enemies. I do not sense any in the vicinity, but one should always use caution.

I sense his apprehension lessen a bit. He has certainly received some of what I have sent, although at this point I do not know whether he perceived the visual images or simply the sensations of emotion. This is not the correct time nor place for experimentation, however. We must share our findings with my people first.

We shall meet at the votary's building. It is inside of what used to be a rather large house. Here he performs routine maintenance requirements and, in return, receives use of a furnished apartment in the old building. In this way, he is able to monitor the minds of the tenants for any nnn-Asi-t influences, as well as have the time at night for actively searching the enemy out. I smile as I envision how easy routine Earther maintenance would be for someone with the capabilities of our people's votary! The votary is extremely skilled, gifted, and experienced in many areas.

We enter the building, and, as we proceed down the hallway, I already sense the presence of the others. I send a very brief flash of myself to them, informing them that I am approaching. Quickly, I position my shield so that nothing further is shared until we are closer. We have been trained to be quite cautious, to avoid having the enemy intercepting any of this. My people do not yet know that I am bringing this Earther. They must see him in order to understand—they must *feel* his power and potential. I will add explanations in words. Then they will totally comprehend.

We will use words rather than thoughts alone. We always do, just in case there might be an enemy within receiving distance. Were we all to project thoughts and feelings and images at the same time, there would a tremendous amount of energy which would be quite difficult to conceal.

I knock softly on the door. They will not open it until I do so. We must appear 'normal' to any possibly prying eyes. The door is opened, and I gaze at the smiling, fair-skinned face of my friend Georgia. It is so good to see her again!

But quickly she looks past me at Jared. She brushes a strand of blonde hair out of her face as her gaze returns to me. I step forward, and pull Jared through the doorway quickly, wanting all of them to experience him at the same time.

Out of courtesy as well as caution, their brief flashes of surprise and doubt are swiftly shielded. I must begin without delay.

"This is Jared," I am saying, my heart beating a little bit faster. "He receives. That is the reason which I have brought him here. He has a very strong sensitivity. He can be of help to us…" I look at the faces surrounding us. There is a continuing light sensation of doubt and confusion which permeates like a murmur.

I hesitate. I take a breath while I organize my thoughts. "You know me well," I continue. "I have considered everything carefully. We need to determine whether Jared's strength and sensitivity are limited to receiving, or if he can *send* effectively as well. If he can, we may be able to increase our effectiveness significantly by working with him. I have—I've—never before come across anything quite like this. We must give careful consideration to our next step."

The room is silent. Although the violet curtains have been drawn shut, they are translucent, and allow the sunlight to seep through to light the room. There is an eerie atmosphere as shadows are cast by some of the furnishings. I gaze around me at the faces of my comrades. There continues to be an undercurrent of confusion—and now, disbelief. My eyes rest on those of my friend Georgia. She seems even more pale than usual. Almost as pale as Jared. This provides a marked contrast to the dark skin of Martin, the votary, beside her. Franco is drumming his light brown fingers against his chin, eyes downcast. Some of the others exchange glances.

I let my gaze travel around our group of seven, then stop to lock with Martin's. I fold my legs and sit down upon the carpeted floor, cross-legged, as Jared follows my example. Without thinking, I find myself extending a hand to place it on Jared's knee, wishing to bring him comfort. Martin's eyes are so deeply brown that they appear almost black, as is his skin. His eyes follow the movement of my hand, then return to meet mine. His mind is shielded, as usual, and I receive no reaction yet from him. From somewhere in my own mind comes the thought that Martin's Earther colour is not that different from his true one. It is just muted a bit. Martin's soft voice distracts me from my musings.

"You're bonded," he says, meaning that he knows Jared and I have crossed the border from friendship and into intimacy. There is no emotion, no judgement in his whispery voice. He is simply stating a fact, an observation.

"Yes." I am not certain whether I should say more at this time. I did not anticipate that this would be his initial response.

His gaze moves to Jared. I turn to look, too, and see blue eyes displaying apprehension and confusion.

"Jared," Martin says in his gentle tones, "we aren't discourteous people, simply concerned. Andrea will have advised you that what she has done in bringing you here, and in making this proposal is extremely irregular. In fact, sharing anything about ourselves could almost be considered as a sort of *crime*."

Well, no. I had not worded it in that way. Theoretically, we have no crime in our world. It simply does not exist. It is more a matter of interpretation than anything else. Jared understands the seriousness of our situation. That is the important element.

Jared begins trying to speak, but his voice is rather raspy. Clearing his throat, he takes a breath, then starts again. "Martin," he says, "it was all my fault."

Martin looks at me questioningly. *Did I tell Jared the votary's Earth name?* I shake my head slightly.

Jared is silent. He has noticed the glances exchanged between Martin and me. We have not projected our thoughts. Jared is obviously quite attuned to our body language, as well. He sighs, raising his eyes once more to meet Martin's. "Andrea—Perka didn't tell me your name. I picked it up from her mind while she was looking around the room. Perka, I know that it's only a name, but if I could pick that up, maybe I can receive words—or more, too."

Jared and I had discussed such, for the extent of his abilities has been a matter of speculation between my bond-partner and me.

Without consciously intending to do so, Jared has given my people a demonstration of some of his skill.

"*Andrea*," says Martin to Jared. "We do not speak our home names aloud. Especially in a group such as this. We are cautious to project as little as possible, maintaining our shields, although we can relax them when we're in a relatively safe environment. Jared, are you able to read the thoughts in Andrea's mind now, at this moment? It would be helpful for us to know."

My shield is already in a tranquil state, as it is certainly not required among the members of this group. I raise it now, although not completely. Although it would be a rare occurrence for an Earther to read the thoughts of my people, it is not entirely unheard of. But if my shield is in place, it should be almost completely impossible.

Jared shrugs. "It's easy," he says softly. "Optimism, a feeling of joy at being with all of you—"

Martin raises a hand to stop him. "I said *thoughts*, Jared."

At first Jared frowns slightly, a bit confused. He is silent for a few seconds, concentrating. He speaks: "*Please, my people, accept this man's abilities with joy—*"

Once more, Martin stops him with a raised hand. He nods in understanding. "Yes, Jared. Of course, Andrea is correct. You are not the only Earther to possess abilities in this area. However, your talent is much stronger than we have seen among Earthers before. And, if you are able to *send* as well, it is imperative that you learn to shield yourself effectively. Now that you and Andrea are bonded, she will be able to receive your feelings and thoughts easily. But we do not know whether you have the talent necessary to purposefully send thoughts and messages to others. We must learn that information, but we must not attempt to find the answer here, at this time."

"He helped me," I add, "when we defeated a strong enemy. I sent a plea for help, and it was Jared who received, rather than any of you."

Martin strokes his chin. His eyes are narrowed as he thinks about the implications. "In what way, exactly, did he assist you, Andrea?"

How very well I recall that night! In my mind, I see it as though it were just yesterday! When I look up, I catch a glimpse of Georgia who gazes at me with interest. I am so glad that she is here to share in this revelation. "I could sense his power and strength nearby," I explain. "I made use of his energy reserves to combine them with my own skills."

It is Georgia who now speaks. "Your bond is strong, then—especially considering that one of you is an Earther! If he was able to augment your own power so effectively in that situation, without any training, he might well be able to greatly increase your strength in battle. Martin, perhaps we should consider allowing other bonded mates to serve together."

Martin takes a rather deep breath, once more considering everything thoroughly. That is one of his responsibilities as our votary. But he shakes his head. "No, Georgia. We have already discussed and considered this at great length. As you likely recall, we have found that bond-mates were *too* aware of one another. And too concerned about each other's safety and wellbeing for focussing on their strength against the enemy."

There is silence for a few moments, each of us considering the implications. Beside me, Jared clears his throat and shifts his sitting position. Sensing his discomfort, I once more place my hand on his leg.

Finally, Martin speaks again. "As Jared is not one of our kind, you and he are not *true* mates, Andrea. Bonded partners, yes, but not true mates. At least, I am assuming that you have initiated nothing like our sharing ceremony…" His dark brown eyes are studying me once more. I shake my head negatively, and he continues. "So, there is, then, more to this than simply your bond. It must be that Jared *does* possess unusual talent. Yet, Jared, you are not one of our kind. This is highly irregular." He sighs again. "As you are not one of us, it is not for me to serve as your votary. Andrea has, I assume, explained the risks to you, should you become involved with us."

Jared once again clears his throat. "Yes."

Martin strokes the thin growth of whiskers on his chin once more. He is not comfortable with this situation, and that is quite understandable. It is so highly unusual. He sighs, then speaks again. "Very well, then. If it is your will and your decision, you may seek to assist us. Obviously, the most effective use of your talent would be through your bond-mate. First, though, we must try to gain a more thorough understanding of this talent of yours. And, if you *can* send as well as receive, we must teach you to shield yourself from doing so when caution is necessary. And we must determine a method for evaluating your sending ability—"

"They could come with one of us," suggests Franco, his fingers toying with the narrow, dark moustache decorating his upper lip.

"Yes," Martin agrees. "In that way, Jared, we would be able to see if you can affect change in another Earther. We must proceed with utmost caution, of course. And we would do this when another of our kind is along with you, too. In that way, should Andrea experience any difficulty and you find that you cannot assist, someone else would be there for her also. What is your response, Jared? Would you prefer to have more time to consider the possibility?"

Jared shrugs his shoulders. I can sense his eyes studying me, but I do not return his gaze. I do not wish to influence him any more than I already have.

He switches the direction of his gaze back to Martin. "When do we go—and what, exactly will we do?"

Martin smiles kindly at him. Yes, it is true that Jared's situation has complicated our mission here on Earth. At the same time, though, he might be able to make our mission easier. And more successful. "Jared," Martin says softly, "no words that you know would adequately describe what we will do. But with your receiving skills, you will, doubtless, perceive what Andrea is sending and, quite possibly, what an Earther is experiencing too. You would simply follow Andrea's example while I evaluate the situation. What are your thoughts, Jared?"

Again, Jared shrugs his narrow shoulders. "Sounds straightforward enough!"

I cannot help but shake my head. Oh, my naïve Earther! You have so much yet to learn!

Chapter Thirteen

Jared put his hand on his stomach. The hot pain was back. It felt like he'd swallowed a litre of acid. And that wasn't all of it. He felt like he'd been split in two. Part of him desperately wanted to simply run away from this whole thing, but another part was anxious to do anything at all possible to help stop this horrible evil threatening his society—his whole planet. Yet the awful fear inside was almost overwhelming. Whenever he thought about himself, Jared David Collins, engaged in battle with some sort of alien, his whole body trembled almost uncontrollably. And *she* knew it. He sensed it, even though she wasn't sending anything from her mind to his. But her skill in transmitting sensations of comfort and reassurance was tremendous, for she seemed able to accomplish this entirely through a touch of her hand or a brief hug, or by simply putting her arm around his waist while they walked.

There was an nnn-Asi-t somewhere in the area and they must not risk it possibly detecting their presence. This being would be *extremely* suspicious, Martin had explained, if it became aware too soon of the approach of more than one of Perka's kind, together.

It appeared that, although Perka and her kind were able to *sense* the presence of the nnn-Asi-t, the reverse wasn't true to the same degree. Her kind's Earther disguises, combined with their skill in shielding their thought-projections from the enemy, allowed them to move about without arousing the suspicions of the nnn-Asi-t—at least, until they became heavily involved in their work. Should they lower their shields, though, they became vulnerable, as a nearby nnn-Asi-t might detect their presence.

Jared was only too aware of his limitations as compared to *their* skills. He had not yet been taught how to keep his own thought-projections safely hidden, when that was necessary. Still, it was vaguely uncomfortable for him to feel the touch of Martin's power inside of him. How awfully strange it was to know that someone else's mind was in constant contact with his own! And how very, *very* strange, to be aware that Martin's presence was strong enough to control him—to prevent him from inadvertently sending any projections of his own. How extremely powerful and skilled Martin must be to shield two minds at once!

It felt like a *physical* presence inside of his head—no, not just his head. It was inside, and almost a new physical part of, his entire body. It reminded him vaguely of when he was a little boy and his dad used to walk along with him, one hand lightly resting on top of Jared's head. Yet, at this time, the thought of happy times with his beloved stepdad did not bring him any comfort or peace. He sighed.

"Here," said Martin in his breathy voice.

They had not known exactly where in the area they would find the enemy. They hadn't even known, when they'd left the apartment, how many of the nnn-Asi-t would be in this vicinity. But they'd felt its presence not too far away. And that had been enough.

Jared stopped. His companions had already stopped, but *he* hadn't felt anything at all, other than Martin's touch inside of him. The others were standing still, rigidly, as though they were listening for something. But Jared knew this wasn't the case at all.

They were *feeling*, sensing for something—carefully, to accomplish this while remaining shielded enough that thought-projections were minimal. It was strange to watch Perka—Jared had to remind himself to think of her as *Andrea*, especially when they were out in the open—and Martin exchange quick glances, and then both look upward at the same spot at the same time.

Jared sighed. Again, he had heard and felt nothing at all. He was beginning to feel kind of useless, like a fifth wheel. *Maybe I won't be as good at this as they seem to think—*

But he pushed that thought out of his mind. He couldn't let negativity interfere with everything. Anyway, he wasn't trying to do something on his own. Martin and Per—*Andrea* were right here with him. Jared turned his gaze to look where his companions did. All he saw, though, was the upper part of a crumbling, old building. But suddenly his companions were exchanging glances once more. And this time there was a more urgent look about Martin's face, as well as on Andrea's.

"Quickly," breathed Andrea, and gave a quick pull on Jared's jacket sleeve. They turned away from the sidewalk to follow Martin as he ducked under the thick overgrowth of hedge, then into a dark and narrow passage between the outer wall and vines stretching their ways up the brickwork of the building. They emerged in a backyard strewn with rubble. A basement window had been smashed, and it was through this opening that Martin began to ease himself, Andrea close behind him.

Jared inhaled. A large part of him definitely did *not* want to follow. He needed to remind himself that his whole planet might depend on this. And, anyway, if Andrea was going in there, he sure wasn't going to let her go without him. "I can't believe I'm doing this," he muttered to himself, as he eased his long frame past the rough edges of the window frame and into what looked like a shadowy abyss…

Grateful to feel something solid beneath his feet, Jared found himself standing on a wooden workbench. As he stepped down onto the cement floor, he had to pinch his nostrils closed to keep a sneeze from breaking the stillness, his other hand waving side to side in front of his face to stir away the dusty air. Ahead, dimly, he could make out Andrea's form. She was motioning to him to follow her. He hurried in that direction, hoping that the air might be less dusty ahead.

But everything in front of him was shrouded in darkness and shadows. It wasn't until he had stepped through some sort of doorway that he was able to recognize the outline of a staircase leading upward. At the bottom, Andrea was again motioning for him to follow as she began to step up.

Jared hurried after her, grateful for the dim light ahead and above that seemed to come from another open doorway. The step *creaked* under the weight from his foot. He clung to the old railing, hoping it would hold despite its looseness. Clinging to it seemed quite necessary, as he couldn't see well enough to be sure each step was secure, and he was fearful of ever finding his way should he lose touch. Finally, he arrived at the top.

Yet again, Andrea was bidding him to follow her. At least, here they were out of the basement and had a faint bit of light from some of the windows to guide them. In the meager moonglow, he could see dust particles floating through the air, gold specks drifting in the lunar illumination. Up another staircase and then yet another. Jared was amazed at the relative quiet, for most of the steps made little or no sound at all, despite their apparent age. He could now see spots in the old, reddish carpeting that were worn through to show the wooden floor beneath.

At the top of the next—smaller and narrower—staircase was a door with a window. Through it, Jared could see twinkling stars greeting them from the night sky.

Martin was at the door. Jared watched as the votary's dark hand reached for the knob. Maybe the door was locked. But something inside told Jared that a locked door would not delay Martin for long. The three of them were together now at the door, Martin on one side and Andrea on the other. It was a narrow staircase, so Jared waited one step down from the others, watching as they exchanged glances and then closed their eyes.

Jared tried to swallow a lump which suddenly lodged itself in his throat. He stood silently, watching them, more and more aware of his heart pounding harder. Then, slowly, he realized that he could actually *see* them as they sensed, felt…and evaluated the nnn-Asi-t.

At first, he thought it was just the light from outside being separated into different colours by the unevenness of the glass or something. Then he realized that Martin and Andrea each seemed to be emanating a different shade. Of course, it was a crimson glow drifting from Andrea and then seeping out through the small spaces around the door. Jared could see that Martin's shade was reddish, too, but with a strong brownish tint.

It seemed like only a second or two had gone by before the—the *whatever it was* drifted back in around the door to soak back in through the skin of Martin and Andrea. Once this happened, the two opened their eyes again and regarded each other.

Andrea turned to look at Jared. She blinked her eyes a couple of times as though orienting herself. She gave him a small smile. But this wasn't enough to keep him from nibbling on his thumbnail. Martin's face was expressionless, yet Jared strongly felt Martin's desire to move *now.* Jared could sense that Andrea felt it too.

The nnn-Asi-t might become aware of their presence…

The door was open instantly, although silently, and Jared stepped after the other two as they disappeared onto a large balcony, their scarlet and brownish-red sensing projections now reaching outward. They'd climbed over a railing to stand on a flat section of the roof. Jared followed, then hesitated. He was suddenly *empty.* No longer did he feel any touch from Martin inside of him. There was no more presence inside to restrain him—

Or *protect* him.

Then, suddenly, over the edge of the greenish roof, he saw it.

The nnn-Asi-t—

A shimmering mass that continually changed its shape as it moved. A greyish, amorphous blob gliding, almost floating, then drifting downward through the moonlight and shadows towards the pavement below. A few silvery patches were catching the starlight as the thing drifted, drifted away…

Then, quickly, the thing began to adopt a more distinct silhouette. In only a few seconds, Jared was staring, open-mouthed, at a slightly built human who then disappeared into the night's blackness. Jared watched, then began to *feel* the presence of Andrea and Martin. Martin's was nothing more than stillness. But he could sense Andrea projecting to the nnn-Asi-t's victim. Suddenly remembering that this was the reason for his presence, Jared turned in their direction.

A young man was standing near the edge of the roof. In his hands was an automatic rifle. He was aiming it in the direction of the commercial area of the city, which wasn't far. When Jared gazed that way, he could make out people lined up to enter a popular downtown bar.

Gasping, he prepared himself to help Andrea. He watched her warm, crimson glow move to surround the young man, who continued to aim the weapon. As her energy seeped through him, though, his hands began to tremble slightly. Jared, too, could clearly feel her peace, as well as the strength behind it. He sighed, letting his shoulders droop, allowing the sensation to enter all parts of him. Then he prepared to take over from her…

Jared closed his eyes, focussing on what was happening inside of him. He could feel the young man—the frenzy inside of him, created by the nnn-Asi-t's amplification of the anger and frustration that had already been there. Also making itself known was the calming and peaceful effect of Andrea's power, gliding smoothly throughout the youth with a silken touch. The youth's frenzy was beginning to ease.

Now Jared moved closer to the young man, to reach inside of him. Jared concentrated on sending calmness, reassurance, tolerance, and maturity. Peacefully yet firmly, he urged it along until it flowed gently from him, all the time reminding himself to relax and not push too hard. As the young man received this, he moved closer to calmness. The weapon was now held loosely in the victim's hands. Finally, almost all traces of the frenzy were gone.

The young man sighed, his shoulders dropping lower while Jared began to withdraw, gently, gently, slowly. He stood for a time, a little afraid of opening his eyes until he was certain that all aspects of himself were back inside him where they should be.

Then, dimly, as though from someplace far away, he could hear Andrea's soft voice as she guided the young man to speak about what he was feeling inside. Jared could sense her touch the victim physically, as well as a small burst of energy piercing deep inside of the victim, sealing and protecting him from any further interference or influence from the nnn-Asi-t.

Through the haze which had developed inside of his mind, Jared was becoming aware of an almost overwhelming fatigue. But then he felt Andrea's essence as it entered *him*. It was wonderful. Incredible.

Her essence and his were locked for a moment, all aspects of their inner beings intertwined—an embrace stretching way beyond physical limitations. Jared saw her, felt her, smelled her, heard her all at once and throughout him, inside and out. She was a part of him as much as his heart or his brain or his skin. And there was a deep sense of warmth and comfort that made him think of a fire in the hearth on a cold winter night…*contentment and peace.* The flames nibbled at the crackling logs happily, glowing in the varying shades of crimson, orange, gold and yellow.

It was beautiful.

Chapter Fourteen

My poor, dear Earther! We were both fatigued after tracking the enemy, and by our efforts with the nnn-Asi-t's victim. But whatever *I* feel must be twofold for Jared, as he has never experienced anything remotely like this. A bit of guilt nags at me, as I am not certain if we were successful in conveying to him just how *exhausting* this might be. If anything, my experience was not nearly as taxing as it often can be, although I ache inside when I consider that we were not quick enough to destroy the enemy. But I reassure myself that it was necessary for us to delay, in order to complete a thorough assessment of the enemy's powers. After all, we were about to include Jared in our efforts for the first time.

It is quite clear to me now. Jared's power to send *had* augmented my own. Together, we had even more energy than we had really required in this circumstance. Jared does not realize it as yet, but when I felt his projection affecting the victim, I withdrew mine entirely. Therefore, he does not comprehend that it was his *own* ability which completed the process and deadened the effect of the nnn-Asi-t. My role had been simply to speak with the victim to give him insight, and to complete the immunization process. If only our interactions with all victims could be as effective as this one was. If only we had the opportunity to be as thorough with everyone. I always feel truly uncomfortable when I have not been able to seal each victim from any possible future manipulation by the enemy.

But sometimes we must settle for simply making them more resistant. Sometimes that is the best that we can do, and we must be content with that.

Jared snores gently, like a purring Earth cat, and I turn my head to gaze at his sleeping form. We are in Martin's bed, as my poor Earther was too exhausted to handle the walk back to his own place or mine. I should have considered this possibility and suggested that we use his car. Martin does not mind, though, sleeping on his sofa. Our people tend to be much more adaptable than these Earthers seem to be. I guess that makes perfect sense, as it is our people who have been travelling to other worlds.

I have already stretched out my limbs. I feel replenished and ready to rise. Gently, so as not to disturb my Earther, I get out of bed and open the curtain slightly, wanting to watch the first fiery rays of this solar system's sun as they kiss the horizon. What a splendid selection of colours! If only such richness could be maintained throughout Earth's day, instead of fading to pale yellow or almost white as the hours of the day advance.

Quietly I dress and step to the nearby bathroom. Then I walk to the kitchen, sit down, and retrieve my LLL-nnnta from its little pouch inside my belt. The tiny ball enlarges and begins to glow, as crimson as the morning sun. As its strength begins to surge throughout my being, my thoughts and memories turn to the sun in my own galaxy, so far away…

It is finished. I feel complete, well and whole. After a deep, invigorating breath, I am filled with confidence and mental strength once more. Suddenly a thought strikes me. There is more now to think about than only myself. My Jared will require sustenance as well! And his needs are so much different from my own! I rise and reach for the handle of the cupboard door, wondering what I might possibly find in Martin's kitchen. Of course. The ritual jar of instant coffee is there. He, too, has become aware of the importance of this social drink one needs in order to pass as an Earther! Our representatives back on my own planet have underestimated the popularity of this coffee.

I wonder if Martin has learned to drink this strange liquid with its stimulant effect...

What else is here? A few boxes of some sort of 'noodle' preparation. Not much else. Only the basics to satisfy any possible prying Earther eyes. In the old refrigerator is a small container of something intended to add flavour to the coffee, but when I check the 'best before date', I see that it has passed. And, as if to prove the point, there is a rather foul odour escaping from the container, and so I empty the smelly contents down the sink's drain. There are other containers in the fridge as well, mostly of fruit juice. Simple props to enhance Martin's Earther disguise.

Well, the most basic morning requirement for Jared is here, at least. While he enjoys drinking coffee with milk added, he sometimes drinks it without—*black*, I believe he calls it. But he also requires food. I read the instructions on the noodle box. Milk must be added. It does not appear to be optional, as in the case of the coffee. However, milk was what I discarded.

A sigh escapes me. I will simply need to go out and purchase some. I had been enjoying the relative safety of Martin's apartment. Anytime one of us ventures outside, we feel the need for vigilance because of the enemy.

I also consider the fact that we were given only a small amount of currency. Our representatives withdrew a bit from the Earther economy so that we could pay one month of rent until we could establish the best possible accommodations. But we are careful to spend as little as possible, so as to disturb the economy minimally. The ideal situation for us is one such as Martin's, where he pays no rent, but performs a service in exchange for his living quarters. It is this type of arrangement for which we all hope. If such is not available, we will take to sharing accommodations, now that we have completed our initial explorations of the nnn-Asi-t and their locations.

The nnn-Asi-t have no such concerns, I reflect. For they exist as shadowy substances until they choose to adopt their Earther disguises. And shadowy substances have no need of such shelters.

I hear a slight noise in the next room, and, assuming that it is Jared stirring, I reach for the kettle to plug it in. But then I feel

Martin's presence behind me. So sensitive are our kind to one another that he does not need to project at all for me to feel him when he is this close.

"Good morning, Andrea," says his deep Earther voice. "Did you sleep well?"

Dear Martin! How adept and correct he is with the Earther customs and greetings! I am quite certain that he must be the only one among our kind who *never* makes any error at all in this regard.

"Good morning, Martin. Yes. I did. Thank you. Poor Jared was extremely fatigued, however. He is still sleeping."

Martin nods. There is silence a moment as he ponders something. "Andrea, it is imperative that we teach him to shield his thought-projections. It's quite likely that his sending can be developed to become rather powerful. He *must* learn control before he can truly become an asset to us."

It is my turn to nod. As always, Martin is constantly assessing our progress, our opportunities, our developments. And setting priorities.

"Andrea, once I've cleansed this body, I'll be busy in one of the apartments. I realize that you will be with the crisis line this evening, so it will be highly important that you work here with Jared today and teach him to shield." His dark brown eyes regard me as he speaks.

I agree with him, and watch him as he walks away. There is a noise behind me, and as I turn toward the counter, I see water splashing merrily from the kettle's spout along with steam. The water is most certainly hot enough! Hastily I unplug the little appliance and prepare to mix the hot liquid with the powdered coffee. As I do, I am contemplating how I might begin teaching Jared to shield. I have certainly never before attempted such with an Earther. But, considering the strong rapport that Jared and I have, surely the process will be relatively straightforward...

Suddenly I find myself standing just outside of the closed bedroom door, my feet having taken me there without any conscious direction from my mind. I open the door, holding the coffee mug in one hand, and watch Jared spread out amidst the heap of bedding. He is emitting a low, strange noise—almost like the contented sound of a kkk-MMM-n back home. I can see his dreams as they drift past me, almost like an Earther television show. Yes. He *must* learn to shield...and soon!

But I find myself pulling the door shut tightly behind me—

I deposit the mug of steaming coffee on a side table, then turn my attention to the bed. It is time to waken my Earther. Sighing, hating to disturb him after his exhaustion last night, I sit on the side of the bed. My hand reaches for his back, loving the feel of his skin beneath my fingers. He murmurs in his sleep and rolls toward me. His hand finds my own. I pull my gaze from our hands to see eyes—as azure as the Earth sky—smiling into mine. He pulls me to him, his arms slipping so easily around me. I let the physical, Earther-like parts of me dominate, savouring the warmth and joy of his caresses. Slowly my clothing is discarded...

Soon the blankets are not the only things enjoying entanglement with my Earther. I open my eyes to see the coffee mug still on the table. Somehow, I know that he will not mind if the drink becomes cold.

We lie quietly. We heard Martin *click* the apartment door closed a short time ago. We have not yet risen. Guilt nags at me, but still, it is difficult to leave the wonderful peace of lying here together. It is truly delightful to allow our physical beings to enjoy a communication such as our inner essences did not that long ago.

"I love you, Perka or Andrea or whatever. I really love you. I've never, ever known anyone so intimately, so deeply, so completely. I love you."

Those whispered words startle me a bit. He has not said them before this, although I certainly know that he cares greatly about me. I want to respond in kind. But I cannot. Is it truly possible for one of our kind to 'love' an Earther? Am I even capable of that? I am simply not sure. I turn to him and put my lips against his forehead, sharing my feeling of joy at being with him. I project my passion, my respect, my delight in him. His smile tells me that such is enough for now.

"Perka—*Andrea*—tell me about the sharing ceremony that Martin mentioned."

My hands are still on his cheeks. I contemplate projecting an image of the feelings involved in it but decide not to. If I use words, I can share the concept more slowly, and he might better understand. "It is—it's the celebration of total bonding. Becoming true mates for life. Both share everything—every aspect of their inner beings. Both are truly in a complete union. All past experiences and every hope for the future—"

"But…*how?* Didn't we do some of that already?"

I smile at the memory and kiss his forehead again. "Only to a small degree, Jared. The actual, complete ceremony is more all-encompassing."

His hands reach up to cover my own. He takes my two hands and presses each, one at a time, to his lips. Then he shakes his head in wonder at what I have said. "I can't imagine it being deeper than it was when we were helping that victim."

One of my hands moves to run through his short, curly, brown hair. "It is—it's hard to explain. But imagine, if you can, that experience a dozen times more intense and deeper. Jared, it's like each partner becomes totally absorbed by the other."

His response is a frown. I know that he is trying to understand. "Do they stay like that?"

"No. Oh, no. But traces…some aspects remain each with the other."

"Have you ever bonded with one of your kind—I mean, taken a mate?"

"No." My voice is a whisper, although I am not sure why. Part of me wants to tell him that, if I were mated I would not have responded to him that first night. But I shield that thought. I turn to him and smile. I lean forward and plant a kiss on his lips. "And now, my dear Earther, we must rise. We have work to do. I am going to teach you how to shield. It is—it's extremely important, Jared."

He nods his understanding and, after a stretch of his long limbs, pushes aside the bedcovers. As he stands, naked, the physical parts of me appreciate his sinewy strength. He has received my thought. Turning to me, he grins wryly.

For some reason I am not aware of, I feel the need to clear my throat. I must focus on our business matters. "Jared, why don't you go and get yourself ready? I will take the bedding downstairs to the laundry room and begin the cleaning process."

As I dress, I hear the water in the shower begin. I listen for a moment to Jared's strange 'singing' as I put the laundry card in my pocket and head for the apartment door.

The need to hurry is strong in me. I am uncomfortable about leaving Jared alone in Martin's apartment. This worry is a new feeling for me. I never cared for anyone in this manner before…

Perhaps I *do* love him. Even as I think this, though, I am shaking my head, unable to really comprehend it.

In my pocket, I have some currency in addition to the laundry card. There is a small store just across the street which sells food. Although it does not offer much in the way of variety, I locate bread and cheese and a small amount of fruit. I am a bit uncomfortable with the fact that I have very little money at all left as I carry the bag back to Martin's place.

Jared is seated at the kitchen table when I return, his phone in one hand, while his other is wrapped around the coffee mug. He has prepared a fresh cup of coffee for himself while I was gone. Smiling wryly, he informs me that he did not bother to make any for me. As I show him the nourishment items which I brought for him, my mind is on the teaching I must do.

Sighing, he has put his phone back into his pocket. He always checks his messages when he rises in the morning, but, apparently, he has not found anything pleasurable today. Jared asked me once why we do not use social media to do our work. My people have no need for phones, as we can communicate with each other without them, should we require assistance or wish to arrange a meeting. And influencing Earthers, in the way that we need to, is simply not as effective through the written word. Unfortunately, though, sharing information through social media *is* helpful to the nnn-Asi-t, as they can use it to tell Earthers about group gatherings at which the enemy can work to arouse the Earthers' emotions. Indeed, the nnn-Asi-t also post messages and videos to negatively affect the Earthers, and therefore use social media to do some of their work for them.

Which, of course, makes the efforts of my people all the more necessary.

Jared appreciates the cheese sandwich. It is obvious when I observe him as he eats it. I pass him a paper towel when he begins to clean the crumbs off his chin with the sleeve of his green shirt. He takes another sip of the coffee and is about to run the back of his hand across his mouth, when I call attention once more to the paper towel in front of him. Watching this leads me to feel grateful again for my people's method of procuring nourishment.

Finally. "Jared. It is time. Come, my Earther." As we head to the living room, I explain to him in words again what we will do, hoping that he is gaining some understanding.

But such is difficult for an Earther to comprehend.

"No, Jared. No. I am sorry. You will have to try again. I *know* that this is difficult. But once you have done it correctly, you will get the feel of it. I think that perhaps you are trying too hard, so you end up pushing outward instead of maintaining all where it is—and that means that you *send* your thought instead of keeping all inside." I lick my dry lips, watching his face. Not that there is any particular need to do so, as I can easily feel his frustration and fear of failure as vividly as if they were my own.

He runs his hand across his mouth, his chin. Jared does this when he is thinking. But it is not necessarily a symptom of frustration, for I know well that he chews on his thumbnail in that situation. His shoulders move, as he tries to relax the muscles, and then he sits back in his chair, closing his eyes.

I can see his thoughts and feelings clearly, as well as his determination and some doubt. He projects to me, then tries to bring his shield into place to stop his projection. Even before it happens, I can feel him prepare to force down the barrier with much more energy than required. I hurry to shield myself, knowing what is about to come—

I can see the blast of energy which he hurls at me in his effort.

It's white. I have never actually *seen* his power before. White is probably not surprising when one considers the paleness of his people. Yet there seems something strange about it. Now Jared is hunched forward in the chair, his head once again in his hands. *My poor Earther.*

Crossing the room, I sit on the cushioned arm of the large chair. My fingers stroke the curly brown hair as I let my support and reassurance slip through them and into his tired being. He slips an arm around my waist and leans his head against me, his forehead damp with sweat.

"I can't do it."

There are two messages as he says this. One is the spoken message, while the other is the true one which comes from inside. This cries out to me to reassure him, convince him somehow, even force him to somehow develop this skill. He wants to be part of our effort here on Earth. He desires so very much to help us to defeat the nnn-Asi-t. His energy and determination are almost palpable.

His energy and power. So vast! How fortunate for us…if only we can help him to master them…

Then I see what the problem is. His *energy*. It is not like ours. So, of course, I cannot assist him in the same way that I would one of my own people. I have to relate to him as though he is one of the most powerful forces we have…

Which he just might be.

"Jared." I stand in front of him, one hand on each side of his face. Our eyes lock, and I project the warmest sensations of peace, contentment, and relaxation that I can. I sense him as he begins to respond, but his self-doubt interferes like air bubbles popping at the surface of smooth water. I send another wave of calm, visualizing it as a soft, light, reddish blanket, falling around his shoulders to caress him, as though it is a living being.

Confusion enters his eyes and his conscious thoughts as he wonders what this has to do with my teaching him. Then, finally, peace and relaxation. I open my mind to him and read his thoughts. He visualizes his relaxation as birds floating effortlessly through the blue sky, with no sound except for twittering and songs.

Then I project a conscious thought to him: *Jared. Shield.*

After a slight hesitation, he begins. His energy is lying low in this relaxed state. I can see the clear sheet slip into place around his thoughts. Then I see nothing but the physical Jared.

I see his mouth drop open in surprise and his face register relief and joy.

Chapter Fifteen

The man walked along the sidewalk, hands thrust deep into the pockets of his denim jacket. It was the beginning of a beautiful evening, the sun sinking slowly downward toward the horizon, decorating the way with a blending of yellows, oranges, golds, and various shades of red. Light reflected from the windows of the little houses, illuminating the area even more.

But the young man didn't see any of this. His downcast eyes were unfocussed, although it looked like they might be regarding the dull greyish tones of the concrete beneath his running shoes. He almost walked into a lamppost, but, muttering a vague apology, stepped around it, eyes still downcast.

Many thoughts were occupying the man's mind. These were confused, and seemed to be constantly swirling in endless competition for his attention. And, although the few passersby could not see this, every once in awhile a clear sheet-like bit of energy would settle like an invisible fence around the confusion. Then, as worry began to nibble away at his resolve, the sheet would shimmer as though undecided, and it would disappear.

And then, with a sigh, he would begin the process all over again.

Jared Collins was frightened. The responsibility seemed awesome. So many were depending on him! He *had* to do everything he possibly could. But all the talk about the vastness of his energy and his power only left him terrified.

If it's so powerful, how can I possibly control it? How can I even shield it effectively?

A long sigh escaped him, his breath visible in the cool air as a long, foggy stream. This was the sigh of a person whose responsibilities seemed so terribly overwhelming that they could not possibly be carried out. With a tremendous effort, he convinced himself to relax enough that he could shield his thoughts once more. Now there were only outward clues to his thoughts, his emotional state sketched only too clearly as deep creases, as well as a frown on his face. The message would be clear to anyone who passed by—this was a young man who felt enormous stress.

There was a shadowy presence in the alley where it met the sidewalk, and the presence was quite aware of the man's emotional state. It could not detect anything at all of the man's *inner* thoughts or emotions, but the outward signs it had seen when it had passed by him identified him as a possible candidate. The greyish mass began to adopt a more recognizable form. As it did, it sensed something like a mixture of fear and excitement inside the man. But this was muted suddenly.

Its metamorphosis complete, the presence now had the form of a slightly-built older lady with grey though her short, brown hair. The dark clothing she wore allowed her to blend easily with the shadows of the alley. She stood near to the spot where the alleyway met the side of the walkway, but she did not need to peer around the corner to determine where the man was. She sensed him as he moved closer.

Suddenly, she stepped toward the sidewalk, quickly. But then he was *there—*

She hadn't expected him to enter the alley so suddenly. She fumbled to respond *now,* but then she saw the man's unshielded thoughts—and his *power—*

A white flash. So fast, so sudden, so strong. And then the nnn-Asi-t was only a mist in the air, slowly dissipating.

Jared stood, watching. His face was expressionless. It registered no surprise, no relief. He'd simply done what was necessary. Sighing, he shook his head to try to fight the fatigue that was creeping in. Somehow, he'd managed to maintain his shield in the correct position, even while he felt like sobbing inside. He stood, back against the brick wall. *Why me? I didn't ask for this! Dammit, now I can't even walk down the street without having to be on guard! Oh, dear God, please help me.*

He scolded himself. He couldn't lose control now! Hurriedly, Jared eased the shield securely back into its place. There had to be some way of experiencing his emotions without losing control of his shield as well as his composure!

There *had* to be.

After what seemed like a century, he finally reached his apartment building. It felt safer here, even though he knew that it really wasn't. Too tired to bother opening his closet door, he hung his jacket over the door handle while he pushed off each shoe with the toe of the other foot. *So...awfully...tired.* He sank into the cushy armchair—too hard, and the loose spring inside reminded his butt how old the chair was. Sitting, he let his head fall against the back of the chair as he sighed, willing himself to relax. Immediately, he was aware of his mistake. He was *trying* to relax.

Jared took a long, deep breath and closed his eyes as he focussed on filling his lungs completely, and then letting the air out slowly, slowly. The sensation of relaxation began to fill his depths as delicate shades of reds and whites forming graceful patterns inside his mind...

And he felt his shield slip into place as easily and naturally as though he'd been doing this all his life.

Maybe he had. And he just hadn't known it. A sigh eased its way out of his body as he closed his eyes. For a moment, he was aware only of a beautiful sensation of peace which began to fill him, then there was nothing at all. He had no idea how long he'd been there. But then he felt *her*. At first, Jared thought he was dreaming. But consciously he recognized it as a brief flash that she must have sent to let him know she was approaching. It wasn't enough, though, to bring him to full wakefulness.

But then she was there. Physically. He was dimly aware of her as she kissed his cheek and touched his hand. Gently, yet with surprising strength, she guided him to his feet and, placing her shoulder beneath his upper arm, she moved him in the direction of his bedroom. But these physical sensations were almost nothing in comparison with the soft caresses of her essence. He was on the brink of waking, yet it was so comfortable as he felt her undress him and tuck the blankets around him. Her essence was inside him now, making him complete. And it was wonderful.

It had been Georgia who'd felt the thing's presence. She had been monitoring it, briefly sensing the degree of its power, yet also careful to keep her own projections still while her shield was not entirely in place. In order for her to explore the thing's capability, her shield needed to be at least slightly open. A delicate situation. Completing her evaluations, she swallowed. Hard.

This was a strong one. And she'd sensed in it a huge desire for destruction, not just of one Earther, but many.

She couldn't risk attempting to learn anything further of its intentions. This thing was quite powerful. It was thus that she had sought the counsel of the votary. If this enemy was as strong as it seemed, the power of *several* of her people working together might be required to stop it from whatever it might be planning. That would be impractical. But there might be an alternative…

"I'm sorry, Jared. But we may well have need of you. You and Andrea together might be the best opposition to a powerful enemy. Eventually, perhaps you on your own. I will go with you, with my shield in place. I'll approach from a different angle, out of sight if possible. Then I can lift my shield and become involved only if such is truly necessary."

Martin's whispery voice stopped. His living room was silent once again. It seemed to Jared that feeling overwhelmed was becoming his new normal. His fingers massaged his forehead. A vague sensation of nausea was developing somewhere in the depths of his stomach.

Then, suddenly, Andrea was standing in front of him where he sat on the rug. She was extending a hand bearing a steaming mug of coffee. Sighing, he accepted it and began to move it to his lips, stopping himself long enough to send a light flash of gratitude to her. Jared wasn't aware of Martin's eyes studying him. But he *did* feel the briefest of flashes instructing him to shield. Jared blinked once and the shield slipped into place. As he sipped the comforting heat of the coffee, he heard Martin sigh.

Martin was nodding. "It has improved, Jared. Most definitely improved. But still, even a little delay like that could mean your destruction. If only there were a way for you to be faster—"

A sudden thought struck Jared as he pulled the rim of the mug away from his lips. It wasn't really a *thought*—more like a memory. At first, it was foggy…

"Martin," he began, trying to sort out his thoughts. "When the enemy approached me, I remember—remember my shield slipping and—and then I felt *it*, and my shield was back in place immediately. Maybe I *can* be faster if I absolutely *have to* be."

Once more, Martin nodded. "A positive thought. Certainly, you displayed sufficient control to defeat the enemy, and that is the most important thing. Yet still I sense your lack of confidence, Jared. We must try to help you as much as possible. But you, especially with Andrea, have the power to defeat it quickly. And quickly it must be, before it can attack us. Prepare yourself, Jared. The sun has been up for awhile and we must get ourselves within monitoring distance of the enemy before it moves in on its victim—or *victims.*"

Dammit, Jared was thinking as he struggled with the zipper on his jeans. *How can I go out there and be some kind of hero when I'm shaking so bad I can hardly dress myself!* Hastily, he washed and dried his hands. But then a tear escaped to run down his cheek and, angrily, he dragged the sleeve of his denim jacket across his face. He hated himself for having such a hard time gaining control over his emotions. *Thank God I'm in the bathroom and I don't have Martin giving me the once-over.*

Then a thought struck him, or maybe Andrea sent it. *You can't keep fighting against your feelings.* And so, sighing, he let the tears have their freedom. Fear and dread seemed to fill his whole body, his entire consciousness. Time to stop resisting—he visualized himself dead, useless to Andrea and her people. As well as his own. He saw the nnn-Asi-t with its piercing stare, and visualized lightning bolts flashing from its eyes, destroying him. Shaking, sobbing, he was scared half out of his wits.

But then it was over. In his mind, he had seen his failure. He'd allowed himself to experience defeat, in his imagination. The feelings had run through him. Now Jared knew he was done with them.

There was no more need to waste energy on resisting them. Breathing deeply, he closed his eyes and, relaxing his grip on the edge of the sink, he let his strength return. He welcomed it, embraced it. In his mind, Jared saw himself reaching outward with his essence to gather all aspects of his strength and pull them inward. He saw himself embrace the bright lights of his power and tuck each one into its compartment like a parent tucking his children into their beds at night. They would be there and ready for him to draw on should he need them…

Opening his eyes, he gazed at his reflection in the bathroom mirror. His blue eyes stared back at him. They were filled with resolve and certainty.

Thoughts completely and firmly shielded, he returned to the living room.

Martin continued speaking, not sensing Jared's shielded presence. Andrea, more sensitive to Jared, felt him first. Her mouth dropped open in wonder, then her lips moved to form a wide smile.

Jared's essence was still shielded—strongly, resistant even to her probing flash. Martin turned to look at him as he entered the room. Even *he* had a slight upward turn at one corner of his mouth.

—∞—

This time, walking along a sidewalk, Jared felt no fear, no doubt. Once in awhile a rebellious emotion—some degree of nervousness—

popped up to demand his attention. Firmly, Jared took it gently and tucked it away until a more appropriate time. Now that his shield seemed to be more co-operative, relaxation wasn't too difficult for him to maintain.

It was all circular, he was beginning to understand. The relaxation contributed to a strong shield, while the strength of the shield helped him to feel more confident—and, therefore, relaxed. And this helped him to save the strength and energy of his emotions for later use.

They had arrived at their destination. It was an old house which had been renovated into an apartment building, along the same line as Martin's. They made their way through the parking lot to the back of the place. Andrea and Martin exchanged looks, while Jared focussed on maintaining his shield. This had all been discussed in advance. It would be Andrea who would sense for the presence of the nnn-Asi-t, as hers was the most delicate touch.

Careful to maintain his shield, Jared watched in awe as her scarlet mist rose from her skin. It looked finer, lighter, than when he'd seen it before, as it seeped quickly into the slight gap around the first-floor window. But then it was back, almost immediately. It surrounded Andrea like a halo around her whole body, then disappeared back inside of her.

"It's gone," she whispered, urgently. "We've got to go!"

Jared swallowed hard, his firmness and control threatened by a mutiny of suppressed emotions.

Chapter Sixteen

Although the small basement apartment was now empty of life-forms, my essence could detect some remaining wisps of the nnn-Asi-t's recent presence. This could mean that it has already used its influence on the victim. One might well imagine it urging the poor Earther victim on, stirring her or his emotions, whipping them up until the victim felt impelled to act—

I have no choice. Although we do not know in which direction they have travelled, we would most certainly have spotted the nnn-Asi-t were it within the ranges of our visual fields. And if it has gone beyond these limits, or perhaps into hiding, we will rely on sensing it. Sighing, I prepare to ease my shield just a bit to try to sense any information which might assist.

When I tell the others what I am planning to do, I am astonished at the words which come from my Earther—

Martin and I exchange looks. The surprise in Martin's eyes is a reflection of my own amazement. I close my mouth and swallow, then find my voice. "What—what did you say, Jared?"

The expression of Jared's blue eyes suggests that *he* is surprised by *our* words. He glances from one to the other of us. "I said—I said that you don't need to move your shield, Andrea. You don't need to do anything. I can see its trail." His voice is almost nothing more than a whisper. Jared appears a bit shocked, as though he has suddenly realized that this means his ability to see trails is a skill that we do *not* have.

Martin urges us to make haste. As we walk along quickly, I ask Jared to describe for us what it is that he sees.

"Well," Jared begins, his long-legged stride causing me to trot to keep up, "it almost looks like a tiny trail of—of dust or something. It's greyish, but there are silvery, shimmery parts to it. It's almost totally nonexistent here, where we are, but I can see it more clearly ahead, and where it goes around the corner of the building. It's not much more than a string, really. But it's definitely there."

We have reached the corner of a garage where the end of the residential street turns sharply to our left. Across the street from where we are is the front of an elementary school building. We are watching, all carefully shielded, as a bell rings. I can hear the laughter and happy voices of children as they spill into a large yard on the far side of the school.

"There." Jared's voice is a hoarse whisper. He nods in the direction of an old, brown pickup truck stopped in the parking lot at the left side of the building, facing the schoolyard. But this particular vehicle is not parked within the lines marked on the pavement, as are the cars. The truck is closer to the side of the building, as though the driver is not concerned about parking correctly.

We hasten to cross the street, and again I struggle to keep up with Jared, while Martin moves quickly off to the right side of the school to approach from a different direction. He has further to travel, but I know that he can be extremely fast when it is necessary.

Now I can see clearly what Jared suspects, and only too well I comprehend the need for haste. A young man steps from the pickup truck, its rusty door creaking. But that sound is mostly drowned out by the joyous voices of the enthusiastic children. Such a young man he appears to be—likely early twenties in Earth years. Too young for all of this. In his hands is what I recognize to be a repeating rifle, for our training included education about the weapons which we might find here.

We have reached the outside of the parking lot, and we have no more time for consideration. The young man raises the rifle, aimed toward the schoolyard, just as I send my first calming projection. It seems that the nnn-Asi-t has found it necessary to remain with the victim for longer than usual. I hope that this might mean the victim will not be terribly difficult to stop.

I can see the nnn-Asi-t as it turns in our direction. It has not yet tried to gauge the degree of my power. But it will attack—

Oh, Jared—my poor Earther! I can see the enemy's blast coming, but the frenzy is still raging inside of the victim, and I dare not yet withdraw from him.

The nnn-Asi-t's blast is strong. It is like a shimmering fireball, but silver, hurtling toward us. I wish I could close my eyes, but I manage to continue to calm the young man and yet witness this strange battle at the same time.

The glimmering silver sphere abruptly stops a few feet from Jared and me. And I know that it is simply coincidence, but still, it seems peculiar to sense the awesome power from Jared as he stops the silver sphere at precisely the same time that I feel the young man coming back to himself. The weapon is lowered. The young man stands, hanging his head while many of the now-screaming children, having seen the weapon, are hurrying back inside to the protection of the building—

And Jared has managed to launch his own attack. Immediately after stopping that silvery ball, his white beam heads towards the nnn-Asi-t.

I feel a need to move closer to the victim. We must, after all, complete our immunization before police arrive. We do not wish for the young man to be punished, and we know that this is most certainly what would happen.

And the surprises are not to end! For, somehow, Jared has already sensed this, and we begin to move forward, stepping around that immobile silvery sphere. Jared's white beam has not yet met its mark. The nnn-Asi-t still has enough power left to fully shield itself.

But it is not able to freeze Jared's beam in place, as Jared did to the nnn-Asi-t's ball. Yet we must not be too confident, for it could be that that was simply not part of its plan.

I touch the victim's arm, my fingers seeking the pulse point just inside of his wrist. A single tear trickles downward, to drip onto the weapon. I speak gently to him, reassuring him as he raises his dark blue eyes to meet mine. I send a strong burst of soothing energy which will warm him and make him better prepared to handle the frustrations which life might bring to him in the future…

And render him immune to further interference from any nnn-Asi-t.

Even as he walks away from me, I am still touching the young, fair-haired man mentally. Trembling, he steps to his old vehicle, gets in, and leaves. He knows what to do with the weapon. He will empty it of ammunition, remove the fingerprints and put it into a dumpster. Martin is near us, and he is watching for the police as we hear a siren coming closer. The votary will plant an idea into their minds, and they will find the weapon not long from now. I sense also the suggestion of a *false alarm* that he is now planting firmly into the consciousness of each of the approaching officers.

My mind touches Jared's, and I am able to send him a thought, even as he continues his battle with the enemy. We need to move away from here, while the police begin to speak with Martin and a man who approaches them from the school. Up until now, the school personnel have been occupied with bringing the frightened children back inside. It is fortunate that all has occurred *beside* the school building, as there are no windows here, and therefore no witnesses to deal with, as that could complicate our mission.

As we move toward a grove of trees at the edge of the schoolyard, Jared sends a strong, white beam in the direction of the nnn-Asi-t, and this one, too, is blocked. Although Earthers are not capable of seeing the actual interactions between us and the enemy, the shelter of the trees will remove distractions, such as the presence of other Earthers. Martin will most capably deal with the police and the school officials, which means that I am free to focus on assisting Jared.

And there is no time to waste, as the nnn-Asi-t is already beginning another assault—

The energy is quite substantial. I can actually *feel* its heat, and this is a bit unusual. A great, searing bolt, silver with jagged edges, leaps from the enemy and into the sky. It makes a graceful arc, leaving bits to shimmer blindingly in the sunlight.

And suddenly, accelerating quickly, it races downward—

But I am confused. The bolt is not aimed toward either Jared or me. I hesitate only for a second, but my confusion is its weapon, as I cannot know whether to shield myself or bolster Jared's defences. Then, oh so quickly, it splits into two and streaks toward both of us at once! I am forced to waste my time reorganizing my power. Angry at myself, I have allowed a flash of fear to distract me...

And now I stare wide-eyed as a transparent, yet definitely whitish, barrier stops that silvery streak of fire much too close to my face. Again, I can feel its heat as it struggles to bore its way through the barricade that Jared created. And that gives me the few seconds of time which I need.

I send my essence toward Jared and learn that he can maintain the protection, so I can now launch my own attack. Totally focussed on the task, I send my crimson thread through the barrier and into that silvery lightning. I am pushing it through, through back in the direction of the nnn-Asi-t.

I can feel it as it slips from me to hurry through the silver bolt. It seems that I can almost hear it as it darts through.

But it stops! Even though I have done this before, I cannot complete it with an enemy of this superior strength! I project to Jared to continue his defence for another moment. I require another few seconds to build my strength. If Martin could only assist, but he is still occupied with the school principal and the police. He will ensure that these Earthers see only myself, Jared and the man (which is the nnn-Asi-t's disguise) off in the distance, quietly conversing. This will not be difficult for Martin, as Earthers are not capable of seeing much more than this.

I am almost ready now for what I hope will be a final confrontation with this vile creature. My eyes are directed skyward, where I focus my thoughts on the approach of a greyish cloud. Into this I direct my scarlet energies, while Jared works on distracting the nnn-Asi-t...

Time is now of major importance, as Jared will not be able to continue his efforts for long at this intense level. I sense the nnn-Asi-t's efforts to increase the energy of its attack, and I direct a protective projection to help barricade Jared from harm. Then, quickly, I send a flash to Jared. I have just sent this, and Jared has instantly acknowledged receiving it, thanks to his superior receiving skills.

Then, quickly, from above comes what seems like a rainstorm of long, narrow beams of red and white. Some are separate, but in some the colours are intertwined. The sky above us seems filled with them, almost like fireworks. More and still more, again and again. Yet they are completely without any noise. All is silent, quite quiet.

The nnn-Asi-t has surrounded itself with a silvery shield that continues to stop our attacks. The first red and white beams splatter against this, then drip like fluid to the ground and disappear.

And still the nnn-Asi-t is unharmed. Should I send an emergency flash to ask Martin to hurry and join us?

But, instead, I send a flash to Jared, and together we send another red and white barrage of our energy, and then another, almost immediately—

And yet more! I am thrilled to feel how truly great our powers are when focussed together! It is even greater than I have imagined it might be! Each is even stronger than the one before it. The sky itself seems to crackle with our combined energy.

I see a section of the enemy's silvery barricade bend inward, just slightly. Instantly, our red and white beams hurtle again into that little dent, pushing, pushing. More and more. I glance at Jared, sending another flash. Then, together, we direct a slender strand of red and white—almost like a long, very thin thread the colour of the peppermint sticks I have seen in the variety store.

Quickly it glides past the others—

And swiftly and directly into that dent and *through* the thing.

Our combined beam then splits into two separate, tiny filaments—one white, one red. Each of them slips into one of the enemy's eyes.

The haze clearing, we stand and watch as the nnn-Asi-t becomes a silvery puddle and begins to dissipate.

It is over. For now.

Chapter Seventeen

Jared lay on his back, staring at the ceiling in the dark. Even after they'd gone back to Martin's place and thoroughly discussed everything that had occurred, even after he'd eaten and replenished himself, even after he and Andrea—*Perka*—had returned to his apartment...and even after they had made love, he still could not quite completely unwind. Yes, inside he was exhausted. His head had begun to ache. Even his bones felt tired...yet he could not seem to quiet his emotions—

Those same emotions that he'd managed to keep controlled during the confrontation with the enemy.

Everything was so strange...so awfully, awfully strange...

The fear, the anxiety, the anger building and building—the anger swiftly becoming hatred...

Blind, raging hatred of the nnn-Asi-t—this eerie, alien presence that would do something as horrendous as taking advantage of an innocent person's feelings of frustration and confusion to try to kill *children!*

Only too well he remembered the fear that he'd lose all control, that he might give in to the intensity of his emotions and ruin everything they were trying to do. It had taken something like a superhuman effort for him to gain command of his energy, and store it away for later use...

And the *exhilaration.* How incredible it had been to find that the energy—that all-important element of his power—was there when he'd needed it! And that he could control it and make constructive use of it when it was required. How absolutely wonderful it had been to feel his essence mesh with Perka's into something that seemed absolutely invincible!

He yawned and stretched. For a moment, he turned off all his thoughts and listened contentedly to the peaceful sounds of Perka's breathing as she slept beside him. Yes, even the exhaustion was magnificent. He sighed and, smiling, allowed himself—just one more time—to feel the thrill of victory. Finally, he slept.

So strange, but even as he dozed, Jared seemed to be in some sort of loose rapport with her. He wondered if—perhaps he dreamed it—she was monitoring him through some sort of projection. Maybe she was making sure he was still okay after all they'd been through…

Somehow, though, he knew this wasn't the case. He was hovering somewhere around the fine line between light dozing and dreamy reality. As he reached his hand toward her, he was reaching out for her outwardly, yet touching her inside as well. His fingers weren't the only aspect of him that felt her presence and the comforting, wonderful closeness.

Together, their essences united in an embrace that was as natural as breathing. She was beautiful…*this* was beautiful.

He heard her whisper something about the sharing ceremony… *or did he?* Maybe *he* had projected the idea to *her*. It didn't really matter. What *did* matter was the awesome experience they were about to share…

They were moving toward becoming true mates—something which was supposedly not possible between their two different species.

Jared could feel Perka's essence as it reached toward his. He opened his mind, his spirit, everything, totally to her. She was inside of him now. Somehow, all aspects of her were. It was breath-taking, exhilarating. He could feel the warmth of her body with his fingertips and yet somehow it seemed like he was also touching his *own* body at the same time. He could feel the wonder of her essence, her spirit, as it all flowed into him, through him.

It was as though she had concentrated herself into a tiny, delicate, yet strong filament, warming him, soothing him wonderfully as it flowed through his veins, his tissues, his spirit, his heart, his mind. He could feel Perka as she passed from one part of him and into another, leaving behind a sensation of the most wonderful relaxation, contentment and peace as she did.

Now focussed on his mind, he could feel her presence as she shared his childhood memories, as she experienced with him all the secret parts of his psyche which he had never shared with anyone else.

Perka knew virtually everything of him now. But no. It was even much more than that…

She had truly *experienced* everything about Jared now. It was as though they had truly been together all of his life. And, with her there, he could feel that there were aspects of his memories that she didn't really comprehend, but she also recognized that this was to be expected, considering the vast differences between them physically and socially. Although similar in many ways, they were, after all, of different species.

As she began to drift away, back into herself, he was struck by the sudden sensation of emptiness. A terrible feeling of oneness, of isolation…of *loneliness* had Jared's heart pounding harder. Fear began to fill him—a horrible fear of losing her. Like he'd lost his dad.

But there was also a realization. She wouldn't let this happen. She wouldn't leave him feeling this way.

As her essence began to slowly, ever so gently, withdraw, he saw in his mind the image of his wonderful Perka, in her glorious deep scarlet, extending one fingertip toward him. Immediately he touched his own pale one to meet hers. She was drifting backward, but the tiny point of contact between them was more than enough for her to pull him with her. Together, they glided from the whiteness of his essence and into the glorious warmth and peace of her crimson one.

It seemed like he had become extremely small and agile, moving smoothly and easily on his own. She was suddenly huge around him as he sailed through every part of the inside of her body, savouring every sinew, every cell. Now he felt his own skin through *her* fingertips. Jared drank in every sensation, inhaled it, totally experiencing and embracing all aspects of what made her kind like his—and at the same time, so very different in many ways. It was wonderful. And it all felt so right. So incredibly right.

There was no other word to describe it but bliss. He didn't think that he had ever experienced anything even remotely like this before. Now he eased himself in the direction of her mind, her consciousness—flowing, gliding there so easily. He looked at his own body through *her* eyes. He saw a human male who had a look of total contentment and of joy.

He turned inward. Beyond the consciousness of her own joy lay the rest of her being. Her desires, her doubts, her fears. Her feelings of success, and of failure. And her memories.

Jared hesitated at the edge of this glorious, deep scarlet sphere…

Was he truly ready? Was he worthy? Was this really *right*? Maybe he should stop right here. But then Perka was beckoning to him, reassuring him. Loving him. He could feel her warm, crimson glow as it edged closer to him. Still, he paused. Something about this might not be right. There was *something…*

But when her crimson crept closer, he reminded himself that he truly loved her. Nothing else mattered.

And he was inside. Now he could see her memories of *her* world. How beautiful it was! It was so much warmer than his own part of Earth. Letting himself relax further, he allowed himself to perceive her world through Perka herself. To her, her world was comfortably warm. And it was so wonderfully bright and alive in the brilliance of its colours.

He must never, ever let himself forget the *feeling* of this place. There was no hatred, no jealousy, no anger. No hidden agendas nor deceit.

Now Jared understood that the close rapport of these people's essences automatically resulted in a sharing of their experiences and emotions, both the positives and negatives. Any feelings of inadequacy or envy would be perceived by all who were involved. True, there was no real *privacy*. But was that important if they all lived in peace because of this?

Their essences, their mental powers, formed their technology. Various individuals developed their skills in different areas. Many, like Perka and Georgia and Martin and the others, had built on their talents that enabled them to perceive threats to other worlds...and to try to help preserve innocent cultures from those who would seek to usurp or even destroy them. Some taught the younger ones to develop and utilize their talents. Others worked exclusively as healers, assisting those who'd been harmed in battles against the malevolent ones.

Still others created visual and musical experiences to comfort the weary and offer them relaxations, to help replenish their spirits.

Jared sensed many other presences, too, that had been stored in Perka's memories as wonderful and glorious items. He didn't have the capability to understand a lot of these, but the love that Perka felt for her home and for her people was quite unmistakable and strong...

As was her love for him.

How truly remarkable it all was. He drifted back into his own essence, savouring the wonder of her lips on his. And it was almost—almost as though their very spirits were embracing as well, at the same time.

They had ventured to the level of absolute and complete rapport. Of totally sharing every aspect of themselves—physical, mental, emotional, spiritual.

They were mates.

Everything was different now. First, there'd been the battle with the nnn-Asi-t—the first time that Jared had actually *participated* in a confrontation with one of the alien things. Then there'd been the sharing ceremony. Now he truly understood Perka and her people. Now he felt like he was one of them. He was in awe of them. Her kind had come from another world to protect Earth from these enemies! Jared still shook his head when he thought about it. So of course, this was his fight too! And now there was a new strength inside of him. Suddenly, he had a true purpose for existing.

Of course, it came at a cost. The threat to his world seemed strange and almost overpowering. Everywhere he went, he was constantly on the alert, always checking to make sure that his shield was in place. No matter where he was, there was constantly that feeling that maybe, just maybe, a being was near that could read his thoughts. The enemy could be anywhere…

But all the while, he was telling himself that these concerns were foolish, unnecessary. After all, not only could he sense their nearness and see them clearly, he could even recognize their trails when they'd already left the area.

Fear. Plain and simple. The idea of confronting one entirely on his own set him trembling. Without Perka by his side, he felt naked and incomplete, even though he knew that he could send her a flash and she'd receive it instantly. Yes, she had told him that if he was uncomfortable on his own, he would be more than welcome at Martin's. Martin, too, had reassured him that this would be quite acceptable.

He wasn't really sure why he'd turned this offer down. Maybe it was male pride. Maybe it was simply that he wasn't sure if he'd want to spend that much time with Martin's dark eyes on him, especially knowing that Martin would be able to pick up his every thought. Still, he knew that Martin wouldn't do that. He was too courteous. No, Jared was determined to adjust to his new life. But he still wished that she wasn't working at the crisis line tonight.

A movement distracted him. He froze in his tracks and checked his shield again. Still not moving, he listened. But all he heard were voices from the shoppers wandering past, the *click-clicking* of noisy heels on the shopping mall's shiny floor. His gaze was focussed on the direction where he thought he'd seen the motion. Something was in the corner, seeking the shadows of the brightly lit open area. He was positive that he'd seen that tell-tale silvery glitter.

Jared took a deep breath to steady himself. After once more checking the security of his shield, he moved toward those shadows, but avoided the urge to approach too quickly or too directly—

As well as the *other* urge—the one that said to simply *turn around and get out of there.*

Quietly he ambled toward that awful shadow, pausing to pretend that he was studying some of the jewellery displayed in the nearby window…

Is this one going to make a move on me, like the one I destroyed in the alley? What'll happen if I just play along with it for awhile?

His heart was beating harder as he moved closer to the patch of darkness. His mouth was dry. Although he tried to swallow the huge lump stuck in his throat, he couldn't seem to manage it. He waited. He pulled his phone out of his inside jacket pocket and pretended to look at it. Everything was so still, except for the few teenagers not far away who laughed as they passed by. He waited, wondering when the nnn-Asi-t might make its move. How long could he stand here and pretend to check his messages before the shadowy thing would get suspicious? Jared was sure it must be studying him, and if it was, did it see an Earther whose heart felt like it was going to burst, and whose palms were getting wet with sweat?

Dammit! What is it waiting for?

He risked a more direct look toward the less brightly lit area. There it was…that silvery shimmer. But it wasn't moving. Was it waiting for him to make the first move? Did it know—could it tell who, or what, he was? Maybe it was *dead.* No, that couldn't be…

He put his phone back inside his pocket and shoved his perspiring hands deep into his jeans pockets, trying to continue looking casual and relaxed. He tried a yawn, hoping it didn't look forced. Turning his gaze to the starry night that beckoned through the glass doors to the parking lot, he stepped in that direction, pulling his left hand from his pocket. Jared glanced toward his sleeve, as though checking for a rip, but let his eyes focus just beyond, toward it…

And now he saw it. He gazed at the sparkly substance. It was there, all right. Leaning down toward it, he was suddenly no longer fearful.

Instead, he felt just plain dumb. Sighing, he picked up the crinkly plastic wrapper and held it in his hand, watching how it reflected the light from the ceiling. A slight breeze from the open jewellery store door stirred it, bringing more of its sparkles to life.

Shaking his head, he stepped over to the nearest garbage and recycling container and dropped it inside.

Why me? Why did it have to me who ends up helping these people? I'm a damn nervous wreck! Dammit, dammit, dammit. I'm not cut out for this!

Jared's mind was suddenly filled with memories of *before.* Sitting at MIKE'S, enjoying a brew. He hadn't been there for ages. He could be there right now with a frosty mug in his hand, listening to—

The thought was gone. Instantly and completely. Jared checked his shield.

There *was* one here somewhere. And he was sure this time. He could see its trail and, just as Perka had described it to him, he could *feel* its presence. Again, he checked his shield. He didn't need to sense it, anyway. After all, he could see its trail.

As he began to walk in that direction, he noted how the older sections of the trail faded gradually from his view. But he could see brighter, more definite parts now, so it was certainly here still in the mall. The glittering and shadowy trail led around the corner, toward one of the other exits. Jared followed, still trying to keep a casual look about him. The size of the trail appeared to be about the same as the one from the nnn-Asi-t they'd battled at the school. But he had no idea if there might be a correlation between trail size and the strength of their power.

The thing had gone into the drug store. Jared was gaining on it. He could see that the trail was fresher here, the glitter more intense and the greyish aspect less transparent. He quickened his step as he saw that it led to the pharmacists' area at the back of the store.

It made sense. *Of course! Just think of the havoc a crazed pharmacist could create!*

More quickly now, he walked past the diapers and the pacifiers, past the deodorants and the dental floss and the hair sprays…

At first, he thought he was looking at the thing itself. It was a moment before he understood that the nnn-Asi-t must've stayed in that spot for several seconds, judging from the thickness of the trail here. It must've been watching the man who was working behind the counter.

But now it was gone. A lesser trail led through the glass door to the outside. Jared hurried to push his way through the double set of doors, the cool breeze slapping his face as he stepped outside.

When he turned, he saw the thing as it changed from a vaguely human shape into a large, amorphous, dark mass. Its silvery parts twinkling in the light from the building's neon sign, the mass floated gracefully upward, into the night and out of sight, the trail gradually disappearing behind it. Open-mouthed, Jared stood on the sidewalk, staring after it. *Should I have tried to engage it? Would there have been time, maybe when it was just beginning to dissipate?* And the pharmacist—

Jared gasped, then raced back through the double doors, trying to look calm as he headed towards the gate separating the pharmacists' area from the rest of the store. He stopped, suddenly feeling awkward as a couple of customers passed, glancing over their shoulders at him. Calming himself, he used his inner vision to assess the emotional state of the pharmacist, while he pretended he was trying to get the zipper on his jacket to work properly. Shield partially lifted, he felt for any possible interference by the nnn-Asi-t.

The brown-haired man looked up from his work, adjusting his glasses. Jared met his eyes and then gently withdrew his essence from the gentleman. Jared smiled at him. The druggist nodded back, a slightly puzzled look on his face. As Jared began to leave, the pharmacist shrugged his shoulders, adjusted his glasses one more time, then re-directed his attention to his computer.

Outside again, Jared watched his breath fog the cold air, thinking that it looked vaguely like an nnn-Asi-t trail. Sighing, he headed quickly to his VW.

He needed to share everything with Perka.

Chapter Eighteen

My poor Earther! My people are so fortunate to have him assisting us, but I wonder about the cost to him. I must do whatever I can to help him accept the reality of what he has—both his power and the awesome responsibility of the entire situation.

When I return from my shift at the crisis line, I find that it is now my mate who is in need of my counselling. After my work with other Earthers, it is certainly not a burden for me to help him. It is so natural and automatic for me to reach inside of him, soothe him, and offer him comfort. Jared has been awaiting my return anxiously, fearful of what more the nnn-Asi-t which he has seen might be planning. He tells me that he stood outside of the drug store and kept watch even after the doors had been locked and secured for the night, yet still he worries.

The degree of his anxiety causes me concern as well. Jared must learn to allow himself to relax when he has the opportunity, or his energy will drain from him unnecessarily, and might not be available when he most requires it.

This provides an interesting contrast between my people and Jared. My people spend their whole lives developing their skills and powers and are therefore quite comfortable with them. Jared—so new to all of this—continues to face challenges with fear and apprehension.

All of this is quite understandable, of course. The great strength of his energies frightens him. I hope that his emotional response will lessen as he becomes more accustomed to his new role.

I touch my finger to his lips to silence him. He has described what occurred quite thoroughly and has begun to repeat himself. It is time now for us to move past words. I run my fingers gently down the side of his face from his hairline to his chin. As I do, I send my own sensation of relaxation and calm. Jared opens his mouth to speak again but closes it once more. I feel his mind and inner being open to me, as if he wants to surround me with his essence in a huge hug that is beyond physical.

But he is an Earther, and his body responds automatically. He reaches for me with both his inner and outer selves. He embraces me with his arms and holds my body to him, his face nestled in my hair. My spirit is inside of him. I see his anxiety and fear as a whitish line with jagged edges, threatening to cut into his very essence—and then my own graceful, smooth, crimson tendril as it floats to join this. My reddish thread touches that lightning-like segment and then gently slides down the length of it. I pull back slightly from it, and then sail gently along it once more. And again. I remind myself to concentrate fully on this, and not allow myself to be distracted by those parts inside of him that I do not quite understand.

I can both see and feel the difference as Jared's sharp edges slowly begin to change from jagged and into softer, gentle curves. Soon his segment is almost completely free of sharp angles, as is my own. I enjoy the peaceful vision as our two tendrils slide delicately around each other, as though mirroring the joy and comfort we both savour as we continue to embrace.

The morning sun lessens the chill somewhat as we walk together from the car in the parking lot and make our way to the mall entrance at the drug store. We are both alert for signs of any enemy presence, but in different ways. I am open to sensing them, while Jared searches with his eyes for trails.

How very strange that this Earther has the ability to see them, while my kind does not possess any skill like this!

We have walked through the store twice. I suggest to Jared that it might be best if we left now. This is not a large store, and I am beginning to feel a bit of suspicion aroused both in the pharmacist on duty and one of the nearby customers.

"Jared," I am saying in a low voice, "we can return tonight. The—um—thing was probably in the midst of planning when you saw it. It would seem sensible that it would try to do something when the place is less busy, like closing time."

My Earther sighs. "I guess you're right, Andrea."

"May I help you with something?" The pharmacist is looking at us from behind the cash register as a customer moves away. The brown-haired man pushes his spectacles back up to the top of his nose while he is speaking.

It saddens me to think of this meek gentleman possibly being whipped into a frenzy of terrible emotions by the enemy. We must prevent that from happening.

"No. No, thank you," Jared says, forcing a slight smile. "We were—we were just looking around. Thank you."

I am concerned that his nervousness might only create more suspicion as he nudges me in the direction of the exit. Nodding toward the pharmacist, I send the man a brief flash of reassurance as Jared opens the door to the outside.

"You really have got to try to relax, Jared," I whisper to him as we open the doors to the old car. My seatbelt buckle clicks as I fasten it. "Your nervousness will only serve to make other Earthers uncomfortable and suspicious."

Jared sighs. He is becoming irritable as he glances over his shoulder, reversing the car from the parking spot. He has to try twice to get the vehicle into the right gear as it groans loudly. "But Andrea! Just standing around for so long was making people suspicious! Who knows? Maybe if we make them suspicious, they'll be *alert* for something strange and then not be as susceptible to enemy influence—oh, I don't know!"

Poor Jared. The anxiety, combined with not enough sleep last night, has left him more emotional than usual. I resolve to be more alert to his needs, even when we rest. I put my hand on top of the one that rests on the gear shift, and, with a little squeeze, send him a bit of calm as well as energy. I am happy to feel him relax a bit. He smiles at me as we approach the exit from the parking lot.

"My love. Let us—let's go and move my belongings into your apartment. Then we will relax awhile. We will—we'll both need all of our energy for tonight when we return to the drug store." As I speak, I study his profile as he waits for the light to turn green.

He gives me a little grin. "What are your people called, anyway?"

I return his smile. "You would not be able to pronounce it, Jared."

It seems strange to move the few belongings I possess into an Earther's home. With such action there seems to be an implication of permanence. This seems so correct and natural on one hand, yet I know only too well that it cannot be so…

Jared and I have never spoken of this. I wonder if he might be assuming, or perhaps hoping, that I will be able to stay with him for always. But no. He *must* know that I cannot stay here. Surely, he would have felt that when we became mates and shared everything. He might have simply been confused when he shared his desire that I somehow remain here with him. Although this occupies my thoughts, I do not wish to discuss it with him at this time. As I have been pondering these feelings, I have been automatically shielding my thoughts. Inside, a tinge of guilt makes itself known to me. This is unusual, as my kind rarely take any actions to inspire emotions such as guilt.

As I ponder, I ask myself if I have been dishonest with *myself.* Could it be that I have bonded, and even mated with this Earther, for the sole purpose of using his power for the benefit of my own kind? No. I have to shake my head when this question pops up in my mind. I am, after all, not an Earther. I have been too aware of my personal thoughts and emotions to allow such to happen. It is something much deeper than that. I must remind him that someday I will return to my own planet…

After hanging my red jacket up in the closet by the door, I walk to the bedroom. I have kept my thoughts shielded; he receives so easily, and I do not wish to disturb him if he is trying to rest. I stop just outside of the room.

I smile as I look past the partly open door and regard my Earther. He lies, sprawled stomach-downward across the bed, his long legs stretching almost from one bottom corner to the other. The bed-covers look hopelessly rumpled, as he is not like some Earthers who 'make the bed' when they rise in the morning. His face is buried in the pillow which he has scrunched into a mound, his arms grasping it from underneath.

Something warm and rather pleasant seems to be growing deep inside of me. In my mind, I visualize it as glowing gently like the embers of a small blaze inside of a fireplace.

And I understand now what it is. It is love. I really *do* love this Earther. And he is not even one of my own kind. Although my mind is now blank, my feet carry me across the room, and I sit on the edge of the bed. Gently, so as not to awaken or disturb him, I touch the inside of his wrist and send a message of love and tenderness…

As well as my hope that we might—somehow—be together for a long time.

Together, we clean up the kitchen and put the dishes away. It seemed important to ensure that Jared have a good, nourishing meal a couple of hours before we return to the drug store. Once again, I muse over how inefficient the Earthers' nourishment systems are. Chuckling, I ask Jared if he is certain that he might not prefer *our* way of procuring nourishment and energy. But he only gives me a doubtful look, one eyebrow raised dramatically. This leads me to laugh more. And this is good, as Jared too cannot help but join in. He needs this little release from his tension and stress.

We practise shielding, then sending and receiving. Our sensitivities now heightened, we are prepared as best we can be.

"Are you *sure* we don't need to bring Martin or Georgia along?" Jared asks this for the second time as he closes his blue jacket, while we make our way down the stairs.

"Jared, from what you described, it does not—doesn't sound any more powerful than the one at the schoolyard. We should not have serious trouble if we are working together. Besides, Martin and Georgia need to be free to pursue other enemies. Try to relax, my love. Remember that we are extremely strong when we use our powers concurrently. I will begin and you follow my lead. Think of our *strength*, Jared."

Jared unlocks the vehicle and leans across the interior to unlock the door for me. As he settles into the driver's seat and turns the key, his blue eyes gaze at me. Despite my efforts to boost his confidence, he looks doubtful. He sighs.

"Anything?" I whisper to him, wondering if he might see any trails.

But he shakes his head negatively. We are inside the car, parked in the parking lot. I can sense only a weak presence, but I do not wish to risk possible detection by lifting my shield any further than I already have. Stepping outside, we walk toward the mall's main entrance. Just inside the doors, I sense something vague that is not close to this location.

Taking Jared's hand in mine, I lead him in that direction. Stopping at a corner, we peer around it. I wonder if we might look like one of the spy or police dramas on television that Jared likes to watch. Now I sense the enemy somewhere, but it all seems hazy. I look upward at Jared's face—

He is completely focussed. "A trail," he says in a soft voice. "It's older, though. The thing must've come in through a different entrance."

Urgently I squeeze his hand. "It might have already gone into the drug store."

Hastily, we move in that direction.

"I can see the trail more clearly now." The colour of Jared's already pale face has faded almost to white. We stop before the drug store entrance, and I slip my fingers to the inside of his wrist to focus on bringing him confidence. When I feel that he has recovered his composure, we enter.

As I smile and nod to the cashier, she returns my greeting, but adds: "Sorry, but this is Sunday, so we'll be closing soon."

Of course, I am thinking. I was not aware that the place closed earlier on Sundays, as the crisis line operates seven days a week, day and night. But the enemy would be aware of this and use it to its advantage. While I paused, Jared has continued to follow the trail. I hasten to catch up to him where he is looking around the corner of the shelves filled with shampoos and conditioners.

"It's there," he says in a whisper.

I gaze around the corner. It is most certainly there. And it has begun its terrible work already—

There is a woman pharmacist this time. She is standing quite still. The light brown skin of her forehead is puckered in a frown, as though she is deep in thought. But I know only too well what will be happening inside of her. She will be aware of a terrible turmoil developing deep inside. True feelings which she might have repressed now return and become exaggerated. She loses her perspective…and self-control. I see her shake her head, her short dark hair losing its neatness as she shakes her head again, in an effort to somehow make the awful, terrifying feelings disappear.

But they will not. I watch as she is obviously losing the battle. The shock and confusion leave her contorted face…to be replaced with hatred and anger. She feels loathing of the very people whom she has been trained to help.

Extremely dangerous, indeed, in the hands of someone distributing medications.

And now I can see the nnn-Asi-t. It has taken the appearance of a grey-haired female. Quite innocent in appearance. She stands just inside of the gate to the pharmacy area. An observer might think her to be simply a 'little old lady', seeking the advice of a professional—

although one might wonder why she has ventured *inside* of the gate which separates the pharmacy from the rest of the store.

We must act now. We should be unobserved, as over my shoulder I catch a glimpse of the cashier busily finishing her work at the front cash register. The floor-to-ceiling gate has already been drawn across the opening from the drug store into the rest of the mall. As I move forward, I send a strong projection to the pharmacist, sending her calm. I must take a moment to concentrate carefully to offset the distance between us.

The nnn-Asi-t has sensed my presence, and turns, its face a sheet of anger at the intrusion. Quickly, I pull away my focus from the cashier, and place a reddish barricade around myself for protection from a possible nnn-Asi-t attack.

I know these vile creatures well enough to anticipate its next move. It has returned its attention to its victim, anxious that its efforts thus far not be in vain. And, just as it focuses on the poor woman who stands trembling behind the counter, I do too. The blast of turmoil from the nnn-Asi-t is rendered neutral by *my* projection of love, calm and peace.

How strange it is to see this poor, confused woman standing silently, while what look like lightning bolts flash into her entire being! And how fortunate that Earthers are not capable of seeing them.

I send a quick projection to Jared, directing him to prepare for the nnn-Asi-t's next attack, while I return my attention to assisting the victim…

But, as I do this, I do *not* feel the expected confirmation from Jared—

There is no time! Just as my projection reaches the pharmacist, the nnn-Asi-t sends a flash directly at me.

Quickly, quickly I reach deeply inside to find an energy reserve. I manage to project a red mist which once again stops the enemy's attack. The nnn-Asi-t stares, as its silvery blast looks as though it is melting in the heat of my mist. Tiny silver droplets fall to the floor and disappear.

I project to Jared to tend to the victim. There is no time to wonder why he did not respond to me the first time.

My attention returns to the nnn-Asi-t, yet all that I receive from Jared are confusion and anxiety. I send a small flash to occupy the enemy for a moment, while I open my shield enough to receive Jared's thoughts…

Marjorie

The name is familiar. I know well who she is from Jared's memories. It is this that has destroyed Jared's concentration. It is left to me to be stronger now. I see the victim as she prepares to put the wrong medication into several vials. She does so deliberately, but with an expression of emotional pain etched on her troubled face.

I must stop the nnn-Asi-t. I will deal with the woman later.

But suddenly, I am distracted by the anguish which Jared is feeling as he tries to project to the woman but fails, his emotions interfering.

Then the nnn-Asi-t sends a sinister flash in the woman's—Marjorie's—direction. A huge blast. Enough to kill. Instantly my own, faster crimson mist is upon it. But the strength of the enemy's blast keeps it resistant to my mist. I must flash more of my power in that direction—

And, suddenly, the silvery blast is gone. My scarlet mist hangs empty. Limp. Hastily, I collect what little remains of my energy back inside where I can store it for later use.

Now the nnn-Asi-t sends its deadly, silvery, flying worms gliding quickly in *Jared's* direction—

I have no time! *No time to counterattack!* My tendril seeks to secure a scarlet net around the enemy's projectiles…

But it slips. I cannot maintain the concentration I need without Jared's help. My energy reserves are too low.

But I will not let my Earther die when his involvement was not his own idea!

As I step quickly in front of Jared, I am able to send a shield upward to protect his face and head—

But I do not have the strength left to cover all of me as well…

The silvery, flying snakes from the enemy burn like fire.

Chapter Nineteen

Jared stood, open-mouthed. Shocked. Here were two women he'd cared for, one on the brink of possible insanity, and the other collapsed in front of him on the scuffed, white, tiled floor…

But in the few seconds he stood there, the part of him that went beyond being an Earther regained control. It *had* to. Closing his eyes, he packed away all his confusion and terror, sending them to a spot inside somewhere out of the way. Strength and resolve filled him. As Jared opened his eyes and straightened his shoulders, his gaze was cool, icy blue.

And deadly.

The nnn-Asi-t didn't know this, as it had turned its attention toward Marjorie once more, sending more of its silvery intent in her direction. Jared didn't move yet. He waited, feeling the strength of his power as it filled him. Intensity and capability seemed to be coursing through every vein, every cell both in his body and in his spirit.

The nnn-Asi-t began to turn toward him, slowly, as though it was just now sensing that something important had changed…

Its grey eyes were opened just a little bit more widely this time. Already, it had begun to surround its Earther-looking body with a strong cylinder of silvery armour that looked almost like smoked glass, covering it from the top of its grey-haired head to the surrounding floor.

Jared's face revealed no concern. He stared with the confidence of one who knows with certainty that he can defeat his enemy.

The cashier had left the store a few minutes ago, and the sliding floor to ceiling gate at the mall entrance had been secured in place. It was eerily quiet, for the only noise came from the weeping pharmacist. The sound of her turmoil was like a stab in Jared's heart. But he could not allow this to affect him now. Gently but firmly, he sent a gleaming white tendril in her direction. It hovered near her, slowly assuming a teardrop shape. Then it entered her, narrow end first.

The crying stopped.

It was becoming obvious to Jared that the nnn-Asi-t had recognized the strength which he possessed. It had had an opportunity to attack him while he'd been tending to Marjorie. But it was still occupied with strengthening its defence.

"It won't do you any good, you bastard," Jared muttered.

He eyed the enemy as it continued to work on the cylinder around and above itself. Hazier and hazier was its surface as more energy was stored there. Jared studied this, evaluating it.

Then he smiled, just slightly. A narrow, jagged bolt of white lightning burst from Jared's right eye to crash against the smoky cylinder's surface. The entire structure quivered a little, the nnn-Asi-t jumping a bit in its place.

Jared took a deep breath, summoning more strength. Then he sent another blast. His blue eyes met the gaze of the enemy, who appeared to try to look away, but didn't succeed. It didn't notice the thin, white filament emanating, thinner than a thread, from Jared's right index finger where it hung at his side, pointing toward the floor. It didn't see how the slender tendril found a tiny crack between the worn, white floor tiles, and how it disappeared beneath them…

Suddenly the nnn-Asi-t's human-looking mouth opened in a gasp. It gazed downward, lifting one foot. Gaping, it watched the white thread quickly rise from the slight separation between the tiles and into the bottom of its orthopedic shoe. And into its foot. It raised its eyes once more to meet Jared's—

Jared stared in awe as the grey eyes began sagging, more and more until the entire Earth-like face became distorted into twice its original length. The entire being faded into grey and dripped heavily onto the surface of the floor, its cylinder barricade with it. In only a few seconds, it was nothing more than a greyish puddle with a few silvery grains sparkling in the light—

Then it was gone.

The emergency over, Jared closed his eyes and took a deep breath. Weariness nagged at him, and he felt a bit light-headed. As he stood quietly, focussing his attentions inward, he searched for his energy reserve. There wasn't a lot left. Then he heard Marjorie sniffling, and he came back to reality…

Perka

His senses felt for hers. His eyes widened when he found only pain.

He gazed downward to where her body lay on the floor. Once again, he had to firmly tuck away the horror and awful guilt that threatened to leave him, too, in tears. Trying to be calm, he knelt by her side. Slowly, he reached trembling fingers to the artery at the side of her neck. At first, he felt nothing, and panic and despair threatened to take all control away from him. Then, with a relieved sigh, he felt a slight pulse.

She was alive, at least.

As an *Earther* she was alive. But what about the rest of her? What about her spirit? All the non-Earther parts?

Jared was frightened for her. He didn't even *try* to put that feeling away. It was too strong. All he could do was reassure himself that she was alive. What he needed to do now should be done in the privacy of their apartment. All he could do at this moment was to project strength to her.

His attention went to Marjorie. But he didn't see her standing behind the counter anymore. He moved around the pharmacy cash register and made his through the little gate and into the pharmacists' area.

Sorrow stabbed at his insides, at his heart. She was sitting cross-legged on the floor, like a little girl. Crying softly, she held her head in her hands, her dark hair falling forward to cover part of her face. Memories flooded through him of the time they'd had together. It seemed like a long time ago, yet also only yesterday…

She'd never cried, he reflected. He'd always admired her inner strength and her control.

His heart heavy with sorrow and concern, he stepped across the floor to her. "Marjorie," he whispered, his throat tight. He sank down beside her, reaching for her. As he had done so many times before—long ago it seemed—Jared put his arms around her. Gently, he murmured reassurances. Suddenly he was angry at himself. This was what he'd do as an *Earther.* Taking a long breath, he regained his self-control, and thought of himself as one of Perka's people. Touching the inside of Marjorie's wrist, he sent calmness and peace to her.

A long sigh replaced her sobs as she pulled away from him to dab at her eyes with her sleeve. She looked at him and somehow managed a small smile. "I—I'm sorry, Jared. I don't—I don't know what's happened to me! I feel so strange." Her eyes widened then as she recalled the horror. "Oh, Jared! I can't believe what I was thinking of doing! I might've killed someone! Am I losing my mind?"

"No," he said gently, reaching forward to touch her pulse point again. Wanting to ensure that she'd fully feel the peacefulness she needed, this time he projected a greater amount of his power. As he did, a bit of nagging fatigue reminded him that his energies were low. "Marjorie, we all have—have feelings that we tuck away because they're not…not socially acceptable. Sometimes, something unexpected can arouse those in us. We have to be aware of that. They're feelings, emotions. That's all. It's okay to feel them, as long as we don't act on our anger or frustration or whatever to hurt someone else—"

"But—but what I almost did—" Marjorie tried to tuck a stray strand of short dark hair behind her ear, but it stubbornly resisted and fell forward once more.

Jared managed a comforting smile. "It wasn't your fault. Remember that innocent-looking older lady who was standing near the cash register?" Marjorie nodded, frown lines creasing her forehead. "Well, I heard her say some terrible things. I think she must've been senile or crazy. That triggered something in you and stirred things up. She—she left when you started to question what she wanted you to do." After a short pause, he added: "And *we* should leave too."

Still holding each other's hands, they rose to their feet.

They were standing together now just as they had so many times in the past. Yet this time was so vastly different…

Jared watched as she completed a couple of tasks and put things away before she turned to face him once more. "Can you drive home okay, Marj?" He reached forward to tuck that stubborn strand of raven hair back behind her ear, but it defied him too. A shiver went through him. *Perka.* His mind was still in touch with her, and she, too, required help. The need for haste nibbled incessantly at him, as he nibbled on his lower lip.

Marjorie sensed the affection and concern in his touch and in his voice. "Yes," she whispered. "I'll be okay. I feel a lot better now. I—I never ran into anything like that before! Oh, Jared! What about your friend? What—what happened to her?"

He followed the direction of Marjorie's stare, where Perka still lay unconscious on the floor. Sorrow and worry flooded him inside. Marjorie was reaching for the store's phone. Quickly, Jared put his hand on top of hers to stop her.

"But Jared, our security guys have first aid training! She needs help!"

"I know, I know. It's okay, Marjorie. She, uh, she has a medical condition. It looks worse than it is. I—I know how to handle it. I'll take her home. She'll be okay, really." As he hurried now to Perka, he continued talking. "You get *yourself* home, Marj. Take care of yourself. We all need some rest." He knelt beside Perka, feeling for her pulse. *Still there, thank God.* From the corner of his eye, he could see Marjorie collecting her belongings as he picked up the limp form of Perka. A shiver of icy cold fear raced up his spine when he felt nothing more from her.

Marjorie held open the door to the outside for him, locking it behind her. Shock still clouded her thinking. Yet, for some reason she couldn't fathom, she continued to feel calm and at peace. This seemed awfully strange, considering all that had happened. For a moment she stood, trying to tuck her hair behind her ear, as she watched Jared ease the woman into his old car. Suddenly she realized that she, too, wanted nothing more than to leave this place, and clicked her key in the direction of her nearby vehicle. After one more glance at Jared, she got inside and prepared to leave.

Gently, gently, Jared eased his burden onto the back seat, and managed to secure the seat belt around her reclining form as best he could. Sighing, he reached his fingers to her wrist and waited—*thank you, God.*

He withdrew, suddenly aware of the pounding of his heart. Easing his long legs awkwardly into the limited space of the driver's seat, his fingers automatically thrust the key into the ignition. He turned the key and tried to shove the gear into reverse, then sighed, collected himself and tried again, more gently this time. As he backed up, he wondered what in hell he was going to do with Perka when he got her home.

Should I try to call out to Martin from here? Of course, Martin would know what to do! After all, others of their kind must've been injured in the past. But…*could* he contact Martin? Yes, he'd received Perka's call that time, but that had been receiving, not sending. And what if an nnn-Asi-t intercepted the message? What then?

Dammit

Anxiety was becoming something more like cold fear, threatening to rise up and take complete control. Determined, Jared blinked away stubborn tears and struggled to swallow the lump in his throat.

I could drive past Martin's. That's it! That's what I'll do! Then I'll be close enough to risk projecting to him.

At last, a solid plan. Jared let go a sigh of relief, feeling somewhat better. He tried to regain total control and tuck his feelings back into their compartments. They could have their release later.

When everything was resolved.

Drumming his fingers impatiently on the steering wheel, he waited for the red light to change. He caught a glimpse of the faces of a couple of teenagers in the car stopped beside him, on the far side. The two—a guy and a girl—leaned toward the VW, trying to get a better look at something in the back seat. Jared glanced over his shoulder and gasped. One of Perka's arms was flung over her head, her hand leaning against the window. The teenagers were laughing, imitating what she looked like, but then they sped away, tires squealing as the light turned.

Jared took a deep breath, imagining a police officer coming to his car and asking him why he had an unconscious woman in his back seat. A honk from the car behind spurred him to give his little vehicle some gas and move on.

Finally, after what seemed like an eternity, they were on Martin's street. Jared squinted, straining to find the right building in the darkness. Ah, there it was! He wanted to pull over to the curb and carry Perka right up there, but there weren't any parking spaces here. He toyed with the idea of going up there by himself and leaving her here, but he couldn't bear the thought of leaving her alone…

But *dammit!* Was it safe for him to project from the street? Jared gazed around the area, at the darkness, the shadows. *Dammit, this place might be crawling with enemies!* He shivered. Then he glanced over his shoulder at Perka where she lay across the back seat. *I've got to!*

Trying to calm himself, he took a long, slow breath, letting the sensation of strength and power fill his being…

And stopped with a gasp. As soon as he'd put his concentration into his role of helping Perka's people, it seemed like he could see every nnn-Asi-t trail there was! And he could see some right now. But, he reassured himself, many of them looked old, beginning to dissipate. There might not even be *any* enemies left in the area now! He put his head in his hands. If he was going to do this, he *couldn't* let himself be distracted by everything! It took him a few seconds to focus his power—

Finally. A little white haze left his mind and began to drift outward, outward. It stopped outside of Martin's windows, hovering just a fraction of a second before it suddenly seeped in around the edges. But it was back quickly, and inside Jared immediately.

Martin isn't there!

"No! Dammit to hell and back! Shit!" Gripping the steering wheel tightly, he let his head fall forward to rest on the wheel, tears burning his eyes. He hadn't even considered the possibility of Martin not being there!

"Perka," he whispered hoarsely. "Forgive me. I don't know what I've done to you. But I swear by everything I am—everything you helped me become—somehow, I'll make you whole again. If I have to die trying!"

The little Beetle coughed once, then continued its journey through the shadows of the city streets.

Jared was nibbling rather viciously on his thumbnail. His eyes rested on the sight of Perka where he'd lain her tenderly on the bed. *We're mates. We've experienced each other totally and completely. We have a rapport that only true mates can have. If anyone can help you, it should be me!*

But fear had him trembling. What if he entered her being only to find that her essence was dead, and that only her Earther body was left? And he was tired, so awfully tired now. He was angry at himself for using so much of his energy uselessly, drowning himself in senseless, useless emotions.

"I have to do this."

Trembling, he knelt by the bed and took her limp hand into his. Touching his fingertip to the inside of her wrist, he felt the faint pulsation. Eyes closed, focussed, he let his entire being meld with this, until everything in his own universe seemed in complete rapport with this important rhythm. *He was inside.* It was like being inside a huge, dark cave while someone outside pounded on the exterior with an enormous, thundering mallet.

Pound. Pound. Pound.

Then…nothing more…

No! He couldn't let that be!

He drifted through her, searching for light. But he saw only darkness, darkness, and more darkness. Emptiness.

There, off to the right. Did he see a glint? There was a spark. It flickered, then stopped. But then it flickered again, and again. *There was a chance*—but either it was, far, far away or awfully, terribly small…

Agonizingly slowly, he inched in that direction. It was as though he were swimming through an endless, black ocean. He swam and swam and swam. It was taking forever! Jared paused and gazed ahead at the tiny reddish light amid the horrible, empty blackness.

I'm no closer! How can this be? Her ember was still tiny in the distance! What if he *couldn't* reach it?

No! As anger and desperation filled him, the image of her little light became more and more cloudy. It was harder to see it at all. He had to concentrate, keep his focus. Dammit, he *knew* how to respond like one of *her* people would, not like an Earther.

Pausing, refocussed and calmer, he could feel his power grow stronger, and he saw her tiny spark begin to grow brighter. *Their connection*—he could feel how very close it was, and then he saw what he hadn't been able to recognize before.

Her little ember *wasn't* off in the distance. It truly *was* tiny, and it responded to the fluctuation of his own energy and focus. Steeling himself, Jared focussed on his power and building his energy store. And he reached forward, seeing himself as a glowing, white thread of the strongest material in the known universe, thrusting through the blackness.

Then he could feel her respond as his power touched her core, her centre. She was a brief, weak flash of scarlet. For a moment he had a flash of sensation that he'd killed her, pushed her beyond, but quickly he shoved the useless thought away, visualizing it being dropped into a garbage can, and the lid firmly pushed down.

Now he sent the wonderful, beautiful awareness of warmth flowing from him, through the glowing, white thread into that little red ember. The power seemed to make his thread pulsate in the rhythm of his heart. It wasn't long before her rhythm began to match his stronger one…

Warmth and peace filled him and now surrounded him as he watched the tiny pinpoint of scarlet gradually, so slowly, begin to stretch outward. For a brief second, it seemed that it would overcome him. Determined, he pushed more, more energy down through his thread and into the reddish ember. It entered her spark as whiteness, then swirled and became a very pale shade of crimson—

Gasping, suddenly he couldn't breathe. He felt like he was *choking*. The energy had suddenly gushed from him in one lump, the red pool instantly soaking it in. How long could he keep this up? How long would he *need* to? Would he have even *close* to enough energy to fill the rapidly expanding void?

A long sigh escaped him, and he tried to force still more power, but he could see his gleaming white thread begin to thin out and come close to breaking...

No! I can't let that happen!

Chapter Twenty

I am dying. Dying…

I can feel my essence as it dwindles away, leaving less and less of me. I have been struggling desperately to reach Jared, but it seems that the constant effort has only served to weaken me even further. And the *cold*. So awfully *cold*. The life spark inside of me must now be very, *very* small. The death process should not take much longer now.

Do I regret the assignment? No, I think not. I understood the dangers and risks when I agreed to participate in this important mission. The Earthers needed our skills, and they still do. The risks had been made quite clear to me, and to the others.

But when I think of regret, my thoughts go to Jared…*my mate*. There can be no doubt that he will blame himself in some fashion for my death. If only I could project something to him. That no longer matters, though. I can no longer focus nor concentrate. My time is most certainly coming to an end.

A jolt, as though I have been struck by lightning! What is happening?

A shock…and then I am dimly aware of the wonderful sensation of precious warmth as it begins to fill me, seep through me and all around me.

Once again, a flood of delicious heat. Energy. It is so familiar. *My Jared's energy!* And oh, oh, he is so strong!

Yet still it comes—more, and even more! This sensation is glorious, for I can feel my spark as it grows to become a flame, licking away the chill of darkness that surrounds it. As it grows, it expands, filled with the power from my Earther. Greedily I drink it in, savouring it, wallowing in it. It is as though I have been lost in the desert county of the th-fff-K on my planet, and someone has put my little glowing sphere into my hand so that I can have the nourishment that I require...

Ahhh... I am growing stronger, stronger, *stronger*. And how gloriously wonderful and tremendous it feels.

Now that I have recovered a bit, I can see the beautiful slender thread which is Jared's gleaming whiteness. I gasp, for the thread has become quite thin in sections—so thin that it is almost gone.

And then I *feel* Jared as well. He has given to me everything he could, and at great cost to himself. I can feel how empty, how drained he now is. *His thread is coming so close to snapping!* And I watch as my own scarlet one creeps forward like an Earth snake. Slithering, it moves from my flame and reaches outward towards that beloved white thread. Curling, it wraps itself around the thin whiteness until it supports and surrounds the entire length.

Now, as we have before, we begin to resemble the peppermint sticks sold by the gentleman in the variety store. Focussing, I send the energy that I can spare over to my beloved and am once again amazed at the strength and power of this Earther. For I have sent him only a little of my energy, yet, somehow, I can see it grow almost instantly as it reaches him.

Again, as I have before, I now feel something unusual inside of him that I still do not understand...but that is not important now.

What *is* important is that we both require rest, and then nourishment. I feel Jared as he slips back into himself, and I send my deep gratitude and love as he departs. Now it is my Earther body which reaches out for his, and, embracing, holding each other closely, we sleep.

Delicious warmth greets me as I awaken. Returning slowly to a conscious level, I savour the feeling of the sunshine caressing me through the opening where the curtains fail to meet in the middle. I can hear Jared as he moves quietly about the apartment. The sound of items being moved in the kitchen suggests that he is preparing food. Now I can smell the unpleasant odour of coffee…

This reminds me of the importance of my own nourishment requirements. I know that the sensations of weakness and fatigue will lessen substantially once I have had the opportunity to enjoy using my LLL-nnnta. Slowly, carefully, I move into a sitting position, closing my eyes against the dizziness. Cautiously, I pull myself to stand, one hand on the window ledge to steady me while I breathe deeply. My eyes quite open now, I turn towards the dresser and see my reflection in the mirror above it.

I am scarlet. I have to chuckle, for it seems so strange to see the skin of my people clad in the clothing of Jared's! So exhausted were we both last night that we collapsed into sleep still wearing our shirts and long pants. Weakly, I manage to propel myself to the doorway. But I stand in hesitation, remembering only too well the awful reaction that Jared had the first time that he had seen my true appearance. *Should I use my LLL-nnnta first?*

He is in the kitchen, sitting at the table, with a sandwich—white bread clutched in hands that seem almost as pale. Blue eyes gaze up at me as he opens his mouth to take his first bite.

Our eyes meet. He stops. Mouth still open in anticipation of what he no doubt considers to be delicious nourishment, his eyes never leave mine as he quietly deposits the sandwich down onto the plate. But slowly and surely, a smile begins to form as he closes his mouth, his lips twisting into a wry grin. As I come closer, he reaches his hand toward me. I take it and sit down on the other chair. Both of us gaze at the sight of our clasped hands—and the rather startling contrast between the deep crimson of my skin and the paleness of his.

"My scarlet woman," he murmurs.

I know vaguely that this is some sort of reference that is based on ancient Earther folklore or a story, or perhaps both. Yet when I lock eyes with the azure ones of my mate, I recognize glorious love and joy.

It may well seem strange to Earthers, but there is no need for Jared and me to discuss what has happened. Even as I think this, though, I am sharing the guilty sensation which I feel inside of Jared as he sees images in his memory of last night. I send him a projection of love and encouragement.

"Jared." I feel a need to explain this part in words. Although we have a powerful rapport, as an Earther, he will likely still benefit if some concepts are explained in words.

He is caressing my hand with his fingertips, and I need to consciously focus on what I am about to say, in order to avoid the human aspects of me being distracted by the physical sensations. I fix my eyes on his. "My beloved Earther, you are in an extremely unique situation. It is my people, and especially myself, who should be experiencing guilt feelings. How awfully difficult it must be for you to join with us, particularly when you see your *own people* being victimized! Certainly, there is always a possibility that one of my kind may be destroyed by the enemy, but we have been prepared for this through rigorous training. You, my dearest one, have been facing this stress and shock without true preparation for the possibility of *my* destruction. And that, my pale mate, is what we must now work on."

Jared nods his understanding, pushing the plate away from him as though he no longer has any appetite. But I quietly push it back to him and encourage him to eat. He requires this nourishment. Sighing, he reluctantly takes a small bite. Relaxed, he has not bothered to shield his inner thoughts, and I see clearly his fear of losing me, as well as his distaste for even admitting that such a possibility exists.

It is my turn to sigh. It appears that this will require more effort than I had initially anticipated. However, I am aware that the intensity of our bond should help to lighten the load. Now I sense a desire for closure as Jared turns his attention once more to my physical appearance.

"You know, Perka," he says with mock seriousness, "you're really rather attractive in this colour, though it's a bit—a bit tricky trying to get used to those eyes!" Then he leans forward and plants a kiss on my forehead. "Nope, I didn't think so," he says as his lips curve upward in a lopsided grin. "You don't taste any different."

I pretend to be offended and withdraw my hand from where it has been resting on the table close to him.

He has raised the cheese sandwich back to his mouth to bite it once again. For a quiet moment, we sit contentedly, enjoying the lightness provided by the humour. Passing a hand across his mouth, he wipes away some stray crumbs. Once more, his eyes meet mine. "What is it exactly that keeps you our colour?"

"In Earther words, it is a pigment-suppressant."

Nodding, he tries to process this information. Then his eyes widen. "I—I saw you using it once. But...but I'd really like to watch you when you use it again. And you sure look like you need it!"

We both smile. That is most certainly quite true!

"I'd—I'd really like to *understand* your people better. What did you say your people are called?"

"You would not be able to pronounce it, Jared." I reach over to curl my fingers around his and give them a squeeze. Then I reach downward to retrieve my pouch from where it is still secured on the inside of my belt. Lovingly, I hold the tiny sphere in the palm of one hand, leaving my fingers open so that my Earther can observe. "LLL-nnnta," I whisper, nodding toward the device. "My nourishment. My source of energy and resilience."

"Ullnawtuh?"

"LLL-nnnta."

His next attempt is closer to the correct pronunciation. As the sphere enlarges and begins to pulsate, Jared's eyebrows arch upward.

After that, I am no longer aware of his reactions. Surrounded by blissful red mist, I am totally immersed in the wonderful feelings of peacefulness and strength. It is as though I am floating on a soft cloud, drifting contentedly...no worries, no fears. It is a sensation that I am reluctant to let go...

As usual, though, once my energy has been replenished, all of this begins to lightly depart as the LLL-nnnta gradually ceases functioning. It will need to regain its own strength and abilities now. Next, I take the tiny pigment-suppressant and, holding it on the tip of my finger, I extend it toward Jared so that he can see it. As he gazes down at the tiny speck, a puzzled frown begins to occupy his face. Before the speck begins to explode, though, I pull it back to me so that I can inhale the little cloud. I raise my other hand in a *stop* gesture to Jared so that he keeps enough distance that he does not inhale the little cloud himself.

He has a questioning look on his face, so I send him an image of himself as an albino. I am not certain whether this would actually happen, but it amuses me and will answer any questions as to why I wanted him to keep his distance. Jared's lips are twisted up to one side. Apparently, he did *not* find it amusing—or, more likely, he does not want to admit so. His eyes are on my skin as the colour begins to fade. He takes my hand and holds it with his own, while we both watch as the contrast between our colours steadily diminishes…

Now the process is complete. My skin retains only a slightly pinkish tone. Flashing through my mind is the thought that I am relieved that my colour will not fade to the level of Jared's paleness. Quickly I shield that thought, not wanting to offend my Earther.

Jared is smiling when our eyes meet again. "Wow," he says softly.

"No, Jared. No. We must try once more. And please, *please* try to maintain your focus." I am growing weary. No matter how hard he tries, it seems that Jared cannot sustain his concentration when I send him deliberate distractions that include possibilities of harm coming to me.

Could it be that I have found a weakness? Could it be that there is a way for the enemy to defeat someone who holds power as great as this Earther does? I do not want to give that thought any attention. And now I can sense Jared beginning to focus on another imaginary enemy and preparing to begin again.

Once more, I send him the memory of that awful moment when I shielded him from the enemy in the drug store, and he saw me collapse. Surely, by now he will have developed some resistance to the shock!

But even now I can feel his concentration waver. It seems that he simply cannot deal with the thought of my destruction or suffering. Yet when I send him images of Marjorie's victimization, he remains strong. It would appear that we have a serious problem, despite my Earther's tremendous strength and potential. He cannot seem to maintain focus or control when he is fearful of losing me or watching me suffer.

I shield my thoughts carefully. Assuming that I survive my experiences on this planet, I will need to return to my own home, eventually. It is my responsibility to ensure that he is adequately prepared for that inevitable occurrence—and that he will be able to cope with the emotions which will accompany it.

Welcome sensations distract me from my serious musings. His arm is around my shoulders, and he pulls me to him, hugging me. My own arms circle his waist and I allow my forehead to lean against his chest. I feel his lips caressing my hair.

"Don't worry, Perka," he whispers. "This is all just *practice*, after all. It's just that I *know* we're not in a real situation, that it isn't really happening. If this was real, I'd be just fine. Really. Don't worry. I've learned my lesson."

I try to look as cheerful as he does as I gaze into those bright, smiling eyes of his. I cannot help but smile too when I nestle against him.

But…if only I could feel as certain as he seems to.

Chapter Twenty-One

Jared watched from behind the glass door in the lobby as the alien female—his companion, his love—walked down the sidewalk in the direction of the crisis line centre offices, a few blocks away. He'd offered to drive her, but she'd been determined to walk. There was a nagging sensation inside of him still that he now understood was worry about her. To him, she just didn't seem as strong yet as she'd been before the awful night with the enemy in the drug store.

She felt his thought and turned, to smile at him and send reassurance. He nodded back at her, sighing, savouring the sight of the setting sun's rays highlighting the scarlet tints in her hair. As her image faded into the distance, he heaved another sigh, his thoughts turning once again to the memory of what happened in the drug store. Although he no longer immersed himself in blame and guilt, there was still something unfinished about the whole thing, something irritating him like acid indigestion…

As turned back toward the inside, he caught a glimpse of the mailboxes under the stairway. Suddenly he realized that he had no idea how long it'd been since he'd checked his. His hand went to his pocket to feel for his phone. But it wasn't there. He hadn't bothered to look at his emails either. Funny to think that not that long ago he seemed to do little more than check both of his mailboxes constantly. His mailbox key was on his keyring with his others, so he pulled it out and checked his mail. Just junk mail, really…and a letter from his mom. He sighed. It would be so much easier if she would just email him more. She did when something really important came up, but she was still more comfortable with a paper and pen.

When he walked upstairs to his apartment, though, he dropped the letter on his kitchen table.

His eyes had a faraway look. The nagging sensation was returning...and he began to realize that it wasn't just Perka who concerned him...

Marjorie. The awful memories came back. *Marjorie.* So strong, so confident. But the experience with the nnn-Asi-t had left her sitting on the floor with tears flooding her face. And the last time he'd seen her, she'd looked so exhausted from the experience. That was when he'd been lifting the unconscious body of Perka into his little car...

Marjorie. Had he done enough to help her? He shook his head. No. He certainly hadn't.

"Marjorie," he murmured, automatically reaching for the closet door handle to get his jacket.

Suddenly, with no conscious memory of even coming back down the stairs, he was in his car, turning the key in the ignition—

What am I doing? Is this just an excuse to be near her again? But he shook his head against the thought. He was just doing what he *should* do. Surely it was the least he could do.

Heading to Marjorie's place. So familiar. How many times have I done this before...back when...

As far as he knew, she still lived in the same apartment. He *hadn't* known that she was working in that particular drug store, although he'd heard that she had found a job right after graduation.

Stopped at a red light, he found himself reliving what had happened in the drug store that night, and how truly bizarre everything must have seemed to Marjorie. But suddenly he remembered that, in a way, he was no longer an Earther, and he must keep his shield in place. Jared had no desire to risk any contact right now with the enemy.

With no conscious memory of arriving, he found himself in her parking lot. He was a little surprised to find that he was in the same visitor's spot he'd preferred when they'd been together. He had no recollection of looking for it. An uneasy feeling in the pit of his stomach nagged at him as he followed the familiar sidewalk towards the building. Jared stopped and tilted his head back, gazing upward at the windows of her apartment. She'd always liked the higher floors because of the views…

Suddenly he gasped. What was he *doing?* He couldn't just barge in! Quickly his hand reached inside his jacket pocket for his phone. Opening it, he saw the texts they'd exchanged the night after the drug store incident. She'd said that she'd be okay, although she still seemed somewhat baffled and confused by what she remembered. Sighing, he pushed her number.

She picked up! She was *there*, at least!

"I—I'm sorry to bug you, Marjorie. I—um, was just in your neighbourhood and thought I'd see—I'd see how you're doing…" He shook his head. It sounded so *lame*, but she'd said it would be okay if he stopped by sometime—and when she said in fifteen minutes, what else could he do but agree?

Well, this is really awkward! Now I have to kill time because I didn't tell her I was right outside her building! Jared, you idiot, she'll think you're stalking her or something!

He stood there, looking through the other recent messages on his phone. A young man passed him on the sidewalk, giving him a backwards glance as he went to the door. Jared stepped after him and entered the building before the door closed again. Inside the elevator, it felt so natural to press the button for the thirteenth floor. As the door opened, he stepped into the corridor. Then he stopped. He sent a projection around the corner and to her apartment…

Jared gasped. He felt her as though she was right here—in his arms—

Taking a couple of steps closer, he wasn't surprised to see the door to her place slowly open. Then he saw her lovely face as she took a tentative peek through the doorway, as though she was unsure whether someone might be there.

A smile lit her beautiful face when she saw Jared. Stepping near, he pushed the door closed behind him as they entered the apartment.

"Oh, Jar," she breathed, and moved into his arms. "Thank you so much for your texts. They really helped. But I'm so glad you came by. I'm still so confused by everything, and it's hard to explain by texts, and I didn't want to bother you! The whole thing just seems too—too weird to share with anyone else, so I called in sick for a couple of days."

The warmth and scent of her in his arms had him wishing they could just stay like this forever. But he was glad that she'd said what she had, as it reminded him of why he was here, of his responsibility. He moved his hands to her shoulders and gazed at her. Focussing on his responsibility helped to offset those old feelings which had been rekindled when they'd embraced. Putting an arm around her shoulders, he eased her toward her sofa. As they sat, he sent a projection of comfort and reassurance.

Relaxation suddenly filling her, her shoulders drooped, and she exhaled. "Jar, I thought of phoning you, but I didn't want to interfere. How is your girlfriend? Is she all right?"

Jared smiled. "She's fine now."

"Oh, good. The poor thing. Well—what really happened, Jared? I know you said that the old lady was insane or something, but how do you know so much about that?"

How much should I tell her? He sighed. "Remember, I studied psychology. It might not be true insanity. It's hard to explain. It—it's like the person's emotions being stirred up to the point of them being irrational."

"But Jared. I would never, ever want to hurt anyone!"

"Of course not. Of *course* not." Jared hugged her gently. *Can I make her completely immune? Do I have the power to do that by myself? If I do, can I control that power? I'm not even sure how to do it—*

"Marjorie, sometimes some emotionally unbalanced people just go around and stir other people up to make themselves feel better—"

"But where did that old lady go? It was almost like she just—just disappeared or something!"

A corner of Jared's mouth turned upward. "Maybe she did."

"What?"

"Nothing really. I was just thinking that it might be good if she did."

Marjorie pulled away from him and studied his face, one hand playing with the strand of dark hair that wouldn't stay tucked behind her ear. "I don't think I really understand what you mean. But I guess it doesn't matter." She sat back against the sofa then and gazed downward at her hands in her lap. "Jar, what if it—if it happens again? I mean—working with pharmaceuticals, I have the potential to really harm someone."

Jared, too, was gazing down at her lap where her fingers twined and untwined. Her whole body was trembling. This distressed him. Marjorie had always been so confident, so self-assured. She'd always been capable of doing anything she might put her mind to. Anger at the nnn-Asi-t surged through him.

Jared sighed, wishing it hadn't come to this. But somehow, he'd known that it could…and that was why he'd felt the need to see her.

Silence surrounded them. He knew that words couldn't accomplish what needed to be done. Yet, even as he reached for her hand, he was wondering if he really *could* do it…

Automatically, she curled her fingers around his longer ones, just as she had done so many times before. Jared didn't do anything to interfere with this. But he reached forward with his other hand until his fingertip made contact with the inside of her wrist. Closing his eyes, he visualized his strength and power as a rainbow against a pale blue sky. Slowly, gently, he pulled the rainbow toward them, until it touched the woman with its brilliant rows of colour. Deep indigo, navy, royal blue, and azure, changing gradually to shades of green fading to yellow, slowly colouring to gold and orange and red. He could sense and see in his mind as each segment of the rainbow emptied its hue somewhere inside of Marjorie, beyond her pulse point.

Eyes still closed, he sensed the inside of her—her returning strength.

Yes, he was capable of this. Now he knew that no nnn-Asi-t would ever victimize her again. Opening his eyes, he smiled into hers, savouring the peace and calm that he could see there now.

As though to confirm this, she smiled. "I'm all right now, Jar," she whispered, her face and all aspects of her a picture of tranquillity.

"Yes. You are." Jared's voice was very soft.

Jared handed the smiling man some coins and stepped back through the doorway to the cool of late evening. Gazing up at the crescent moon and admiring the brightness of the twinkling stars...

Closing his jacket at the neck, he continued to study the sky. *Which star is she from? Can I even see it from here?* A sudden breeze emphasized that the temperatures were falling, and Jared found himself hurrying to do up his jacket only to find that he already had. Almost time for winter clothing.

He stopped, emptied his mind. Had he sensed something? Was he about to have another battle with the enemy?

But no. Now he saw them. It was just shadows over by some garbage cans in his peripheral vision. Shaking his head, he chuckled at himself. This must be what it was like for war veterans on their return home, or maybe for a cop who's off-duty—feeling like they have to be constantly on the alert or on guard.

Adjusting the position of the folded newspaper tucked under his arm, he mused about how he'd never bought newspapers before he met Perka. Before that, his phone had given him all the news he needed. Hands in the pockets of his blue jacket, he continued in the direction of his apartment building.

But, just outside of the building's front door, he stopped. There was *something.* And it was something different. Not like one of the nnn-Asi-t. It'd been just a very quick flash, but nebulous, vague. Yet it'd been definitely *something.* He opened the door of the three-storey walk-up and moved to the stairs. He took them two at a time, thankful that Perka would be home soon. Maybe she could clarify things.

Opening his apartment door, he pushed off his shoes and tossed his keys and paper on the nearby table. Running his hand across his mouth and chin, he crossed the room to the window and stared outside, wondering what it could be that he'd sensed. It must be some sort of projection, some sort of message from Perka's people. But he couldn't make anything out of it. Closing his eyes, he massaged his forehead to get rid of the stress, wishing he could just turn the channel, like on TV. A sound from behind made him jump a bit. With a little gasp, he turned, half-expecting to see an enemy poised for battle—

Perka! She was early. But his grin faded as he sensed disquiet emanating from her.

"What is it?" He was whispering, as though several nnn-Asi-t might be within hearing distance. "I felt something too. But what *is* it? I couldn't make anything out of it."

Cautioning him to silence with a finger across her lips, she projected to him. They were at such close proximity now that a projection should be quite safe from enemy detection. At first, Jared only felt and saw a strange, amorphous thing, like a cloud. But then he began to recognize a *code*, hidden inside. Suddenly it was clear, like something he'd understood all his life—

A general alert. It was Martin. Something serious was at hand and they were all to meet at his place—

Carefully shielded.

Despite the fact that Jared was inside his apartment and still wearing his jacket, a strong sensation of cold wormed its way through him. He wasn't aware that it was the biting edge of fear until he sensed the warm reassurance from Perka—*Andrea*, he reminded himself—as the pleasurable comfort wrapped around him like a soft blanket, slowing his shivers. Then he felt her presence withdraw from him and saw her shield slide gently, but firmly, into place. Automatically, he followed suit.

"We must go now, Jared," she said quietly, her face serious. "We should take the car this time."

Nodding, he tried to feel as businesslike as Perka—*no! Andrea*—looked. *Use her Earth name.* Focussing, he managed to start putting away the aroused emotions into their little compartments, visualizing his mind as a computer. Inside the little car, he wondered what on Earth the nnn-Asi-t might be up to now—something that would necessitate a hastily-called meeting! Had Andrea experienced occasions like this before since she'd come here?

Angry at himself and cursing, he found that he was automatically on alert for the enemy, for their trails, every time the VW came near a dark or shadowy area. Maybe there was just one, but it could be a great, gigantic, colossal silver-and-shadow creature, just waiting for them.

Chapter Twenty-Two

I am very aware of the anxious expression on Jared's face. Yet, at the same time, I am rather pleased with him, for despite his trepidation and concern, he has managed to maintain his shield quite effectively. Not needing to be concerned about him is quite a relief. But I, too, feel trepidation lurking inside of me. I have sensed no presence at all of any nnn-Asi-t during the days following the drug store, and Jared has mentioned the same thing.

But now there is *this*. This was not a cry of fear, nor a signal for help like the one I had sent and Jared had received what seems now like a long time ago. The new message was a *coded* request for us to come. It must be a serious matter affecting each of us, and perhaps also our entire mission—

Something affecting the very reason we are here.

Experience and training advise me that something quite different must have occurred regarding the nnn-Asi-t. I have turned over all sorts of ideas in my mind (shielded)…and I am concerned about the possibilities which I see. We have long suspected that the enemy might try to alter their usual approaches, once they had come to realize that my people were arriving here in increasing numbers. But we have no idea just what to expect. It is unnerving not to be able to prepare oneself for whatever might occur.

What this development suggests is just how very much the nnn-Asi-t want this planet. I suppose that this would seem quite strange to Earthers like Jared. Why, they might think, would anyone else want this third planet, with its polluted air and waters and all of its other problems?

What the naïve observer might not think of is the fact that, even with its surface somewhat spoiled, as long as any capability of sustaining life remains, there is hope. And inside and below the surface of the planet are precious metals. Other planets in this solar system have them, too. But the climate here is better suited to the nnn-Asi-t.

And the nnn-Asi-t have the means to persuade the innocent Earthers to work for them, to provide the enemy with what they will need in order to live here and make this planet their own home. They do not care at all if Earthers might suffer in the process.

They want to have the Earthers use their Earth technology to obtain the metals and process these…for the benefit of the nnn-Asi-t.

My own planet, too, could benefit from the metals which the Earth possesses. But my people are not greedy and cruel. We are not willing to ruthlessly steal this planet for its metals and for the technology that these can help to create.

We have developed some of our own technology. Our power comes from a combination of our own innate abilities and substances like the one from which my LLL-nnnta has been fashioned. It is our hope that one day we might engage in trade with the Earthers so that we might all share the bounties from our planets and civilizations. We wish to preserve this Earth and help it to be all that it can be without the interference of this terrible enemy.

The way it *should* be.

The car stops. So engrossed was I in my thoughts that I did not at first realize we were here. All is quiet. Martin's apartment house is just across the street. I am watching the profile of my Earther who sits between me and the apartments. His expression is extremely serious, as it should be. We exchange glances and open our doors, closing them quietly again. The chilly wind has picked up, and once more I have to fight it in order to keep my hood up. I begin to take a step, but then I notice Jared in my peripheral vision. He stands beside the vehicle, his eyes in constant movement as he turns his head slowly to take in the surrounding areas. His thoughts are well-shielded as he uses that skill which he possesses and—for some reason—my people do not…

Jared is looking for trails, but the continuing movements of his eyes and head suggest that he has not found any. Oh yes, the nnn-Asi-t are most certainly up to something. But I have absolutely no idea what.

"Nothing," Jared murmurs as he steps in front of the car and extends a hand to me as I move toward him. As he holds my hand, his eyes meet mine. "Nothing at all."

Inside of him I feel a longing to understand, but also a desire to be reassured that everything will be all right. I cannot give him what is not yet there to give. I reach a hand to touch his pale cheek. I can feel his trepidation, and also my own. Sensing this, he gives my hand what he wishes to be a reassuring squeeze. Slipping his arm around my shoulders, he whispers into my ear. "We'll be okay, Andrea. I promise."

It is interesting that he feels sufficient confidence to make such a promise. Hand in hand, we cross the street to the old building. As we enter, I understand his true message. What he means is that he would willingly die before he would allow anything to harm me again. He is being valiant, which is most kind. But such a frame of mind would not be constructive to our efforts.

Softly, I knock on Martin's door.

Silence dominates the room as we all consider the information. We have been comparing reports. None of us has sensed any nnn-Asi-t activity within the city during the past few days—

None of us except for one. Franco has been monitoring the area around the university, and he reports that he has sensed strong traces of nnn-Asi-t there. And this has been steadily increasing during the past few days.

Something is happening, something involving several of them. They may well be preparing for some sort of major attack.

Of course, we had considered this possibility before leaving our home planet. What we must do is obvious to us. In order for us to defeat combined nnn-Asi-t powers, we must combine our skills as well.

But all of this seems to be occurring rather quickly and suddenly. Theoretically, I am prepared. Yet still I am rather aware of the increased pounding inside of my chest. As I regard the others in the room, their concern becomes quite evident, too. Especially Franco. His fingers toy constantly with his thin, dark moustache, as though at any moment he might begin removing it hair by hair. This is most understandable, as he is the one who has been monitoring the unsettling situation and its progress.

"What about the others?" It is Megan's voice. Although she has been working near the other side of the small city, this development will likely concern her as well. When I look at her, I instantly think of Jared. Her colouring is quite similar to his, almost as though they were related. Her body does not react as smoothly as mine does to the pigment-suppressant, leaving her almost as pale as my Earther. The light from the nearby lamp catches the blonde strands of her hair.

Her question is a good one. We need to know whether this enemy development is isolated to this area. And so we look to Martin.

His dark face seems heavy with the responsibility. "Yes," he says softly, "we must check with the other votaries throughout this country—and perhaps the entire planet." He sighs then. "Yet we must also keep our communications shielded. To do so will require a great deal of our energy—energy that we might be called upon to utilize at almost any time."

I study the drawn faces surrounding me. *Have they forgotten?* But then I sense Martin's dark eyes focussing now in my direction, and I return his look with a nod.

"Yes," he murmurs. "Of course. Jared has the ability to send, with likely more strength than my own. That would spare the rest of us for shielding. Jared, of course the decision is yours."

My Earther gazes first at Martin, then at me, nibbling continually on his thumbnail. But then he shrugs a shoulder, and grins wryly. "I really have no idea what I'm agreeing to, but why should today be any different, right? So just tell me what I have to do!" His apparent lightheartedness is a sharp contrast to the seriousness of the power that we can feel in his voice.

Martin regards him with a look that is almost mournful. After a quiet moment, he nods with a sigh. He smiles warmly at Jared. "I wish that all of this wasn't necessary."

"No problem, Martin," Jared replies. Again, we can clearly feel the power behind his words.

Martin nods in my direction, and I turn to Jared, his blue eyes meeting mine. I take a deep breath before I begin to explain. "Jared, you will send a slender thread of your power upward to the thermosphere. From there you must project your question around the Earth, over and over. The rest of us shall, together, shield your projection from enemy senses up to the highest level of the thermosphere. Beyond that, the enemy will not be able to read it. They might be able to pick up some sort of signal from one of our kind to another but will not be able to make sense of it. You must open yourself to projections from the other votaries in this country and beyond it, letting them combine with your thread. Then, allow yourself to return. You might feel as though you are falling downward, as though through some sort of tube. But do not be alarmed. You will be seeing our protective shield." I lean forward to put my hand on his. "I—*we*—will not allow anything to interfere with, or to harm you in any way."

His eyes hold mine for what seems a long time. Then they drop and he nods to himself. After a moment, he raises them to meet Martin's.

"I'm ready."

I move away from Jared's side and join my compatriots as we form a circle around my Earther. My people and I interlock our fingers as we join hands. This physical contact will help us to avoid inadvertently sending projections that the enemy might detect. As we do this, I feel our togetherness, our readiness, and our combined strength. Although the enemy might sense some sort of shield, that is absolutely the limit of what they might be able to recognize.

My scarlet mist rises upward, upward to the ceiling and well beyond it. Georgia's yellowish/orangish shade blends into mine on one side and into the deep brownish black of Martin's on the other. My other compatriots add theirs, each in its own unique hue. A tall, transparent cylinder of varying shades surrounds Jared now, although if he can see it, it is not through his eyes, but rather his inner senses. Deep in concentration, he has closed his blue eyes.

Finally, I can see it. My entire being fills with pride, as well as a deep respect and admiration for my Earther's unexpected abilities. Quickly I shut my own eyes to ensure that my inner strengths are properly focussed. But I know what I would see if I were to open them once more. I would be watching a long, deceptively thin, whitish thread of Jared's power as it rises upward inside of our protective cylinder. His strength is once more so great that his filament will seem to glow. I concentrate on my part of the shield, imagining my scarlet mist blending with Georgia's and Martin's. *Upward, upward, higher, higher still.* Yet each, individual segment must be strong. There must be *no* weak areas…

We have reached the upper section of the thermosphere. I do not allow myself to think at all about Jared now. The greatest contribution that I can make is through focussing on my area of the shield so that it is as strong as it can possibly be. Nothing else can equal this in importance. Together, we maintain our massive shield for what seems like ages. Every now and then, I am aware of a couple of enemy attempts to pierce our cylinder. But they amount to no more than little nudges here and there. And each time one of us senses this, we send greater strength to fortify that section.

Such requires great concentration and focus from every one of us. Yet it is also far easier for us than it would be if we did not have Jared to do the sending and receiving.

Finally, I feel him as he begins to slip back downward, and we follow him, gradually relaxing more and more until we become aware of our powers as they slip back inside of our Earther-looking bodies.

Although this process is completely natural for my kind, it feels wonderful to be without those constraints once again. I open my eyes. Some of us will have had their eyes open the entire time, although I felt a need to close mine to enhance my concentration—and not allow myself to be distracted by concerns about my Earther. I blink, not yet quite functioning as a totally separate being.

Suddenly, something about Jared seizes and holds my attention. He appears to be even paler than usual. I reach for him physically. I shield myself from sending a projection, as I do not yet understand what the problem might be. My hand finds his and grasps it. As I grip it gently, a shiver of concern goes through me.

Has the procedure harmed him in some way that I had not anticipated? Did it sap too much of his power? My mind is brimming with questions, yet I sense that it is important for me to remain silent for now. Our hands are still joined. I watch him closely as he sits, head hanging, eyes closed. He is frowning, taking frequent breaths, as though he is attempting to either relax or recover, perhaps both. I glance toward Martin, who gives me a reassuring nod, motioning to me to give Jared time...and space. Releasing his hand, I sit back, seeking to calm myself, and wait for him as the others do.

I am powerless to help him while I remain completely shielded, but I understand that Jared requires some moments without interference. Helplessness is not a feeling which I enjoy. A sigh escapes me. How can I find calm when my mate gives me no clue as to what state he might be in? The difficulties which I am experiencing seem to confirm the logic behind not having mated pairs working together.

Jared covers his face with both of his hands for a few moments. But finally, his eyes still closed, he speaks. "I have—I have the messages from the votaries," he says in a hoarse whisper. Finally, his eyes open, but he does not focus on anything or anyone. Instead, he simply stares straight ahead toward the wall. However, his long fingers edge in my direction until they curl around mine. At last, I feel a bit more at ease. The great strength which I can feel still inside of him is reassuring.

He takes a long breath, and shudders as he exhales. "There is activity, like what Franco has found, in a couple of other locations. In some countries, there have been no more of the enemy reported. It looks like many of them have been defeated by our—*your* people."

Despite this report, my Earther does not appear to feel pleased or relieved. As he hesitates to continue, a look of distress clouds his face. He gazes around our circle, seeking eye contact with each one of us. After a sigh, Jared continues: "There's a build-up, like Franco said, at the university." Pausing again, he sighs again deeply. "It could be even bigger than we thought. It looks like the rest of the enemies from the surrounding areas are gathering there. Great Britain is now completely free of the enemy. But…but there seems to be a gathering in the Middle East—and—and—"

Jared shakes his head and nibbles on his thumbnail. He swallows, then continues. "There is a rather large group coming together in what we Earthers call Russia."

Chapter Twenty-Three

Perka had explained the situation more than once to Jared through words, as well as projections. Yet still it seemed that nothing could soothe him. Nothing truly helped to ease his worries and his fears. Yes, Perka's people realized the importance of this development in these particular parts of Earth. Yes, they understood that the politics and cultures of these areas were drastically different from those of the part they were in. They had tried their best to reassure Jared. After all, they had said, Perka's people, too, were stationed in many places around the Earth, and these places included the Middle East, as well as Russia.

Even now, their spacecraft were moving some of Perka's people's strongest warriors from one place to another, ensuring that their talents would be used most effectively where they were needed most. The situation was not simply a matter of having an equal number of Perka's kind to the numbers of the enemy, as Jared had assumed.

The best weapon, they had tried to explain as clearly as they could, would be to have their most powerful warriors working together against the enemy...*and that meant having Jared working with Perka.*

Still the tall Earther shook his head, anticipating a world-wide crisis that would be far greater than he'd be capable of dealing with...

In the middle of Martin's living room, he sat—a solitary figure, despite being surrounded by individuals who were ready and more than willing to lend their support and assistance, in any way possible.

He was sitting on the rug, its brown hue paling to nearly white in places as though to complement Jared's pale colouring.

Jared's heart was beating *hard*, his head filled to bursting with confusing thoughts and emotions constantly threatening to escape his control. His situation was not helped by the fatigue nagging at him after his contact with the votaries in other parts of the world. He leaned his forehead against his knees, hugging his long legs against him. It looked as though he was trying to curl himself into a ball, seeking somehow to maintain control of those new aspects of himself that he hadn't known he possessed until he'd met Perka and her people.

Again, he sought information, hoping once more that further knowledge might help to lift the cloud of confusion muddling his aching mind. "But—but how can your spacecraft move around undetected?" His voice was quite soft, as though speaking at a low volume might suck less of his energy from him.

Perka sat beside but facing him, her hand resting on his shoulder. "Oh, but they are," she replied, her voice equally soft as she smiled patiently. "They sometimes show up on your radar screens. But they have been treated with a substance from our world's plant life that allows them to blend with the background colours of your skies. At night, they just appear as darkness with white stars. Your people tend to think of them as 'glitches' in the tracking systems. And they are not large, as well as being very much aerodynamically designed."

The Earther did not return her eye contact. His mind was entirely focussed on the details, as well as the gravity of their situation. Finally, he sighed, and his shoulders sagged as a bit of calm began to return. It was simply too difficult for him to comprehend everything. He needed to stop trying.

After all, *he had no choice in this matter.* If these people believed that his involvement was vital in preventing a world-wide catastrophe, well, it looked like it would make no sense for him to refuse. He couldn't simply say *no* if his help was as important as they seemed to think! And, anyway, it was his own Earth people that he would be protecting.

But still, he wanted to understand everything that this might involve! He felt awfully insecure about simply following their instructions without really knowing what the hell he was doing! Having the weight of the world on his shoulders was not something that he had ever contemplated…and it was sure something that he didn't want.

Jared turned the key in the ignition and took a long breath. With the engine turned off, everything seemed awfully quiet.

Still looking straight ahead rather than at the woman beside him, he gripped the steering wheel hard. "How much *time,* Andrea?"

Perka didn't need to use any unEarthly abilities to sense the anxiety that once again gripped her mate. It was good that she'd monitored him to ensure that he'd rested during the afternoon. She shook her head at the seemingly endless number of questions he continued to ask. Her own face remained a picture of complete calm. No matter how she truly felt inside, *calm* was what her mate needed to see.

A long sigh left her. This helped her to find the patience which she needed, to assist her Earther in making himself ready for what lay ahead. "If they are preparing for something on a large scale, as we believe that they are, they will require time to set and enact their plan, just as we need time to get ourselves ready, and to learn whatever we can. I know that you find this difficult, Jared, but please try to maintain control." Reaching across the space between their seats, she pulled his right hand away from the steering wheel to hold it between both of hers. "You must not allow anxiety to control you. My people need you, which of course means that your own people do, as well. We must find out whatever we can, and then rejoin the others."

Only too aware of the fact that she was right, Jared turned toward her. She was *always* right, it seemed. He nodded, opening the car door as he did. As he walked around the car to where she was, he held out a hand. She took it, and they stood quietly, eyes on each other. No, the reassuring smile on his mate's face did not lessen the gravity of the situation for him. But he still enjoyed seeing her lips turn upward at the corners of her mouth.

A deep sigh misted the cool air, then became long, slow, more relaxed breathing as he felt the comforting warmth seep through her fingers and into the depths of his being. Closing his eyes, he could *see* her strength flow gently, like a little scarlet stream, from her and into him. Jared sent his own whitish tendril to meet hers, wrapping it around and around her crimson one. Joy and peace began to fill his inner being, and, smiling contentedly now, he slowly withdrew. Ever so gently, he gave that wonderful red filament a nudge back in Perka's direction. She too, would need her strength, after all.

When he opened his eyes, the inner peace remained with him. Maybe it had something to do with the beauty of the autumn late afternoon. Maybe it was the vision of the woman he loved, surrounded by colourful leaves drifting delicately to the ground, many the colour of her glorious deep-reddish hair. Suddenly he was filled with gratitude that they were physically close enough to share like this, without having to worry about arousing the suspicions of their enemy.

Mostly though, he could feel that it had something to do with the beauty of this woman's entire being—the fact that all these people from her planet were here to risk their lives to protect his Earthers, who had never done anything at all for them. His people didn't even know that hers existed.

He sighed once more. *It's time to set things right.*

Neither one spoke now. There was no need. They turned toward the main campus as she put her arm through his. While they walked, they both increased the shields surrounding their conscious thoughts. Leaves swirled around their feet as they left the VW behind in the visitors' parking lot.

"Use your vision as much as you can for spotting trails, Jared. I do not want to take any risk of their feeling my presence if I try to sense them. It is unlikely, but with others of us in the vicinity trying to sense their locations—well, I do not want to take any unnecessary chances, in case some of them are especially perceptive."

Jared nodded, his head turning away from her so that he could scan the area more thoroughly. Cursing softly, he was a bit unsettled by the thought that had suddenly struck him: *If the enemy is planning something, what if they're developing a way to intercept our thoughts more effectively? What if they learn to do it even if we're close together, or even touching each other?* He sighed, refocussing. It didn't matter right now. It was important to concentrate on what they knew, not remote possibilities. He could feel Perka's eyes studying him. She and her people were depending so much on him. Closing his eyes, Jared steeled himself, visualizing his spine straightening, strengthening.

Returning to the reality outside of him, he opened his eyes. His gaze took in the surroundings. The campus was beautiful, with a mixture of older buildings and modern ones amid grassy open areas and tall, mature trees, shedding leaves of yellow, orange, and gold. The breeze was cool, stirring and swirling some of the leaves gently through the grasses.

But that was all. Although this was the general area where Franco had sensed enemy presence earlier, Jared neither sensed nor saw anything of the nnn-Asi-t, even though his gaze still travelled around what he could see of the campus.

A thought struck him again, but maybe this one could be more helpful. He stopped looking into the distance, a frown suddenly etching deep creases in his forehead.

Perka touched his hand gently, saying nothing, relaying patience and leaving him free to think.

Jared was looking at the leaves that were scattered or swirling in some places, and heaped in other areas beneath the big trees. Suddenly the creases left his face, and a small, wry grin appeared. His gaze travelled downward, and he squatted, studying the fallen foliage as the memory of tracking a previous nnn-Asi-t sparked an idea. Reaching forward with his hand, he moved some of the leaves around...

But they revealed nothing out of the ordinary. Standing up once more, he nudged at the leaves with his running shoe. Glancing at Perka, he saw that she was already doing the same. Together they moved to another spot, closer to the building. Nothing. Then another, between two buildings.

"Wait! Back up a little bit and do it again!" Jared's voice, although thick with emotion, was little more than a whisper.

She stepped backward, then shifted the leaves in front of her with her foot, gazing at his face as she did.

"*There!*" Jared strode toward her, nodding in the direction of something he'd noticed beneath the yellowish foliage on the ground. Automatically, Perka looked downward, although she knew that whatever Jared had seen was something that she could not.

To Jared, though, their efforts had been quite worthwhile. As clearly as they could both see the colourful leaves at their feet, this was a sight for him and him only...a silvery glitter hidden beneath.

Gazing at his mate, he smiled. His voice was very soft. "I'm thinking that the enemy's trails might hang suspended in the air for a few seconds—maybe even minutes—before they fall to the ground and begin to dissipate. Some of the leaves covered this one. Maybe... maybe the leaves keep them from disappearing as quickly." His blue eyes now scanned the surrounding areas—*could there be more?*

"We know, then, that this is definitely one of the areas where Franco sensed them." Perka sighed. There were still many uncertainties. She, too, cast a glance at the vast surroundings. "We cannot know how old that trail might be. I will need to sense for their presence. Otherwise, we might find ourselves searching for the enemy in places that they left some time ago. Anyway, before we had you, we relied on sensing for them. None of us have ever been able to actually *see* their trails."

Dammit. Although being involved in this whole affair had Jared feeling almost overwhelmed much of the time, there was still a part of him that wished he could play the part of the big hero. But here he was with nothing more to offer. He was pretty sure that the trail wasn't fresh. So...what alternative they did have?

Perka sent a small and very quick flash of energy to feel for enemy presence in the immediate area. Although he'd witnessed this before, it still seemed eerie to Jared to be able to see the crimson mist as it left her, like a puff of smoke, and return almost immediately.

She was shaking her head.

Jared nodded in the direction of the two older buildings. They knew that the enemy had been where they were standing. Maybe they'd find something *inside*...

They walked to the area between the two structures. Gazing downward, Jared saw something. Squatting, he moved aside some small sticks. *There!* "A bit of a trail," he said softly. But it was between the buildings. Rising, he gazed at one building, then the other. Jared nodded in the direction of the closer one. "Let's try inside."

He opened the door, then the second one, just inside. Welcome warmth struck their cheeks as they left the chill of the autumn breeze behind them. Ahead of them and to their right were wide staircases, one leading up and one down. Closed doors were on the left side. Jared's eyes busily took in the surrounding details as he searched hungrily for traces of trails. At this moment, he was not unlike a dog thinking there might be a bone somewhere nearby.

"Dammit," he whispered. The only thing that greeted him was nothing. And there were no leaves here to prevent trails from dissipating quickly.

"We should look further," Perka suggested.

Her mate sighed. In front of them was a long corridor, the length of the entire building. And Jared saw nothing that might help. There were only a few students visible, now that the supper hour had begun for most of them. He looked back toward Perka as she nodded to the stairways on their right. Once again, he watched as the crimson mist rose from her body. This time, it hung in the air for just an instant before taking the form of two long, red tendrils. On the end of each, Jared could see an arrowhead shape develop.

Then they disappeared, one up the staircase and the other down.

Although they'd only been gone for a couple of seconds, impatience began to nag at Jared again. Giving Perka one more quick glance as he nibbled on the inside of his lower lip, he slipped down the stairs, his long legs easily taking two steps at a time. It seemed almost obvious to him that the thickness of the shadows at the bottom would offer shelter and hiding places for their enemies.

Reaching the bottom of the stairs, he opened the door which he found there, just in time to watch as Perka's crimson arrow sped past him on its return journey. Fascinated by the sight, he gazed over his shoulder to see it disappear back up the stairs. But then, quickly, he returned his attention to the corridor stretching off to the right. He found himself squinting in an effort to squeeze every possible bit of acuity from his vision, but—

Nothing! Dammit to hell and back! No trace of any trails whatsoever, not even old ones! Was all this for nothing? Shit, shit, doubleshit!

Cursing out loud this time, he hurried back up the stairs. Thinking about heading up to the next floor, he paused to share eye contact with his companion. Her red mist having once again become part of her, she just looked like an ordinary Earther. And she was shaking her head negatively, a serious expression on her face.

He'd been about to say something aloud, across the hallway to her but stopped in response to her warning frown. His long legs covered the distance between them in only a couple of steps. Puffing a bit from his exertion—and concern—he whispered hoarsely to her: "How can this *be*? How can there be nothing here? The remains of the trail outside were definitely closer to this building!"

At first, she just shrugged silently, but then she met his eyes with hers. "You could not determine, from what you found outside, whether the trails were arriving at this building, or perhaps leaving it. Perhaps the enemy was here awhile ago, and—and has left to go to the other building. According to the signs outside, both are used by the chemistry department."

A deep sigh escaped Jared as he closed his eyes to collect himself, trying to keep his impatience in check. "You're right," he said after opening his eyes again. "Let's go."

They made their way hurriedly back to the doors leading to the outside. As Jared pushed the second one open, the autumn coolness once more greeted them, and a shiver ran through Perka. The Earther's eyes were instantly scanning the leaf-strewn ground, searching for trails, or clues—*anything* that could help.

Both were shoving the leaves around them with their feet, while Jared constantly studied the ground revealed by the leaves' removal.

Suddenly, the sound of a throat being cleared nearby startled him from his concentration—

A man maybe fifty years old stood in front of him. His light brown hair was streaked with blonde and a bit of white, and he pushed his glasses up the bridge of his nose. He was wearing the uniform of a security guard. "Lose something?" Thin lips curled upward on their corners in a wry attempt at a bit of a grin, as he studied Jared's face.

It was Perka who took a step closer to reply. She smiled broadly, her face a picture of warmth and sincerity. "Yes," she said pleasantly. "Um…there is a possibility that my boyfriend could have dropped his phone here somewhere."

"Well," said the security guard in a gentle voice. It seemed that he couldn't help but smile when his attention was on Perka. "I'll be around. If you don't find it, just let me know, and we'll do what we can to help. My office is in the community centre, just back there near the parking lot." Smiling again, he watched while they continued to look, and began to study the ground himself.

Just what I need—an audience! Exhaling sharply, Jared forced himself to focus. But everything just seemed so muddled. Yes, he could see silvery and grey indicators of the trails here and there beneath the leaves. And what Perka said was certainly true—he couldn't tell whether the trails were leading *to* or *from* the buildings.

Jared turned toward the second chemistry building. Nodding to Perka, he took a step in that direction—then, after a thought, he nodded graciously to the security guard, who returned the nod, and began to move away. Pulling open the heavy door, and then the next, Jared was grateful for the warmth inside, and mused that his mate would most certainly welcome it, considering how the cold affected her.

The layout here was quite similar to that of the first building. They were greeted by upward stairs and downward stairs and another long corridor. The Earther stood and carefully peered down the hallway—

There it is. For one ridiculous second, he felt like he'd won the lottery.

"Bingo," he said to no one. Quickly, he was moving down the corridor, heading toward the promising silver shimmers.

But then he was slowing down. Thinking. *How strange.* He hadn't seen trails like these before. These looked like they'd been etched, somehow, into the walls! Shaking his head, he tried to make some sense of it all. Maybe the old age of the building's walls caused them to be more porous, absorbing the trails or something...

But all that didn't matter. He couldn't care less, if he'd found *something* to follow—something to tell him that he was at last heading in the right direction to get those bastards! Jared turned, then, to follow the shimmering silver where it looked like a shiny snake climbing the wall alongside the staircase leading up. Quickly following it, at the top of the stairs he jerked open the door and rushed through to the next corridor.

For a few seconds, he stood blinking, not daring to believe his eyes.

There, ahead of him, it stretched. Along the wall near the base. A shimmery trail. It continued along the empty corridor and appeared to turn a corner to the right, not far ahead. He sped after it, oblivious to the voice that softly called his name.

Chapter Twenty-Four

Softly, I call to him once again but again he does not seem to hear, so intent is he on locating the enemy. My insides ache for him, as he will be so disappointed! Yet still I must be careful to keep my thoughts firmly shielded in case an enemy is in the vicinity. I open my mouth to call to him again but close it once more. I do not wish to call attention to us either through projecting or through voice.

Ahead, I see him as he hurries out of sight around a corner. I do not wish to run after him. Such will sap the energy of this Earther-like body, and I am certain to require much physical, as well as mental, stamina in our efforts. Can I *dare* to risk flashing a quick projection to him? If what I now suspect is completely true, this enemy might be even more of a challenge than my people have anticipated.

And, if such is the case, I do not wish to imagine what they might have in store for my Earther.

Very quickly, I send a brief flash, telling him simply that something is not right, and that he must stop. I receive nothing in reply, and I am hoping that this is because Jared is using good sense. This will be the case if he is keeping his own thoughts shielded until he can understand more completely what is happening. If the enemy has done anything harmful to him, I would know because of our close rapport. Still, I hurry in his direction, distracted from time to time by the sight of those silvery threads along the wall. Then he turns back around the corner, into the main corridor, and we come face-to-face. His is an urgent picture of excitement, concerns, and questions.

"Andrea, listen!" It is more of a demand than a request. So certain he is about what he has found!

I shake my head and lock my eyes with his. "Jared." Although I speak softly, I know that he will hear the firmness in my voice. My hand is on his arm. "*I* can see them too!"

My Earther frowns, deep creases forming between his eyebrows. His blue eyes now move restlessly as though searching somewhere for a possible explanation. I can see that he is beginning to understand the implications of this. "Per—Andrea! If that's true, is it a trail at all?"

Once more, I have to shake my head. "I have never seen one, so I have nothing to compare it with. But… I do not think that it *can* be." If I can see it, too, then it is certainly not something that I—or any of my people, for that matter—have ever seen before.

I step around the corner into the smaller hallway, hoping to avoid the prying eyes of *any* species. Moving close to the silvery shimmer, I reach out a finger toward the nearly invisible marking. Watching as a tiny crimson thread emerges from my fingertip, I find myself holding my breath as the filament makes its way forward to mingle with the thing which stretches along the base of the wall.

But it *is!* I gasp as I crouch there. I can feel that this *was* left here by the nnn-Asi-t as clearly as an Earther would recognize human footprints. It *is* a trail. Yet somehow it is also *not.* My kind *cannot see trails!* I am left shaking my head again, this time in confusion…as well as trepidation.

"Jared. Do the trails usually look just like this one? Or is this one different in any way—any way at all?"

So great is the frown on my Earther's face that he looks as though he is angry. He sighs impatiently. "No. I—I mean *yes.* Yes, it *is* different! It seems—it seems more *silvery* somehow. The other ones looked more like—like grey mists or something, with *parts* of them that were silvery. And…and this is first one I've seen that looked like it was actually—actually *embedded* in a surface—"

"Embedded," I echo him as various possible explanations drift through my conscious mind for consideration. Now it is my turn to sigh. "*Embedded,* Jared. Almost as though they have been planted here. Placed here deliberately."

"Deliberately! Deliberately? Like they…like they *wanted* us to find them. *Dammit.*"

"Yes." A long exhalation of breath makes its way from me. I raise my eyes to meet his as I rise to stand beside him. "And that means another thing too, Jared. They must…they must *know* that one of our group can see their trails. They must have *known* that one of us would recognize this. And, oh Jared, that would mean that they must know about *you* because my kind cannot see the trails."

He looks away and begins to chew on his thumbnail. This news is, quite understandably, unnerving for both of us. Because this suggests that the enemy may well be prepared for Jared.

My hand is on his arm as I continue speaking, careful to keep my voice low. "My—my people are used to thinking of them as not being as intelligent as we are. To a large degree, it has always been my kind who have outsmarted them. We have not before seen much in the way of planning or scheming from them…at least, not before *this.*"

"So," Jared whispers. There is a faraway look about his eyes. "Is this a—a *trap* then? I mean, if they wanted to make sure it wouldn't fade before we…or before *I* got here to see it?"

As we stand in contemplation, a shiver makes its way up my spine. Suddenly, I am feeling cold. "Jared, how much did you see of it when you entered this smaller hallway?"

"This is as far as I got." He turns his head to look toward the rest of the corridor. "Let's go."

But my hand still grips his arm, and so he turns his gaze to meet my eyes. He must feel me trembling, and he puts his hand on top of mine. The comfort this brings warms me. I study his eyes that match perfectly the colour of the sky peeking through the small window at the end of the hall. Now, glimmers of gold from the setting sun bathe our surroundings. I admire the bravery my dear Earther shows…and I am also quite aware of the fact that I do not want to risk losing this mate. "Perhaps we should meet with the others before we take any other action." Bravery is always more effective if it is accompanied by at least a bit of caution.

But Jared shrugs. Yet again, I can easily sense his impatience. And I hope so much that this will not be his undoing. He directs his gaze down the rest of the smaller hallway, stepping in that direction, but stops. Shrugging again, he turns back toward me. "I don't see any *real* trails, Andrea. If they were waiting for *me,* you'd think I'd see something like a real trail—"

"No. Not necessarily. We do not know how they would set these—these *false* trails. And it could be a trap in the form of a human whom they have victimized. That is always their primary goal."

Jared nods when I say this. The firm way that he has set his chin tells me that his mind is quite made up. "Then it's only too clear what we should do next." Stepping past me, he returns to the larger corridor. As I follow him, I am sending out tiny sensing projections to ensure that there truly are not any nnn-Asi-t waiting for us in the immediate area. Jared has made his way back to the staircase, and quickly begins to make his way up. Following him again, I wish that my own legs were long enough to take the steps two at a time.

We have reached the top. Now we are on the third and highest floor in this building. Jared has turned to the right and begun moving down the hallway. But he has stopped in his tracks. An alarm seems to go off inside of my head—

Have they somehow stopped him? Is he in danger?

A quick flash between us tells me that this is not the case. He is looking at something, and as I near him, I can feel both disappointment and puzzlement. Once again, my hand seeks the touch of his forearm as I gasp for breath. And now I can see what he does…

The end of the fake trail. It is an abrupt end.

Too abrupt. It leads nowhere.

Why?

Our group has gathered beneath one of the large trees. All that remains of the setting sun is the upper half of the reddish sphere as the rest sinks below the horizon. Franco believes that he has caught a glimpse of the enemy through a downstairs window in one of the older buildings. Jared and I exchange looks as Franco points out which one—

It is the same one where Jared and I found the fake trail. We have explained our finding of the fake trail to the group, and we have discussed possible implications. Martin, Georgia, and Franco gaze at Jared and listen carefully to his words. There are three more of our people who are working in the city, and we will contact them if their assistance is required. With the enemy apparently so close, we do not want to risk sending any projections unless we are certain that such action is worth that risk. For now, Franco will guide us in the correct direction, and it will be my Earther who will search for true trails.

We now head back to the second of the chemistry buildings, this time following Franco. Darkness is beginning to fall as he opens the first door, and we follow him inside. This time, though, we take the staircase leading downward. At the bottom, one of the overhead lights is not functioning correctly, and it fizzles out, leaving the bottom of the staircase in ominous shadows.

This seems to be a most appropriate atmosphere in which to conduct our search for the nnn-Asi-t. There is no longer enough light through the small window to offer us helpful illumination.

Franco has stopped. "I am quite certain that I saw it drift down these stairs," he says softly. "But beyond that…" He shrugs his shoulders.

Immediately, Jared steps forward. We all understand what is needed from him. The tallest of our group, he bends forward to gaze through the window in the top part of the door in front of us. Looking back at us over his shoulder, he shakes his head. He sees nothing helpful. But he pushes the door open and steps silently through, into the corridor. We watch from behind as he turns his head from one side to the other, upwards and down, searching, searching…

Shrugging his shoulders, he moves down the hallway to a junction. Stopping, he gazes down the corridor to his right. Although the rest of us automatically look with our eyes too, we must accept that this will likely be of no help. I resent this helpless feeling. It seems we are all blind to the one thing that we need to find.

Jared has turned back in our direction. "It's there," he whispers. "And it's a mixture of an older trail with a newer one, like it's been moving around this whole area."

As he heads down that corridor, we follow him once more, all of us preparing ourselves for what might be a challenging confrontation. I am quite aware of my feelings for this special Earther—and of the imperative need to keep any such feelings under complete control.

No matter what.

Jared stops just outside of a doorway. We walk quietly over to him, trying to appear as casual and inconspicuous as possible, although we have seen only a couple of people moving around the building at this hour. This is, indeed, a good time to be here. It is quiet, oh so quiet. Along the hallway are some doors, but they are all closed. If Jared had not followed the trail, we would have no clue at all as to enemy's whereabouts without sending projections.

So certain is Jared that the enemy is in that specific room that he puts a hand on the door handle and very, very quietly opens the door, just a bit. We are all holding our breath in an effort not to break the stillness. Finally, we can hear faint talking from somewhere inside of the room…

We stand, silent and still, and Martin manages to soundlessly close the door behind us. After several unhelpful exchanges between the two speakers, we finally hear something important.

"No," says the strained whisper of a young male. "You're crazy! If I did that, it could poison the water supply!"

And then we hear a despairing moan as the young man wrestles with what we know will be overwhelming urges of hatred and anger. The low voice sounds rather tired, as though this unfortunate victim has been trying to resist this terrible enemy for quite awhile now.

We cannot delay any longer. Martin nods, and he and I step inside. I am already sending a projection of comfort to the poor young man who sits trembling, a small capsule of some sort in the palm of his open hand. His hand is glistening with perspiration, a tribute to the length of time that he has apparently been resisting the enemy's urgings. Of course, the nnn-Asi-t is well aware of our presence now, and already it begins to strike. Its gentle-looking false face is that of an older gentleman who has brown hair with a bit of white at the temples, and it is furious to see its lightning bolts bounce easily off the barricade which I have quickly erected.

And now a stronger blast, but it is slower. I have an opportunity to quickly send a second projection to the victim, before I protect myself once more. As I do this, I sense that Martin is ready and waiting to assist, although I know that he will not interfere unless this is quite necessary. Unneeded interference can sometimes cause problems. I send a flash toward the nnn-Asi-t in order to assess its defensive skills. Although its barrier is up, it does not respond as quickly as some enemies with whom I have dealt in the past. I watch my reddish blast as it drips down the enemy's transparent barricade, like little droplets of human blood.

Quickly, quickly, before it has a chance to respond, I send tiny crimson knives to descend like red rain from above, as though from some invisible cloud. If speed is this enemy's weakness, then I must use speed as my own advantage.

But it has created a barrier which is adequate to fend these off, too. Another approach might be warranted. Fortunately, I can focus easily. I do not need to be concerned further about the victim, as there are others here who are well prepared to do just that.

Yet I have no time to consider another attack, as—quite suddenly—a glowing ball of fire moves in my direction. So far in our battle, we have been fairly evenly matched. As long as my energy level is sufficient, I should be able to strengthen my barricade to handle this attack without incident. I direct my concentration, drinking thirstily from my pool of strength.

Soon the outside of my barrier is dripping wet, as I have created something like water to cascade downward. It is as though I am standing behind a steep waterfall. There is a great burst of steam as the fiery ball is destroyed by my defence.

As I begin to drop my barricade to prepare my own attack, something from off to the side distracts me—

A second one! There are *two* of what Jared would call *those bastards!*

One attack is stopped by a powerful blast from Martin. And, nagging at the back of my mind, I can feel Jared's longing to defend me, even though it is not necessary…at least not yet…

Now I see an innocent-looking silvery snowflake materialize and dart in Martin's direction. As it moves, it grows to a larger size.

Cold! I can feel the frigid temperature of the thing as I send a long, reddish tendril to touch it—and then I send a flame along its length to melt the thing before it can come any closer to my mentor. From the corner of my eye, I see Martin as he moves, so, so swiftly, deftly delivering his brownish-red arrow against the other enemy's barricade.

Now I sense doubt from my own opponent—and I respond quickly to dispatch a crimson tendril to render it helpless.

But, momentarily puzzled, I stand still and ready with my barrier continuing to surround me…

My blast did not feel sufficiently strong to destroy the nnn-Asi-t. Perhaps I have struck a vulnerable spot strictly through good fortune…

Chapter Twenty-Five

Welcome relief flooded through Jared as he watched the two nnn-Asi-t collapse into silvery puddles. Finally, he relaxed his hands. They'd become clenched fists as he'd been struggling more and more to stop himself from interfering. Frustration had been eating at him when he hadn't been asked to work as a team with Perka. After all, *he'd* been the one to find the damn enemy.

Gratefully he watched as Perka's and Martin's shoulders visibly sagged, relaxation finally greeting them once more. They were all now at peace, Georgia moving to the victim's side to complete the process of immunization.

But all relaxed feelings left Jared when Martin spoke in his velvety-smooth voice. "This was too easy."

Perka nodded in agreement, frowning. Her eyes were on the nnn-Asi-t puddles where they lay on the tiled floor like pools of silvery rain.

"They haven't begun to dissipate," Franco observed.

Suddenly, with a surprising burst of speed, one blasted like a rocket, shooting upwards, a trail of greyish silver remaining behind as, like a puff of smoke, it disappeared inside the air vent.

But, just as the second of the two puddles began to move, something else happened. From somewhere out of nowhere, a barricade suddenly appeared to cover the ventilation grate. The cover now looked like something from a chamber of horrors—a strong, metallic thing with long, sharp spikes, and needle projections. Open-mouthed, the group watched as the second enemy, which had already shot up to the grate, impaled itself, silvery sparks disappearing into the air. Then it and the barricade were gone—

And everyone turned to stare at Jared, who simply shrugged as though creating the cover was nothing special.

Martin was speaking in his soft, whispery tones: "They managed to present us with the illusion of their deaths while they were still alive."

Silence hung ominously in the air as each member of the group gazed toward the dark-skinned man. Georgia was shaking her head, eyes closed as she breathed deeply. "They are—they are evidently more intelligent…and much more *capable* than we've been thinking."

"That's not the only thing we should be concerned about," Jared added thoughtfully. "The one that escaped is obviously going to warn any others about us." He sighed deeply. "We're going to have to shield awfully carefully if we're going to keep them from picking up our whereabouts—"

"We'll all have to be especially vigilant, and rely more on physical signs of them," Franco said in a low voice. When he mentioned physical signs, some heads automatically turned to look at Jared. "It could be that some of them are acting as sentinels."

Silence returned to hang in the area again as everyone considered the implications. All of this had been unwelcome news, as the enemy had never before been known for these sorts of actions.

"Jared," came Martin's smooth tones as he stroked his chin thoughtfully. "Jared, how is your energy level? We've managed to spare you from involvement in the confrontations, but is your physical stamina sufficient for you to continue, after creating that barricade? Will you be able to recognize enemy trails and assist us again? Or should we rest awhile? You are, after all, not one of our kind." Now Martin smiled kindly. "Although you have certainly become one of us, in a way."

The Earther could see the concern in those deep, brown eyes. Jared closed his and took a moment to sense inside of himself and try to gauge his physical state. It was hard to be sure, though. He could still feel the adrenalin pumping through him, and the feeling that he could climb Mount Everest right at that minute. But he returned Martin's smile. "I'm okay, Martin. And anyway, if they're alert to our presence, we won't have a lot of time."

The votary nodded. "We must find them. And stop them." Martin began to rise—

But suddenly Jared was moving, cursing himself for not thinking of this before. He seized a chair and positioned it immediately beneath the air vent, where his barricade had impaled the enemy. Climbing onto the chair, he found that his ample height prevented him from standing erect. Awkwardly, he fished in his pocket for a dime, and used it as a screwdriver to work at removing the cover from the air duct. Succeeding suddenly, he had to put a hand hard against the ceiling to brace himself from falling. Cursing softly, he managed to poke his head inside of the air duct as far as he could, wishing the opening could be bigger—

But he gasped. Jared could see enough. He could see all that he needed to. There it was. A trail. A true nnn-Asi-t trail, not a fake, he was sure. Or, at least, he *wanted* to be sure… *Okay, you bastards. Maybe you're right. Maybe I* can't *track you all the way through the air shaft. But I'll find a way, you bastards. I'll get you. I'll damn well find a way.* Peering down the narrow passage, he followed the greyish trail with his eyes. He could see where it turned out of sight far ahead, but there was no way that he could tell just *where* inside the building it might have gone.

Yet suddenly he *saw* it. No, no, he didn't *see* it. There was no way that he could have. *What the—*

Somehow, he found himself looking ahead, from *its* body—through *its* eyes, or whatever in hell it used to see. He couldn't take the time to wonder why or how it happened—he just assumed that this was more of his strange, undiscovered, unexplained ability that was beyond anyone's comprehension, Earther or alien.

Jared watched ahead as the thing—and somehow, he was part of it—glided along, turning this way and that. How bizarre it was to feel the rush of warm air around him as he seemed to fly through the air, as light as a feather—

Then, like a slap in the face, a blast of cold air struck him. After the warmth he'd been careening through, this felt like pure ice. And, although—somehow—he was one with the nnn-Asi-t, he felt *free.* Floating through the cold air like a bird, beneath him the rooftops of the campus buildings…

How incredible.

Through it, though, he was aware of a sense of urgency. Deep inside, he could clearly feel a need to alert the other nnn-Asi-t to the threatened interference. They had to hurry, *hurry…*

They didn't go all that far, though. As they began to make a gliding descent through the chilly night air, he made out a sign about *Biochemistry Laboratories.* From the overhead vantage point, he could see that this structure was only a short walk from the building they'd been inside. They slipped inside, through a sliver of an opening between the window and the surrounding material—

Now! I've got to do something!

Jared began his own battle, wondering just how strong he truly was. Focussing all the strength he could muster, he reached for the consciousness of the thing that he was inside, seeking the source of that urgency to complete the mission. But that consciousness in turn reached for Jared's own, like hooked talons, curving and razor sharp at the ends. He could feel the things come closer, closer to all that made him who he was while he struggled with all his might to push them away.

He couldn't—

There was most definitely a limit to his power, but still he struggled. *What choice do I have?*

But…somehow there was a part inside of him that wanted to *respond* to that driving urgency—something that *understood* and even *felt* the nnn-Asi-t mission—

And now he knew what he had to do. The driving urgency inside of him grew in power as Jared relaxed his own controls and stopped fighting. He allowed the urgency to grow, let it get bigger, stronger.

The nnn-Asi-t consciousness felt this and reached toward Jared's inner being, eager to use this unexpected power to help it in its mission. As the nnn-Asi-t consciousness came closer, Jared sent mental images of how great their forces could be if combined. Closer came those claws to what remained of the true Jared inside of the nnn-Asi-t, and, with a tremendous focus of energies, and a monumental effort, he took what remained of his true essence and sent it *out*, back behind them to trail behind, a tiny thread of white glowing in the cold outdoors and beyond, through the dark corridors, while he projected as strong a cry for help as he could.

Now inside the nnn-Asi-t's greyish form, all he could make out was a confusing mist, and all he could feel was the desperation of that urgency, the importance of the mission. Then came the terrible claws as they began to rip and tear at the tiny bits of Jared that still remained and hadn't yet been absorbed by the awful urgency…

Heat, heat, and pain—the nnn-Asi-t directed its talons to rip the true parts of Jared away, to allow everything that remained of him to merge completely with its own consciousness.

More power! Jared needed more *strength*! Even *he* couldn't maintain this situation—the tiny bits of him inside the enemy would be totally absorbed, while the rest of him reached out fervently for some sort of help…

Oh, Jared, you've really done it this time.

Suddenly—something—*something* through his thread out behind.

His filament was warming. It was beginning to feel stronger. Now he could sense the others as they wrapped their own essences around his, fortifying it. Swiftly, some of them wound around and around his thin thread, while yet another raced at lightning speed up through his filament and toward him.

Reaching back, he strained in the direction of that wonderful reddish thread to touch it with his own—

And he was going back, back out behind the amorphous grey of the enemy.

Finally, he let himself relax, letting Perka's essence carry him home to his own body. He gazed inward as he felt himself leave the nnn-Asi-t. There it was—a part of him that *understood* the nnn-Asi-t—almost felt an awful sense of kinship with it. Disgusted, he gave that part of him a mighty shove. The nnn-Asi-t could keep it—he didn't want that part of himself.

But it wouldn't stay behind. It was like trying to take off a glove but leave one finger inside at the same time. It was part of him, and it wouldn't stay away.

Now he felt his entire *self* merge, wrapped tenderly yet firmly in Perka's strong essence, coursing through her thread. As he glanced back at the already fading image of the nnn-Asi-t, he was relieved to find that he had at least a bit of strength left. Because Perka's energies were with his. The enemy exploded into a billion tiny segments of grey, black, and silver as soon as Perka's gleaming crimson arrow, which had flecks of white throughout, struck it…

Chapter Twenty-Six

My impetuous Earther! I marvel at your bravery and determination. Yet those very traits may well have alerted the other nnn-Asi-t to our presence, even though you risked your own existence to prevent the one from informing the others.

It is certainly true that the one nnn-Asi-t escapee would most likely have given the others of its kind some sort of report about us. But it is also true that we do not really know whether the nnn-Asi-t would have sensed the destruction of one of their own kind. Truly, though, they will now have sensed our activity. We will have to move quickly and maintain our shields once again. But, my Earther, we are grateful to you.

What you have done has enabled you, and therefore all of us, to learn the exact whereabouts of the enemy.

I watch Jared's face as all aspects of him become one again with his body. His face is relaxed once more, although he looks somewhat tired, and more than a bit confused. But he will be all right. I reach over to him where he sits, leaning back in the chair, and I lay my hand against his cheek to send warmth, love, and gratitude. Even with physical contact only, I can feel the question that burns now inside of him. And he has a right to know the answer—he *must* know the answer. Eventually. Not now. Not just yet.

Through the warmth of our physical contact, I send a request for patience. He nods his understanding. Then, suddenly, his arms are around my waist, and he pulls me into his lap, holding me tightly against him. More reassurance...he seeks still more reassurance. As

I put my arms around his neck, I rest my cheek against his stubbly one. Knowing this will be for only a short time, I allow both of us the welcome opportunity of a peaceful moment.

"We must hurry," comes Martin's gentle voice. He is not impatient, simply informative.

Sighing, Jared nods, recovering his composure. I stand, holding his hand, and send him my brightest smile. His eyes lock with mine. "Let's go," he murmurs hoarsely as he rises. Without any further delay, Jared heads for the doorway, past the others.

Quickly, we move out of the old building and follow Jared away from the two nearby structures. After a moment, he pauses, then heads in the direction of a brighter, newer building. Just outside of it, we stop.

Jared closes his eyes in an effort to focus his thoughts. "When I was with the enemy, we went in through a gap between some windows. But where *is* one that would have some sort of gap around it?" He gazes upward, his eyes darting from one sight to another, and we all join him to search for a way inside the building which is accessible from up high. We spread out and circle the building to continue our efforts.

Then, suddenly, I am distracted by a small figure hurrying amid the shadows. It moves quickly, but silently. It bears no resemblance whatsoever to the security guard we had met. Now I can see that it is heading in the direction of my Earther. Quickly, I step forward from my spot, anxious to move to Jared's side. But the other being is faster than I am. The shadowy figure lunges forward and reaches toward Jared's arm. He turns toward it, and, breathless, I too am there.

In the light illuminating some of the surroundings, we see who it is. *Georgia.*

"Jared," she says, pausing to catch her breath, "look at the top floor across the back. There are three windows that look newer, and have a slightly different design—"

"That's it," Jared exclaims in a hushed voice. "I remember now! It was the middle of three, near the corner! Top floor. Let's *go!*"

Hastily we make our way to the door. It is challenging to try to move as quickly as possible yet try to remain unobtrusive. Fortunately, the corridors and lounge areas are mostly empty. Of course, it only makes sense that the nnn-Asi-t would select a place and time with no evening classes scheduled. We see only six or seven students reading, studying, using books, laptops, and phones. Some socialize over drinks—no doubt their coffee—from the nearby vending machines. The lights automatically dim in this area unless the presence of people causes them to brighten. But, when they brighten, they are much more luminous in here than the ones outside. Conscious of this, we try our best to appear calm and unhurried, although we move more quickly whenever we enter a more shadowy section again.

How strange it seems that we are fighting to save the world which belongs to these people, yet they remain serene and contentedly oblivious to the danger.

Unless they become victims.

Outside of the elevators, Jared pushes the top button. Almost immediately, he is muttering expletives and pushing it once more. Then he jabs it again and again. We do not interfere, knowing that this Earther requires such emotional release, if he is to be able to maintain complete control of his impulses when it is essential that he do so. However, I am not the only one in our group who glances behind and around us, hoping that no one in the vicinity might consider his actions to be unusual.

The door opens after only a few seconds, although Jared exclaims *finally* as we step inside. It is not the most comfortable ride, as we are not alone. I cast a sideways glance at the young student who stands beside me as she stares at her phone. Perhaps it is *her* victimization which we are hoping to prevent.

Fortunately for us, she is completely absorbed in her phone. She does not seem to see what might, indeed, appear to be a rather strange group: Martin, Georgia, Franco, and me with faces displaying nothing but calm concentration, and Jared puffing like a bull readying for an Earther bullfight, his reddened face a vivid display of his concerns and determination. Yes, quite a strange group we might appear. Here we are at the university without any books, laptops, or backpacks, or even phones to look at. The only exception might be Jared, who keeps a phone in his inside jacket pocket. But a phone is the last thing on his mind as he stares at the lighted number above the elevator door, displaying at which floor we have arrived.

The young woman exits onto the third floor. The door closes once more and then we hear a little *ding* as it opens onto the fourth floor.

As we step into the corridor, Jared takes a moment to orient himself, concentrating on the memory of where the nnn-Asi-t had been heading. Then he turns, and we can see from the expression on his face that he is quite certain. He says nothing. Walking ahead of us, he hastens through a narrow hallway, past what look to be offices. Once more I am becoming breathless. It is a challenge for me to keep up with this Earther and his long legs. He pauses outside of a door. After checking over his shoulder to see if we are all there, he opens it and steps inside.

It appears to be empty. I look at Jared, studying him for clues, not wanting to sense for enemy presence unless absolutely necessary. To do so could alert it, or them, to us. We can all see that Jared is concentrating. Now he touches a finger to his lips and gazes at us meaningfully.

We must be ready—yet remain completely shielded.

Closing the door quietly behind him, Jared crosses the room. Slowly, silently. The room consists of countertops, sinks, computers with stools in front of them for seating. Various types of equipment stand inactive, most of this on the far side of a windowed area. The only light comes through the window in the door to the hallway.

The shadowy darkness makes it easy for us to see the illumination, seeping in from under a closed door on the other side of the large room.

Slowly, carefully, not wishing to make any noise, we make our way through the area. Automatically, I am checking the shadows. *Shadows. It seems that I have been taught all of my life to watch for the presence of possible enemies which might be lurking within them.*

Ironically, we are following an Earther who is the only one of the group who knows for certain just where the enemy is. Now we step after this man who beckons ahead of him toward what looks like empty darkness. But he mouths the word *trail* to each of us.

Just outside of the closed door, we stand silently, patiently, and listen together to make out whatever we can from the muffled voices. But this proves difficult and ineffective. The words are indistinct behind the door.

Jared gazes back at us and, after taking a long breath, reaches for the doorknob. Slowly, so slowly, he places his long fingers around the knob, then closes his grasp. He tries turning it gently to the right. Then to the left. Opening his fingers, he slowly moves his hand away, his shoulders moving downward as he finally relaxes once more. He has done well. There has been no sound which might warn the enemy.

But the door is locked. Gazing at us, he opens his hands palms upward as though to question what to do next.

The next step will depend on my people. I give Jared a smile of gratitude, and nod. Closing my eyes, I prepare myself, ready to discard my shield when the time is right. Martin will remain with me, and once I have relayed to him, Jared. Georgia and Franco stand to the side and behind us. Adjusting their stances, they prepare themselves, and exchange looks. Franco nods. Now we all turn our attention to that closed door…and whatever lies beyond it.

Our next move is quite important, for not only can it afford us access to the enemy, but it will also allow us to display our strength as we—hopefully—catch the enemy off guard. Although they might have sensed our activity in the other building, we hope that our secure shields have prevented them from knowing just how close to them we have now become.

A thin, orangish beam emanates from Georgia, joined immediately by a filament from Franco. Melding together, these stretch forward to touch the lock which secures the door. The enemy might sense our presence now, but it—or they—will have about one or two Earth seconds to prepare. I flash to Jared that our battle has begun.

That is all he requires.

In two seconds, the locking mechanism on the door has become nothing more than ice, and immediately crumbles into a million or so tiny pieces.

As the door suddenly opens in response, two nnn-Asi-t—possibly defenders—immediately move to attack Georgia and Franco, who quickly attempt to barricade themselves. But they are not fast enough, as they have just launched the attack on the lock. Jared is quite prepared for this eventuality, though, as he sends what resembles a solid metal wall to prevent the enemy blast from touching Franco. Martin's brownish-red beam stops and spreads into a murky pool in mid-air. Into this, the other silvery nnn-Asi-t crashes, becoming stuck in the hopeless mire.

All of this has happened in an instant. I have been left free. Quickly I send a strong flash to the bearded student who is seated at a table, and send him strength to help him withstand the enemy—

But my flash is stopped. There seems to be a transparent wall surrounding the student.

Hastily, I erect my own barrier. But a silvery blast seems to come from nowhere. I cannot see its source. And I am unable to sense its whereabouts when my barrier is in place. *How did the enemy do that?*

Casting a quick glance to the side, I can see that Jared and Martin are faring adequately, while Franco and Georgia monitor the situation and prepare to contribute further when needed. I step in the direction of the student at the table, concentrating on maintaining my all-important barrier. Were an Earther able to observe any of this, I might look as though I am walking while I am surrounded by a bubble. My eyes constantly scan for the enemy while I move toward the victim. Suddenly, rain seems to begin falling on my barricade. I can see innocuous-looking clear droplets as they make contact with my protection, some rolling off like rain from an umbrella. I have never before seen anything exactly like this.

A gasp escapes me as I watch the droplets become acid, eating away at my barrier. Quickly, I reinforce my bubble from inside to block the weapons from entering. But this enemy is strong. More and more of the little droplets fall, again and again. I resent needing to expend so much energy and concentration on defence when there is an enemy to be defeated!

Suddenly it stops. Now I see a white glow not far from me. It is very quick and quite strong. The nnn-Asi-t attempts to barricade itself, but it is no match for this attack from Jared.

My bubble begins to dissolve—at *my* instigation—and I watch as the enemy falls from its vantage point where it was up near the ceiling. It will be a puddle soon.

But there are still more—

Shadows and more shadows are rather difficult to see in the dark corners of this room. I cannot feel for them unless my barricade remains down, but then I see a silvery snake as it lunges forward, and I slice off its head with a crimson knife before it can get any closer to my Earther. Wishing to intimidate these enemies, I push more energy into this one, sending an image of torrents of scarlet blood pouring from the enemy's serpent.

Instantly I must reinforce my barrier, for most certainly another attack will be on its way. In my peripheral vision I can see a dissipating nnn-Asi-t at Franco's feet. Now that the enemies are fewer in number, I might be able to assist the victim once more. As I turn in his direction, I maintain my barricade in case of another enemy attack. A few seconds go by, although it seems like an hour or more. The others who are engaged in battle do not appear to require any assistance, so I do not intervene. Extremely cautiously, I drop one layer from my barrier. There is nothing. I wait another second or two...

One more second to inhale deeply and collect as much of my energy as I can. Then I drop my barrier and push outward to flash to the student who still sits at the table, head in his hands amid books and computers and various sizes and shapes of vials and bottles. Frustrated, I watch yet again as my crimson tendril drips down the invisible barrier which blocks us from the victim.

So, there is something more.

There is most definitely something more in this room—somewhere—which, despite all of the interference and the attacks by my people, still maintains this enclosure of some sort around the victim. Carefully, I use my vision to scan the long, narrow room as I surround myself once again with a cautious barrier. Not wanting to be *rained* upon once more, I make certain that I include the dark corners of the ceiling area as well as the shadowy corners.

Yet I continue to find nothing—nothing except for the four or five enemies dissipating on the floor, and the other four which my people continue to engage in battle. *Why did the enemy select this particular young man, anyway? What can there be about him which warrants the attention of so many of the enemy?* But I have no further time to consider the possibilities.

Wherever can this last enemy, or enemies, be hiding? My choices right now are severely limited. I have no options. I *must* defeat this nnn-Asi-t, and I cannot defeat it if I am unable to even *find* it—

I steel myself, inhaling deeply while I prepare myself for speed. Very quickly this time, I drop my barrier. Instantly I am sensing every corner of the long room, every shadow, including the air vents. It *is* here. Why can I sense it yet not be able to *see* it? Still I feel its presence, yet my eyes tell me absolutely nothing. *Could it be invisible?* Surely not!

And, if somehow it *is*, how will we ever be able to defeat the thing? But…if it is maintaining a barricade around the victim, it cannot also be completely barricading *itself*…

As I turn once more toward the student, I send again a flash of crimson. And once more the invisible barricade stops me.

Quickly, urgently, I turn and send quick blasts into all of the dark corners, each and every little hidden place where it might be cowering. One. Two. Three. Four. Five. Six. Seven lightning bolts of power—again and again, until I gasp for breath after the exertion. But, yet again, as I scan the room, I see no nnn-Asi-t remains, other than of those defeated by my companions.

How can this possibly be?

Suddenly a blast from Martin distracts me, as he counters an attack directed at me by this mysterious enemy—

As I turn, the largest nnn-Asi-t I have ever seen takes shape as it begins to drop its barrier. The barrier is something the likes of which I have never before witnessed. It perfectly matches the colours and textures of the walls and floor of the room. Invisible? No. Just the most thorough and complete barricade I have ever beheld. And *fast*, too, for this enemy must have managed to re-barricade itself as soon as I had stopped my efforts with the victim.

But its blast of fire is stopped by Martin's thick, syrupy pool. Already I am barricading myself, knowing that Martin will be dropping his own barrier to leave him free to attack.

Barricaded as I now am, I am powerless to intervene as it sends the fastest attack I have ever seen toward Martin—

No! I feel in myself some of his agony as everything that is Martin now becomes raging flame. Suddenly the entire room explodes into a hundred thousand different colours. We are now surrounded by shrill screams and ear-piercing whistling sounds which only my kind and the enemy—and likely Jared—will be able to hear.

Chapter Twenty-Seven

Jared's head felt like it was spinning on his neck. "But what—but *what?*" He was sputtering, trying to make some sense out of the alarming confusion that filled his brain. "I—I didn't see anything strange."

"I know, Jared." There was an uncharacteristic urgency in Perka's voice. If she'd been an Earther, it might have sounded almost like panic. "Jared, it was the most powerful nnn-Asi-t I have ever experienced...or even heard tell of. It has taken that victim somewhere to do something important and we *must* stop it!" She pulled on Jared's arm so that it was over her shoulder and attempted to help him to his feet, but it was a daunting task when Jared was so groggy.

The earnestness of her voice alerted him, and he managed to stand, somewhat unsteadily. Automatically, he shook his head to clear it but was rewarded with only more dizziness. It was so confusing—everything had seemed to be going so well, or at least as well as it had the other times that he'd been assisting Perka and her people...

Jared massaged his temples with his fingers while he waited for the damn room to stop spinning. Then he gazed around him at Perka and her people. But, instead of the usual calm and reassurance, he saw faces that looked tired and drawn, exhausted and anxious. When he glanced to the side, he gasped—

Martin! *Martin? Could that be Martin?*

Where Martin had been standing was now a smouldering heap of brownish-red...*something*. But whatever it was that was dissipating into the air was not affecting the smoke alarm or the shower system—*of course, he's not...he wasn't an Earther,* Jared reminded himself.

Jared let go of the breath that he hadn't known he'd been holding. "Martin."

Perka nodded, taking one more glance in that direction before turning back to Jared. "There is nothing that we can do to help him, Jared." There was more urgency in her voice. "*But*, if we hurry, there might be a chance that we can stop this enemy before it makes another attempt at destruction."

Georgia had put Jared's other arm across her shoulders, distracting him from the sight of what remained of Martin.

But still Jared stared. *It just doesn't feel right to simply leave him here.*

"We *need* you, Jared," Georgia was saying as she and Perka guided him toward the doorway and the corridor beyond. "We need you now more than ever before. This is a huge, powerful enemy. And, if you can see its trail, we might just have a chance to get to it without being detected. If we have the element of surprise, that will give us at least some hope."

"Yes," Perka agreed. "If we can get to it undetected, and if you and I combine our energies."

Jared sighed, trying to find the strength to stop leaning so much on these two. As they reached the elevator, he put a hand against the wall to steady himself. Closing his eyes, he managed to stand to his full height.

"Can you *see* anything, Jared?" Franco's voice seemed to echo the urgency and impatience of Perka and Georgia.

For a blank moment Jared didn't know what the hell Franco could be talking about. Shaking his head, he forced himself to focus. He breathed deeply. As he let the air out once again, he scanned their surroundings, wondering at first why he didn't see anything. Then he gasped—*it was here, right here!* "Yes," he muttered. "There's a trail, all right. *They* took this elevator too!"

Franco nodded, his fingers seeking contact with his moustache. He thought for just a second, then pushed the *down* button, intending to go directly to the first floor. This was taking a chance if the enemy and the victim had simply moved to another storey of the building. But it would be faster than simply stopping to check for trails at each level. And, if this was a major move for the enemy, it would seem likely that they would be leaving for another, and more important, location. The door opened with a *ding*, and they stepped inside, Franco immediately pressing the first-floor button. Fortunately, there was no one else inside to have to share the ride with this time.

"I think—I think I have an idea what it was all about," Perka whispered, licking her dry lips. She was silent a moment, trying to sort out the confusing mass of images in her mind. "There were two vials on the table in front of the student. There were others around, but only these two were in front of him. I—I cannot remember what exactly was on the labels. I couldn't see them clearly—some sort of Earther chemical symbols. When the nnn-Asi-t took the student away, they must have taken the two vials, because they were no longer on the table when we left the room."

"If only...if only we knew what those contained," suggested Georgia, "maybe we'd have some way of knowing where they would go with them."

"Well," Jared put in, "remember—the other victim was going to poison the drinking water. And if this nnn-Asi-t is as powerful as it seemed, this time they might be planning something even worse than that." He sighed then, his breath coming out as a shudder.

As the elevator door opened, Perka was eyeing him with concern. The light shining into the elevator seemed to emphasize his tired and pale appearance. A vending machine off to the right caught her eye. "Would something in there help your energy level, Jared?"

It seemed like his stomach suddenly grumbled as soon as he saw it. "It might. It just might." He fumbled in his pocket, then deposited some currency into the machine. As a large chocolate bar appeared in the opening at the bottom of the machine, Jared's lips twisted into a wry grin. Under other circumstances, this could have been a welcome treat. Hastily he peeled back the wrapper and sank his teeth into sticky chocolate and caramel.

"What do you see *now*?" Georgia's voice suggested impatience.

Focussed once more on their situation, Jared scanned the surrounding area while he chewed.

And he nodded, stepping toward the corridor, chocolate bar in hand. They hurried down the hallway after him, then to the outside through a side door. The chilliness of autumn evening struck them, but for perhaps the first time since coming to this third planet from its sun, Perka was grateful to feel the refreshing coolness of the breeze.

Jared stopped. Eyes still scanning the surroundings, he muttered something incoherent.

"What?!"

They had to wait a few seconds while he managed to swallow some of the sticky stuff. "I said, they went over that way, towards the student parking lot."

Georgia sighed. "How can we *find* them and keep our shields in place if they've gone in a car?"

"It's okay." Jared sounded confident as he licked chocolate from the corners of his lips. He turned to Perka. "Remember when we followed the enemy to the schoolyard? The trail was a lot fainter when the thing was in the victim's truck, but I could still see enough of it. Maybe—maybe the truck's windows were open or something, I don't know, but if this thing's as great as you say, I'll still find its damn trail. If we go fast, maybe it won't have time to set up a decoy trail."

In her desire for haste, Perka had already begun to move. "We do not have to worry about that, Jared. Remember, *we* can see the decoy trails too! We need to get your car and we can meet the others at the closer lot—*hurry!*"

Quickly they rushed across the grassy area, Perka slipping on the damp leaves, and Jared catching her arm in time to prevent her from falling. At the car, he tried to jam the key into the lock, but fumbled, the key ring falling to the ground with a clatter, then sliding downward into the top of a ditch.

Jared's head moved from side to side as he looked down, trying to see where it had fallen. "Dammit to hell and back!" On all fours, he patted the damp ground and leaves for something that felt metallic. He was half-expecting some unseen nnn-Asi-t to attack them from the increasing darkness. *Finally*, something cold and hard.

Thank God! Quickly, the key was in the door, then the ignition. He sighed with relief as the engine started on the first try. With a cough and sputter, the little car took them in the direction of the students' parking lot.

"Jared!"

Perka's cry had him pouncing on the brakes. *Is there an enemy?* He turned to her, his heart pounding. For a second, she stared at him, surprised, then she understood. For the first time in a long while, she gave him an understanding smile. When she spoke, it was in a soft voice: "Jared, you were searching so hard for a trail that you drove right past the others!"

"Dammit!" Jared glanced into the rear-view mirror. The old car's gears ground like the VW was in agony, but he managed to put the vehicle into reverse.

Franco and Georgia clambered into the back seat. "Can you see any trail?" Franco seemed to have gotten the question out before he'd even climbed inside.

"Yes. Yes, I can," Jared replied as he eased the car forward. "It's fainter than most of them, so they're probably inside a car. But I can still make it out." The rusty green Beetle chugged along, following the signs that only Jared could see.

"Maybe...maybe we should stop and send for help. If this thing is so tremendous, maybe we should get Megan and Paul."

But Perka shook her head. "We can send a flash to them from wherever we are going. We should not risk being detected or deviating from the trail in case it gets fainter, or darkness interferes. Besides, if you and I work *together* from the moment we arrive, we *will* be stronger than it is. I promise."

"Are you saying—*dammit to hell!*" The traffic light turned red and the taillights of the car in front suddenly lit up as it stopped abruptly, forcing Jared to jam on his brakes. He banged his hand against the steering wheel and swore. Perka turned her head toward him to meet his stare. "Wait a minute, Perka. Are you saying—are you saying that you made a *mistake*, that we should've been working together as soon as the door was open in the lab?"

She let go a long sigh. "Possibly. At the time, it seemed that there were enough of us to handle the enemies effectively, without needing two on one. Yet…if we had called out to Megan and Paul at the beginning of all of this, perhaps Martin—"

As Jared eased the gearshift into first, he glanced into the rear-view mirror and met Georgia's gaze. When Georgia spoke, it was in a very soft voice: "Our people, too, are imperfect, and we do not always make perfect decisions."

"Dammit, dammit, *shit!* The trail—" The little vehicle lurched into the end of a driveway. Still cursing, Jared looked over his shoulder for traffic, then backed out and retraced their route to the intersection where he'd last seen the trail. "Stupid *lights!*" He banged on the steering wheel again, hating the glittering and flashing neon that made the silvery-grey trail almost impossible to see in several places.

"This one definitely seems to be showing signs of higher intellect," said Georgia. "Going through the downtown area certainly provided camouflage for its trail."

Franco was nodding in agreement.

Perka was watching Jared. If they'd been in different circumstances—less than a life-or-death situation—she would be concerned by the Earther's anxiety and frustration. But now his shoulders sagged as he relaxed a bit, which suggested that he must have found the trail once more. "Per—Andrea," he murmured softly as he stared ahead at the roadway in front of them.

"Yes, Jared," she replied gently, continuing to study his face. She knew that he was deep in thought and…that he was going to ask the question that they both knew he must.

"Andrea." Taking a moment to think, he nibbled on the inside of his lower lip. "Why—why was I able to…to get *inside* that nnn-Asi-t like I did? Why did it feel so natural, s—so *familiar* somehow? You *know*, don't you. I know you do."

"Is this the best time?" It was Franco's voice from the back.

"I was asking Per—*Andrea*." Jared's voice suggested irritation.

A gentle yet firm touch was on his shoulder from behind him. "This concerns *all* of us, Jared," came Georgia's voice. "This affects everything we're doing. And it could affect the outcome."

Jared sighed, twisting his fingers tightly around the steering wheel. Wasn't there *anything* that could be just between him and Perka? But even as he thought this, he knew it wasn't really justified. After all, the fate of the Earth—his home, his entire planet—could be at risk. "Okay then. Dammit." Closing his eyes as they stopped at another traffic light, he took a second to breathe deeply, trying to calm himself at least a bit. "*Is* this a good time to answer me? *And I resent not having any say in it!*"

"Perhaps—perhaps," but Perka wasn't speaking to him. Her head was turned as she studied the two in the back seat. "Surely true knowledge of his strength and power could be more of an asset—"

"Can the Earther cope with the information adequately?" Franco's voice was impersonal, factual.

Jared glanced to his right to see Perka's eyes on him.

"Yes," she said with confidence.

The Earther swallowed a huge lump which seemed to have lodged itself firmly in his throat. There was something about the way she was looking at him. The traffic light changed to green. Putting on his indicator, he eased the VW to the side of the road. He pushed the gearshift into neutral and pulled on the parking brake. Turning to Perka, he said softly but firmly: "Tell me."

With a sigh, Perka licked her dry lips. "For you—for you to have the power that you do…and—and some aspect inside of you that blended with the enemy… Jared, I was just thinking about when you and I completed the sharing ceremony. There was something strange and unfamiliar…something—some *part* of you that I could not touch at all. And it seems to make sense now. That part—that part of you was a small…but *greyish* area, Jared."

"A small greyish area," he repeated softly. His heart was beginning to beat harder as a sickening feeling developed inside of his stomach. "Then—then there's an nnn-Asi-t inside me…"

"Not quite, my love." There was affection in her gentle voice, but something else—something like resignation. "It is not as bad as that. And it is only a very small part of you—"

"But...*how?*"

"Jared, you told me a bit about when your father died, but you said that he was actually your *step*father."

He nodded, gazing ahead, although his eyes were not focussed on anything. "My biological father died when I was just a baby. I never really knew him. My mother didn't talk about him much. Apparently, they didn't along well."

"Jared, I think that *she* never really knew him, either." Perka's hand was on his forearm.

He could feel the sensations of love and comfort which came to him through her touch. Despite this, he ran his other hand through his hair, and then began to chew again on what remained of his thumbnail.

Perka's touch on his arm tightened, and wonderful love moved from her fingertips and into his aching heart. When she spoke, her voice was as smooth as velvet. "Jared, my love, we do not have much time." Despite her words, she paused to lick her lips. When she resumed, she did so gently, yet firmly. "Your biological father must have been an nnn-Asi-t. It is unusual for different species to procreate together...but my people and the enemy, as you know, have mental abilities which your people either do not have, or have not learned how to fully develop. And, as you also know, these abilities are not always used for the common good. Your mother may well have been an unsuspecting victim."

Once again, Jared found himself struggling to swallow a lump in his throat. Sadly, what she said made sense. Now he began to realize that he had been suspecting something like this but hadn't wanted to acknowledge it. Well, they had an important mission to focus on. Glancing into his mirrors, he checked the traffic, then pulled away from the curb. He pushed the gas pedal to the floor. They had to make up for lost time.

Chapter Twenty-Eight

Haste is rather important now. As Jared pulls into the parking lot of the airport, I send him love and reassurance, and when the car is parked, I remind him that he might be able to use this nnn-Asi-t part of himself to help us. *Somehow*. I hope that his new knowledge might be of use to him. We clamber out of the car and watch Jared as he scans the area for the trail. When he gestures toward the terminal, we hurry behind him in that direction, all of us watchful for any sign, any clue.

Entering through the doorway, we search for any signs of the bearded student, or of the enemy. Fortunately, this is not a huge city as some are on this continent, and so the airport, too, is not large. We are in the only terminal building. Jared turns to his right, and we follow.

Suddenly he stops. His face twists and contorts, his forehead puckering into a frown.

I step beside him and hold his fingers with both of my hands, soothing him. If only he could keep his emotions in check! "Jared, use your sensitivity to scan for it, but do *not* allow your shield to weaken or move—not yet!" He is the only being I know of who can feel the presence of an enemy even while fully shielded.

His blue, blue eyes hold mine for a moment. "I can't—I can't feel *it*, exactly, but I can *read* the trail, sort of."

Then, without another word, his consciousness is somewhere else. He stares blankly, seeing with his senses rather than his Earther eyes. My own eyes study Jared's face as I wish that I could see what he does. Shielded as I am, I cannot simply slip inside of his mind to see for myself.

Now it is my turn to close my eyes. I am beginning to *feel* what he does through our physical contact.

Urgency. Mission. Must complete the task.

My Jared is there, feeling what the enemy does. Opening my eyes, I see him look downward at the floor, then step slightly to the left. It appears that, if he walks in the trail and focusses correctly, he can feel what the enemy did when it was here...or is it what the enemy feels *now*? Glancing around me, I watch the small number of people who are checking in at the counters or snacking or talking among themselves. I hope that they do not regard Jared's behaviour as terribly odd.

As he moves once more, we follow our Earther. There is a door not far ahead leading in the direction of the runway. But of course, this must be locked. Just before that, we turn a corner. There is nothing much here. Just a staircase leading upward—

And an alcove beneath the stairs that is in the dark shadows and almost invisible from human view. A hole. At floor level, just large enough for a being of average human size to fit through. The windowpane has been pulled out and propped up against the opening, which might allow it to be overlooked by human eyes. As I gaze at it, I can see how the nnn-Asi-t would have used its skills to soften the material of the frame in order to remove the windowpane without setting off an alarm.

Or am I seeing this as it actually happened? I glance down at my fingers intertwined with Jared's—we must maintain this contact! Carefully, we maneuver ourselves through the opening, Jared snagging his jeans on something and pausing to pull the material free. Outside, we step to our feet and slip around a corner, Franco and Georgia following.

Ahead of us, amid the increasing darkness, we see a small jet plane. Its engines are not yet running, so there is still some time. The student, now clad in a dark shirt rather than a lab coat, is speaking to whom we assume to be a pilot. Beside them is a man who has an air of authority about him, wearing what looks like some sort of uniform...

But we can see him as a silhouette of greyish silver. Its power might be something we have not seen the like of before, for we can see glitters and sparks emanating continually from it.

My hand still holding the Earther's, I can feel a cold shiver running through him.

We watch as the student hands a small package to the pilot. An alarm seems to go off inside of my head, for the student is no longer resisting at all. Unfortunately, this suggests that he is now completely under the control of the nnn-Asi-t.

Shields discarded simultaneously, my Earther and I send a bolt of red and white lightning directly toward the thing's back—

I feel Jared as his mouth drops open in shock. Our bolt has simply dropped away—*the enemy has already barricaded!* Its power must be tremendous for it to have already created a barrier against our attack, when others of its kind would not have even known yet that we were here! Now it turns to face us as the two Earthers continue their discussion.

An assault is blasted at Georgia and Franco both at once, forcing Jared and me to intervene. Even with both of us together it is not easy, but finally our companions have stronger barricades, reinforced by our energy.

It is imperative that we break through this enemy's barrier. As the thought enters my mind, it is shared with Jared's consciousness. Suddenly I feel him being pulled away from me—torn away—yet when I glance toward him, I see that we have not physically moved—

Gasping, I realize that the enemy is *inside* of Jared, trying to separate us, but as I try to send energy to my Earther, the enemy sends a lightning bolt for me to contend with, and my attention must be focussed on maintaining my barricade. I struggle to try to keep open to Jared yet not allow that *thing* inside of me, as well.

I still have a touch on Jared's mind, and I see the images of what the nnn-Asi-t sends to him—

Images of me dying, dead. Visions of my body crumpled here on the pavement. My skull crushed. Blood, blood everywhere, seeping into the cracks of the concrete. One eye hangs limply from its socket, dangling from a dripping thread, smearing my cheek with red liquid as it lolls from side to side...

NO! As long as I still have a touch on Jared's mind, I will NOT allow this enemy to rob him of his concentration. I direct a slender thread of strength upward and in through Jared's ear. Now I am in the midst of the horror. The awful stench of the nnn-Asi-t seems to fill my nostrils as it invades Jared's consciousness with more images of my destruction and death.

Cold determination streaks through me, and I create a great, clawed hand and reach for the horrible presence and seize it with all of the strength that I can muster.

A sudden blast of grey—

I'm gone—*I'm out*—

But *no*. I am on the ground with the picture of my own death vivid in my mind. Everything around me seems to be tilting, rotating. Now, through the haze, through the blinding flashes darting constantly back and forth between the nnn-Asi-t and the other two of my kind, I begin to see some sort of answer.

Jared knows it too. Despite the grasp on his mind which the enemy plans to use for his destruction, my mate has enough energy and strength left to ease his foot forward, in my direction. Gasping, my physical energy and control almost gone, I manage to flop myself toward him. I can see the energy within him that makes him seem to glow and I stretch my hand toward this, my own remaining power gleaming red along my fingers. Straining forward, I have my hand across his foot, trying to grasp his ankle—

But I am flung back by the force that holds my Earther.

It seems that we are in the midst of a typhoon, but I yell in Jared's direction. "We do not need it!" His eyes still have a glazed look. "Jared, we do not *need* to touch! We can do it. You are *open* to it, so you are open to me too!" And I throw everything remaining of my essence into Jared. Into my mate.

I feel the coming force as it turns momentarily from Jared to fling me aside.

AS IT TURNS FROM JARED TO FLING ME ASIDE…

As it turns from Jared—

And Jared is quick. Our essences swiftly embrace as Jared pulls me in. Immersed now in my Earther's essence, I pull up all the feelings of urgency for the enemy mission. I pull up all the greyness of the nnn-Asi-t—*Jared's biological father*—and I pull up the horrible images of my death which this nnn-Asi-t has planted inside. Now Jared joins me, and we mix this together with our own power.

Our barricade is thick and huge. The enemy would require endless energy and power to penetrate *this.* Barricaded, together we create our weapon.

Jared opens himself once more to the enemy. Quickly, *so quickly*, he uses his memories of the horrors planted in his mind by the enemy, and the nnn-Asi-t greyness which we have melded with our own power. As the enemy releases its blast, Jared directs a mirror image of it back toward it, instantaneously. I back it up with ten thousand tiny, red, razor-sharp needles, each one dripping searing flames.

We are now unbarricaded. But we will remain this way for now, in order to use all of our combined power for speed.

It is unknown whether it was Jared's mirror image of the enemy's weapon that killed it, or my tiny needles, or both. It does not matter, although I will reflect on this for possible future use against other enemies.

What *does* matter at this moment is the poor, frightened victim who, sobbing, stands gazing at the vials in his hand, gasping and shaking his head. What *does* matter is the comfort that we provide to the pilot when he, too, comes to realize the horror of what might have happened. They will both forget and recover. We do not always remove complete memories, but sometimes it is necessary.

What *does* matter is that two vials containing liquid which would produce gases capable of murdering tens of thousands of innocent Earthers will *not* be dropped from any plane over the Middle East or Russia.

We hope that our companions in those countries have been successful in their efforts, as well. At this time, though, I cannot help but worry about that. They, after all, had no Jared to assist them.

Chapter Twenty-Nine

Jared moaned. Wakefulness nagged at him like a constantly itchy mosquito bite, threatening to pluck him from the comfortable nothingness of his dreamless sleep. Memories began to play inside of his mind, like a continual light display, somehow connected to throbbing noises and intense pain.

He had to focus, to put determined effort into setting these distractions aside. Those parts of him that the sun's rays caressed, through the open section where the curtains didn't quite meet, felt tremendous. The quiet, the delicious silence surrounding him was as comforting as a mother's cradling arms. Rolling onto his side, Jared could feel something wonderfully warm and precious against his fingertips. Taking a deep breath, he opened his eyes as he let the air out slowly.

Beautiful scarlet greeted him. She was farther from the window than he was, so he had the opportunity to caress her with his eyes, loving the lighter tones of the colour where the sunlight met it, as well as the deeper crimson which lay in the shadows. Gently, almost holding his breath in his desire not to waken her, he ran a finger lightly along the curve of her cheek, then let it linger awhile in the deep, intense, ruby shades of her hair.

Smiling, his eyes half closed, he inhaled the wonderful, peaceful, serenity of lying in the warmth of the morning sun beside the woman he loved. After a few minutes, he allowed the memories from a couple of nights before to play through his mind, like he was watching a movie on TV.

How amazing it felt just to be alive! Still, he found it hard to believe that they had defeated the strange, mutant nnn-Asi-t—and that, somehow, *he* had had something to do with it. And the memory of the exaltation when, so exhausted from the battles that he thought all his power and energy were gone, he'd begun to receive the messages from around the world. One, two, three, four, and then five at first. From all different places on the globe, and they all said basically the same thing—

Perka's people had defeated the other nnn-Asi-t that were on the planet. Jared's world was free of them—at least, for now.

Every time the thought, or the memory of it all, crossed his mind, Jared was filled once again with the joy of victory…and relief. It was wonderful to know that his world was free from the enemy influences. He found it difficult to understand why Perka and her people weren't completely relieved.

Instead, they were concerned. Of course, Jared could comprehend that to some degree. After all, it was true that the nnn-Asi-t were changing, further developing their power and their cognitive skills. Perka's people could no longer afford to think of themselves as intellectually superior to this enemy. And Jared's involvement had really thrown them for a loop! The fact that the nnn-Asi-t had sent their most powerful being to Jared's area suggested that they must have known more about Jared and his skills than anyone had suspected.

Perka had enjoyed sharing his elation, of course. But she and her people were now preoccupied with thoughts about the *other* nnn-Asi-t which they would likely face on other worlds. If these enemies, too, were developing greater skills and cognition, then they could well be superior even to the mutant her people had confronted with Jared's assistance…

Hard to imagine.

But here, right now, all was wonderfully well. Jared wanted time to stand still. He wanted the rest of his life to be just like this. *Quiet. Peace…*the contentment of lying beside his mate while he savoured the warm sensations of sunlight and relaxation. Stretching forward, he caressed her radiant hair with his lips. Scowling, he banished an unwanted thought from his mind. Right now, he didn't want to think. He just wanted to enjoy the wonder of sharing this peace and tranquility with the woman he loved.

Dammit! He was too awake now. Thoughts kept bursting into his brain like popcorn popping. Each time he thrust one aside, another would take its place—

Dammit, dammit, dammit!

Still lying with his lips and cheek against her soft hair, he felt tears begin to fill his eyes. *Dammit.* If only he could turn her into an Earther, somehow. She looked enough like one when she used her pigment-suppressant. But she'd said that this simply wouldn't be possible. Or practical—or justified—when her people still had work to do to protect other planets from the enemy.

Sighing, he rolled away onto his back, but kept his fingertips in contact with her. A sour feeling began to simmer inside of his stomach when he thought of her continuing to live the way that she and her people did. How could they keep defeating the nnn-Asi-t if the nnn-Asi-t continued to increase their own power and intellectual abilities? And if they couldn't defeat this enemy, what would happen to them? It ripped him apart inside when he thought of her possibly dying...somewhere out there. Without him.

Jared didn't know how much more time they would have together. But he knew that it wouldn't be much. Some of their kind had already left the planet. They needed to begin tracking the enemy on other worlds *soon,* before the nnn-Asi-t had a chance to increase their power—

What would he do when she left? How could he *live?* How could he possibly go on without her?

Rolling back onto his side, he moved close to her once again. As he put his hand gently on top of hers, he brushed her earlobe with his lips and his cheek, savoured the glorious sensation of his lips against her hair. "I'm so glad you were able to stay a little longer," he whispered softly. A lump formed in his throat. He set some of his tears free as he lay against her.

I honestly don't know how I'm going to stand it when you go.

They were sitting in the living room while the glorious sunshine bathed both of them in golden light. Outside, a gentle breeze stirred the falling leaves as they decorated the ground with wonderful yellows, oranges, and reds.

Jared was sitting on the sofa, and Perka in a chair facing him, close enough that their knees touched. He was holding both of her hands in his, as he had been for some time.

"My love," she whispered. "There is no further need of my people here now. It really *is* time for me to go."

A heavy sigh escaped him. Yes, he knew it. She had been preparing him for nearly a week, reminding him that this time would come. Now she and her people had made certain that everything had been set right here on Earth. There were no traces of poor Martin anymore. And where there might have been suspicion on the parts of some of the people in the university, there was no physical evidence to back any of it up. Her people had taken extra care with the bearded student to ensure that his memory of the nnn-Asi-t consisted only of some weirdo who had strayed by mistake into the biochemistry building, muttering nonsense. All that remained at the airport was some confusion, as some people had *thought* they had seen something. Georgia and Franco had been able to scramble images on any recording devices involved.

"But you *can't* go yet," Jared said, his voice grave.

It was her turn to sigh. After all, everything had been explained, and explained again when necessary. She gazed at him questioningly, her head cocked a little to the side. A frown twisted her lips as she tried to understand what objection or question he could possibly still have.

And his thoughts were shielded this time.

"Because you *lied*, Perka. And you told me that your kind does not tell 'falsehoods'. So, I can't help but wonder if maybe some of the other things you've told me might not be quite true."

Her mouth dropped open in surprise. "Jared! But—but I could *not*… I *would* not. What are you talking about?"

A pang of guilt hit him when he saw how concerned she was. He had a hunch that he knew the answer he was looking for, yet he couldn't resist teasing…just a bit. "Remember when we were looking for trails at the university? The security guard?" When she nodded, he continued. "You told him that we were looking through the leaves for my cellphone. Wasn't that a 'falsehood'?"

Perka sat back in the chair, silent. Jared nibbled on his thumbnail while she searched her memory. Then she smiled slightly. "I remember," she said softly. "Do you recall my exact words at the time, Jared?" She leaned forward to hold his hands once more.

He frowned. No, he didn't remember them *exactly.*

Perka's smile grew broader. "I said to him that there was a *possibility* that you *might* have dropped your cellphone in the area. Is that not true?"

Chuckling, he shook his head. She had him. "But weren't you just wording things to avoid the truth?"

"Yes. Yes, Jared. I was. Although we do not tell falsehoods, at times when we deal with other cultures, we have to choose our words quite carefully in order to avoid misunderstandings. In that situation, time was quite important—we knew that there were likely to be lives on the line. My dear Earther, among my own people, falsehoods do not exist. But when we are among other cultures, or the enemy, we must be extremely cautious about which words we use." Perka gazed downward at their hands, caressing his fingers with her own.

His eyes, too, focussed on the sight of their hands. A twinge of sadness touched him now that her colouring was more like an Earther's. He'd grown to love the sight of her when she was in her natural state.

"Jared," she said softly, still holding his hands. Their minds touched then, all shields forgotten, and she read the question in his mind. "Yes. There *will* continue to be social problems here on Earth. But your people will survive, now that the nnn-Asi-t are not here to interfere with your people's development. Some of your people's social issues will be resolved over time, and new ones will develop. The important thing is that your culture, and the other cultures on your planet, can be free to develop as they may. Your people need to focus on listening and respecting each other, so that you can work on social problems in a positive manner. With your skills as a counsellor—and your mental abilities—you can help your people directly to deal with problems constructively."

"What'll happen if you're...if you're pregnant?"

Her eyes met his, and she smiled warmly at him. She opened her mind to him, and he knew that she wasn't.

"Our people have learned to control aspects of their bodies with their minds. Your people, too, have abilities in this area. With practice, they can develop this skill further."

"But what about *me?* My biological father was one of *them!* How could that be? Did he *mean* to impregnate my mother?"

"Possibly. And, if he did, that is even more reason for my people to continue fighting this enemy! We hadn't thought that they had the cognitive abilities to do such planning. My people still have much work to do."

"You said that you wouldn't come back." A lump formed in his throat again. His voice sounded hoarse as he tried to talk past it. "Is there...is there *any* possibility that you or your people might?"

She shrugged her narrow shoulders. "As your people develop and your culture goes through changes, perhaps if it seems necessary. If your world moves too close to destruction, it may be that my superiors would deem it appropriate for us to intervene, perhaps not. It is not my decision." Her eyes became unfocussed.

The thought of her superiors brought a memory of Martin to her mind, which Jared picked up.

"Martin," he said softly. "Does—did he have a family?" Then, suddenly, his consciousness was filled with beautiful peace, tranquility...and he knew that this was what Martin experienced now. He closed his eyes, savouring the sensation.

"We are all Martin's family," Perka said gently. "He never took a mate, desiring instead to give himself entirely to this important work. And now he is free to attain total peace in the True Universe."

Whatever that is, Jared mused. Whatever it was, it must be wonderful, judging from the serene smile on Perka's face.

For a moment, he considered projecting his next thought to her, but decided against it. For some reason, he felt a need to speak again. Maybe it was an Earther thing. "When you go—will you… will you change my memories of you?"

The faraway look in her eyes disappeared, but the warm smile on her face did not. Her inner being reached to him, sharing a wonderful sense of peace. "We almost always do with Earthers," she whispered, "but considering your skills, I will not unless you wish for me to do so."

There was no need to speak now. Sighing deeply, he savoured the sensation as his essence melded once more with hers, amazed yet again at how such a blissful union could be completely non-physical. But there was a twinge of pain, too.

Jared could feel her desire to leave and to return to her own world, and to her people's mission. He saw his pain as a smouldering fire, but as he watched, she extinguished it with a sprinkling of joyous raindrops. Then he began to feel her total and complete joy in knowing that his world and his kind were no longer in immediate danger…and that hers awaited her.

That is as it should be. But his sorrow was as much a part of him as his memories and love of her. He knew now that it could not be denied, and so he took it, and stored it away, deep inside of his being. This he put near the nnn-Asi-t parts of him, carefully sealed like a locked safe.

Exhaling deeply, he wriggled his arms into the sleeves of his blue jacket. He was relieved that this was to be a fairly long walk that would allow him to have at least a little more time with her. Of course, he'd offered to drive her and some of the others. But they wanted to leave the city in just the same way as they'd entered it.

A chilly blast of evening air struck his cheeks as he stepped through the door of his apartment building. Running a few steps, he caught up with the woman, noting the joyous look on her face. Although inside of himself he felt a deep sadness when he thought about her leaving, he was also quite aware of her enthusiasm and excitement about making her way to the same place where she'd begun her assignment here. Jared was so incredibly lucky to have shared this experience with her, as well as her happiness as she anticipated returning to her home. His gaze travelled upward as he eyed the stars, wondering which one was hers, if it was even visible right now. What would her spacecraft look like? So hard to believe that it could arrive and leave undetected...

Then he was distracted by the sight of Franco, who was moving in their direction from a few streets over. The dark-haired alien said nothing as he approached them. There was no need, Jared understood now. Communication without words was, once more, easy between them, now that there was no enemy to pick up their thoughts. Franco didn't even look in their direction, simply falling into step on the other side of Perka, his eyes sweeping upward toward the sky, as Jared's had done. Jared slipped inside of Perka's consciousness, wanting to share as much of her experience as he could in the limited time together that they had left. Now he enjoyed her immense happiness at the thought of making her journey once again through the stars.

Caught up in her excitement, Jared wondered about going with her. But even as he thought this, he found himself automatically dismissing the idea. He was an *Earther*, and this was his planet. Could he even *survive* on her world? They didn't have any *food!* They sure wouldn't have any coffee! She had never suggested that this was a possibility so, evidently, she didn't consider it realistic or possible.

At the outskirts of the small city, they were joined by Paul. As Franco had, he said nothing, simply falling into step with them. A chill ran through Jared as the wind blew harder, with no buildings to shelter them from it. The bushes and few trees were powerless against it.

But the night was beautifully clear and, although the breezes prompted him to pull his jacket zipper up as far as it would go, all seemed still and peaceful out in the field. The crescent moon looked like a cheery smile in the dark sky as Jared followed the others into the dampening grasses. The others were here. Georgia, conscious of Jared's Earther ways, gave him a welcoming smile before turning her gaze upward as the others had already done. Jared followed suit. He frowned. He could see nothing other than the sky.

Then suddenly it was there—simply *there*, as though it had just dropped out of the overhead sparkling darkness! He recalled what Perka had told him about how well the vehicle was camouflaged, both from human eyes and radar. But still it was incredible to witness this.

"Wow," he said aloud.

Fascinated, he watched as the others headed in the direction of what looked to Jared like a vague, amorphous, dark bluish mass. He assumed that they were boarding the craft, although all he could see was each individual disappearing from view.

Perka was in front of him now. Her hand was on his cheek. Then her essence was inside of him, caressing him with wonderful scarlet ribbons that wrapped around and through his entire being, completely filling him with warmth and joy. Captivated, he closed his eyes just for a minute—

When he opened them, he was *alone*. Yet he could swear that he still felt her touch on his cheek. His fingers went to his cheek, feeling for traces of her…

Panic began to surge through him. *He hadn't seen her go. Hadn't even watched her as she'd stepped aboard the craft.* Still savouring the warmth of her presence inside him, he gazed at their spacecraft, the dark bluish mist-like substance, as it slowly rose and disappeared. His hand fell from his cheek to drop at his side. A moan escaped from him.

She was gone. Just like that.

An almost overwhelming emptiness was all that he had left. Automatically, he found himself trying to project to her. But he found nothing. Jared was completely, totally…*alone.* With the back of his hand, he wiped a tear away, then thrust his fingers deep into his pockets.

Gasping, he pulled out his hand and studied the little sphere which had been inside his pocket. His fingers caressed the smooth exterior, his heart filling with gratitude that she'd left him something to help him remember her. At least, with something tangible, he'd know that everything hadn't simply been a dream.

Placing the sphere carefully back into his pocket, he blinked through the tears blurring his vision as he made his way back through the city. His heart seemed impossibly heavy, like a lump of lead hanging suspended inside his chest. This was more than a heavy heart. A heavy heart was what he'd felt when Marjorie had left him, and when his dad—his *step*dad had passed away.

This seemed to be much more than that—a terrible, aching emptiness, as though a part of *him* was gone, too. Automatically, Jared kept reaching out for her, projecting to her, only to find emptiness.

Dimly he recalled the suicidal thoughts he'd had what seemed a long time ago. The thoughts that had led him to the crisis line… and to *her.* Yet, if he called that same line now, she wouldn't be there. Sighing, he pulled out a tissue and blew his nose, stuffing the tissue back into his jeans pocket. His eyes continually blurring with moisture, he stumbled his way back through the chilly city streets, wondering but not caring if passersby might think he was drunk. As he trudged up the sidewalk to the front door of his building, he paused. He'd seen something from the corner of his eye.

Freddy. The orange cat was gazing at him from the brick corner near the parking lot. He opened his mouth and meowed in his strange, raspy voice. Jared chuckled at him. For a moment, he simply stood. Then he looked back at the feline, who was rubbing his back against the brickwork. Jared shook his head and sighed.

"Okay, buddy. Let's do it. I thought about this before—but maybe it's time to *do* something." Jared knelt so he was at a level closer to the ground. "C'mon, buddy. Come here." He moved his fingers back and forth, and the feline hurried eagerly to join him, gratefully rubbing his back against Jared's hands. Chuckling again, Jared stood, holding the happy cat in his arms. Freddy purred loudly, joyfully rubbing his face against the man's hands, then chin.

Back at his apartment, Jared laughed at the cat, and struggled to unlock the door with his arms quite full. Kicking his shoes off, he shoved the door closed behind him and, not bothering to take off his jacket, he sat on a chair at the kitchen table. Distracted, he sat for a minute, cat still in his arms, oblivious to his ring tone…

His *phone—*

As the cat jumped down to explore his new surroundings, Jared pulled his phone from his inside pocket and mumbled: "H'lo?"

"Hello. Uh—Jared Collins?"

The voice wasn't familiar. "Um…yeah?"

"I know it's after business hours, Jared. Sorry to bother you, but I wanted to speak to you. Do you mind?"

"If you'll tell me what this is all about!"

"Oh! Of course! Jared, this is Keith O'Brien. You had an interview with me a few months ago. At the Belgrave Centre, the youth treatment centre. Remember?"

"Oh!" It seemed like another world and another time. "Yes. Yes, I remember."

"Well, I hope that your job hunting is going well. But our funding for an additional counsellor didn't come through. So, I'm afraid there isn't a position that we can offer you…"

Jared just chuckled.

"*But* I wanted you to know that I thought highly of you during our interview, Jared. And, if you're still available, I'll keep you in mind if something comes up. Would that be okay?"

"Sure," Jared said softly. "That would be great. Thanks."

After their conversation, Jared sat for a moment with his phone in his hand. There was someone else who he should talk to. For now, though, he put his phone down on the table. He reached into another pocket and retrieved the little sphere.

"Thank you, Perka," he said softly, caressing the small ball with his fingertips.

Then he gasped. The thing was becoming warm—and now it was *glowing* a bit, like Perka's sphere had. It became a bit warmer, then began to turn various shades of crimson, then pink, then crimson once again. And slowly it grew in size, stopping when it was as large as an apple.

Now it seemed to emanate peace and relaxation, vibrating slightly with a pleasant sound reminiscent of Freddy's purrs. As its exterior changed, he could see some sort of image, or moving picture like a video. Fascinated, he held his breath in awe.

Perka! There was her *face*, somehow—

"Jared, my Earther!"

"Perka! I can *hear* you!"

"Yes! And I can see and hear you too! There is too great a distance now between us for us to project to each other. But you can try to contact me through the LLL-nnnta whenever you wish. If I am not free to respond, I will wait until I am. Then you will feel the LLL-nnta become warm…"

"Almost like Skype," Jared chuckled.

She smiled. "I suppose. Jared, you need not worry about being alone. I owe you this much at least for the tremendous efforts you have made on behalf of my people, and me. But, if you wish to be alone, simply put this sphere aside. No one else will be able to make it respond."

"Perka. I should be thanking *you*."

The bright smile continued to light the image of her face. "Jared. If you ever sense or see any indication on Earth of any presence other than that of your own kind, contact me. I doubt that the nnn-Asi-t will return to your world, but if they do, you have the ability to sense them. And now you can contact us. Would you do this, please, for your people and for mine?"

"Of course! By the way, what are your people called, anyway?"

She chuckled. "You asked me that before. Do you remember what I said?"

"You wouldn't tell me."

"I said that you would not be able to pronounce it!"

"Try me!"

She laughed again, then said something that sounded like a mixture of growling and tongue clicks.

It was Jared's turn to laugh. She had him this time! But he didn't mind. Not at all.

After her face had faded from view, the sphere faded in colour and began to cool. He placed it carefully on the table with his phone and sat silently, his mind thinking about all that had happened over the past weeks, and all that it meant.

There was a faraway look about his face as he picked up his phone and held it in his hand.

Then he opened his list of contacts and touched a number.

Smiling, he placed the phone against his ear as Freddy hopped up on the table in front of him and gazed at his new human. Jared scratched the cat's ears.

"Hi mom! I've been thinking about you—"

Epilogue

I am called Perka. But no. Not anymore. My name is once more pp-KKK-uh. Finally, I am in our small craft, travelling home to my world. I watch contentedly as we leave the area of the third planet from its sun. As we increase our distance, it becomes a bluish and white ball, smaller and smaller behind us.

And I see a free world, a world which can now evolve as it will. There remains a possibility that it will perish before it should. After all, its inhabitants seem to have a violent streak even without interference from any enemy. I hope that they will learn to have tolerance and respect for one another, and that the inhabitants might eventually think less of themselves, and more of how they can benefit each other. Perhaps with assistance from Jared and others like him, they will find their way.

But, for now at least, they will reach their own destiny, rather than one selected for them by an interfering enemy. Vividly, I recall my arrival here. It seems like this was a long, long time ago, although I know that it was not.

All had gone as expected, at first. We certainly had not anticipated, though, to find that the nnn-Asi-t had been involved in some sort of program to increase their strength and their skills in communicating with each other. And I certainly never anticipated the possibility of mating with an Earther...especially one with aspects of the enemy as part of his inner being!

Yet, without him, we would not have been able to defeat the more highly-developed nnn-Asi-t.

My people. Do they resent me for becoming 'involved' with Jared, as some Earthers might? No. My people realize that there would be no purpose in such emotions. What has happened, has happened.

But now my future is clear to me. Having mated with an Earther, I will not take one of my own kind. And that is as it should be.

I shall carry on as KKK-rr would have—Martin Kramer. I shall devote the rest of my existence to protecting the planets in our universe. I shall continue to protect innocents from any interference from the enemy.

I am pp-KKK-uh. And I am a warrior, a protector. A zzz-o-LLACHT.

IF YOU ENJOYED THIS BOOK, PLEASE CONSIDER LEAVING A REVIEW OR RATING ON AMAZON.

About the Author

When Lynne Armstrong-Jones started writing novels and sending out manuscripts, eventually finances dictated that she return to full-time work. Now that she has time to write once more, she has completed most of her *On the Trail* fantasy series. Check her website www.lynnearmstrongjones.com for more information on these novels.

The first version of ASSIGNMENT: Earth was written awhile ago. It has evolved into the current novel. Lynne lives in London, Ontario, Canada with three cats and one husband.

Printed in the USA
CPSIA information can be obtained
at www.ICGtesting.com
LVHW041928220923
758883LV00001B/126

9 781637 840740